THE WINTER'S TALE

（中英文双语对照）

冬日故事

【英】威廉·莎士比亚 著

孙大雨 译

上海三联书店

WINTER'S TALE.

DRAMATIS PERSONAE

Leontes, King of Sicilia
Mamillius, his son
Camillo, Sicilian Lord
Antigonus, Sicilian Lord
Cleomenes, Sicilian Lord
Dion, Sicilian Lord
Polixenes, King of Bohemia
Florizel, his son
Archidamus, a Bohemian Lord
A Mariner
A Gaoler
An Old Shepherd, repated father of Perdita
Clown, his son
Servant to the Old Shepherd
Autolycus, arogue
Hermione, Queen to Leontes
Perdita, daughter to Leontes and Hermione
Paulina, wife to Antigonus

剧 中 人 物

里杭底斯，西西利亚王
曼密留诗，王子
喀米罗 ⎫
安铁冈纳施 ⎬ 西西利亚四贵人
克廖弥尼司 ⎪
第盎 ⎭
包列齐倪思，波希米亚王
弗洛律采尔，波希米亚王子
阿乞台末史，波希米亚一贵人
水手
狱卒
老牧羊人，哀笛达之闻名生父
小丑，老牧人之子
老牧人之仆
奥托力革厮，棍徒
候妙霓，里杭底斯之后
哀笛达，里杭底斯与候妙霓之女
宝理娜，安铁冈纳施之妻

Emilia, a lady attending on the Queen
Other Ladies, attending on the Queen
Mopsa, shepherdess
Dorcas, shepherdess

Other Lords and Ladies, and Attendants, Officers, Satyrs, Shephers and Shepherdesses, &c.

Time, as Chorus

SCENE: Sometimes in Sicilia; sometimes in Bohemia

爱米丽亚，陪侍王后之贵妇
其他陪侍王后之贵妇数人
瑁泊沙，⎫
桃卡丝，⎬牧羊女郎

其他贵人与贵妇数人，侍从数人，公吏数人，山羊人
　　妖仙数人，牧羊人与牧羊女郎数人，等

　　　　　　　　"时间"老人，作为歌舞者

剧景：有时在西西利亚；有时在波希米亚

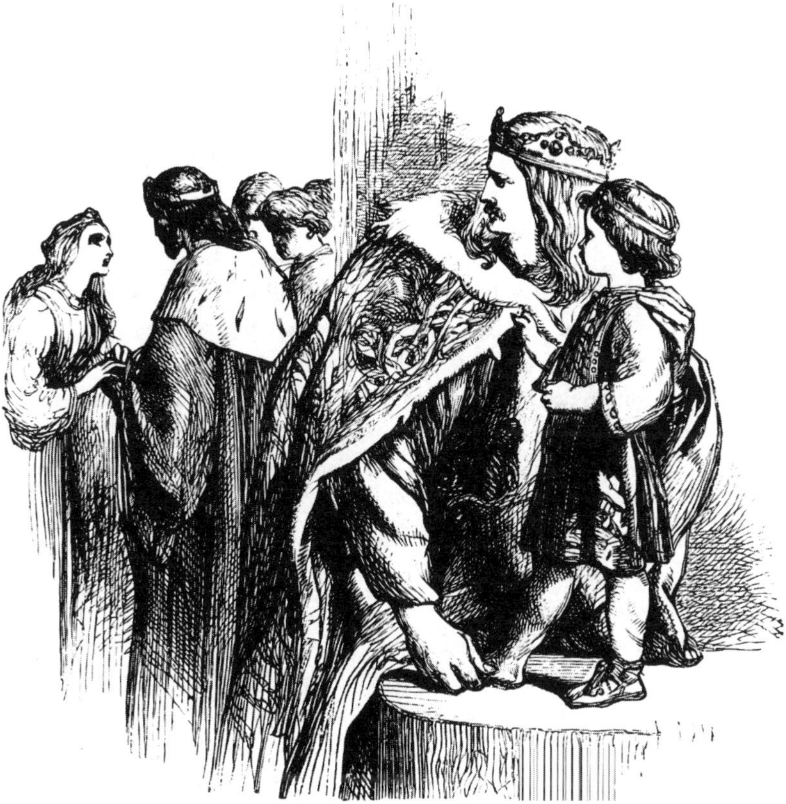

ACT I.

SCENE I. Sicilia. *An Antechamber in Leontes' Palace.*

[*Enter* Camillo *and* Archidamus.]

Archidamus If you shall chance, Camillo, to visit Bohemia, on the like occasion whereon my services are now on foot, you shall see, as I have said, great difference betwixt our Bohemia and your Sicilia.

Camillo I think this coming summer the King of Sicilia means to pay Bohemia the visitation which he justly owes him.

Archidamus Wherein our entertainment shall shame us we will be justified in our loves: for indeed, —

Camillo Beseech you, —

Archidamus Verily, I speak it in the freedom of my knowledge: we cannot with such magnificence — in so rare — I know not what to say. — We will give you sleepy drinks, that your senses, unintelligent of our insufficiency, may, though they cannot praise us, as little accuse us.

Camillo You pay a great deal too dear for what's given freely.

Archidamus Believe me, I speak as my understanding instructs me and as mine honesty puts it to utterance.

Camillo Sicilia cannot show himself overkind to Bohemia. They were trained together in their childhoods; and there rooted betwixt them then

第 一 幕

第 一 景

［西西利亚。里杭底斯宫中一前堂］
［喀米罗与阿乞台末史上。

阿乞台末史 您若是有机会，喀米罗，到波希米亚去，像我现在这样肩负着使命，您将会见到，我已经说过，我们波希米亚和你们西西利亚大有不同。

喀 米 罗 我想来年夏天，我们西西利亚王上将有意对你们波希米亚王上作一次他确是欠下了的访问。

阿乞台末史 到时候我们招待不周，只有用热情欢迎来弥补欠缺了：因为，当真，——

喀 米 罗 请您，——

阿乞台末史 说实在话，我知道确是如此才这样说：我们做不到这么隆重——这样宏壮瑰丽——我不知说什么才好。我们将飨你们以催眠的酒浆，于是你们的知觉将感受不到我们的不足，也许就不会责备我们，即使你们本来不可能称赞我们。

喀 米 罗 对我们的招待，您过奖了。

阿乞台末史 信任我，我只是照我所了解到的来说，而且一秉至诚地说出来。

喀 米 罗 我们西西利亚王上对你们波希米亚王上无论怎样热情招待都不过分。他们孩童时期是在一起受教养

such an affection which cannot choose but branch now. Since their more mature dignities and royal necessities made separation of their society, their encounters, though not personal, have been royally attorneyed with interchange of gifts, letters, loving embassies; that they have seemed to be together, though absent; shook hands, as over a vast; and embraced as it were from the ends of opposed winds. The heavens continue their loves!

Archidamus   I think there is not in the world either malice or matter to alter it. You have an unspeakable comfort of your young Prince Mamillius: it is a gentleman of the greatest promise that ever came into my note.

Camillo   I very well agree with you in the hopes of him. It is a gallant child; one that indeed physics the subject, makes old hearts fresh: they that went on crutches ere he was born desire yet their life to see him a man.

Archidamus   Would they else be content to die?

Camillo   Yes, if there were no other excuse why they should desire to live.

Archidamus   If the king had no son, they would desire to live on crutches till he had one.

[*Exeunt.*]

SCENE II. *A Room of State in the Palace.*

[*Enter* Leontes, Polixenes, Hermione,
Mamillius, Camillo, *and* Attendants.]

Polixenes   Nine changes of the watery star hath been
The shepherd's note since we have left our throne
Without a burden: time as long again
Would be filled up, my brother, with our thanks;
And yet we should, for perpetuity,
Go hence in debt: and therefore, like a cipher,

的；他们彼此间种得有这么多友爱的深根，到今天便不禁要枝叶扶疏起来。自从他们身居尊位而年事稍长，以及为君的需要使他们分袂以来，他们的接触虽不是亲自的，但却是以礼品、书翰、友爱的使命交相来往，由钦差大臣们显赫地进行的；于是他们虽天各一方，却似乎在一起，像超越着广漠在握手，又仿佛从风向四面八方的来处凑合拢来在拥抱。愿上天使他们的友爱绵延不尽！

阿乞台末史　我想这世上不会有恶意或任何原因能改变这友爱。在你们这位年轻的曼密留诗王子身上，你们有说不尽的安慰：以我所注意到的来说，那是位前途不可限量的都雅君子。

喀　米　罗　我非常同意您对他的希望。这是个光彩显赫的孩子；他当真振奋臣民们的心志，叫老年人心胸重新少壮；他们当他还未出生时已经持了拐杖的，如今只想活到能见他长大成人。

阿乞台末史　若是没有他，他们可愿意死吗？

喀　米　罗　不错；若是他们没有别的借口愿意继续活下去的话。

阿乞台末史　如果王上没有世子，他们会愿意挂着拐杖等待他生一位出来。　　　　　　　　　　　　　　　〔同下。

第　二　景

〔宫中一朝堂〕

〔里杭底斯、包列齐倪思、候妙霓、曼密留诗、喀米罗与侍从等上。

包列齐倪思　自从我们离了御座一身轻，
　　　　　　牧羊人见到水上的银轮已有过
　　　　　　九度的盈亏：我们将化来表道
　　　　　　谢意的时间，王兄，会同样地悠长；
　　　　　　可是我们告别后仍然将长此
　　　　　　负着欠：所以，像个计算上的零码，

Yet standing in rich place, I multiply
With one we *thank you* many thousands more
That go before it.
Leontes　　　　　Stay your thanks a while,
And pay them when you part.
Polixenes　　　　　　　　Sir, that's to-morrow.
I am question'd by my fears, of what may chance
Or breed upon our absence; that may blow
No sneaping winds at home, to make us say,
This is put forth too truly. Besides, I have stay'd
To tire your royalty.
Leontes　　　　　We are tougher, brother,
Than you can put us to't.
Polixenes　　　　　　　No longer stay.
Leontes　One seven-night longer.
Polixenes　　　　　　　　Very sooth, to-morrow.
Leontes　We'll part the time between 's then: and in that
I'll no gainsaying.
Polixenes　Press me not, beseech you, so,
There is no tongue that moves, none, none i' the world,
So soon as yours, could win me: so it should now,
Were there necessity in your request, although
'Twere needful I denied it. My affairs
Do even drag me homeward: which to hinder,
Were, in your love a whip to me; my stay
To you a charge and trouble: to save both,
Farewell, our brother.
Leontes　　　　　Tongue-tied, our queen? Speak you.

它本身虽无足轻重,但居于要位,
我用一声"多谢您",将以前的感激
平白增加了几千倍。

里杭底斯 　　　　　　　　请暂停道谢,
等临别再致吧。

包列齐倪思 　　　　　王兄,我明天就走。
我被自己的疑惧所问起,当自己
不在时什么意外会发生,会滋长;
我但愿家中不会刮一阵寒风
啃得皮肤痛,好使我们能说道,
"这可产生得太早了!"而且我待得
已太久,使尊驾感到了厌倦。

里杭底斯 　　　　　　　　　　王兄,
尽您怎样严峻地来考验我们,
我们总是强韧得不会有动摇。

包列齐倪思 不再稽留了。

里杭底斯 　　　　　请再多留一星期。

包列齐倪思 煞是当真,明天走。

里杭底斯 　　　　　　那我们把时间
且来分一下;那样办我倒不反对。

包列齐倪思 请您莫再敦劝了,就这样。但凡能
言谈的唇舌,没有了,这世上再没有,
会像您这样,能迅速赢得我同意:
如果您这恳请里有绝对的必要,
当会赢得我,虽然我必须拒绝。
公私丛脞在极力拖我回家去;
阻拦对于我将是个责罚,虽然
施鞭挞您出于衷心的友爱;我不去,
对您是个负担和烦扰:为避免
这两件不快,再会吧,王兄。

里杭底斯 　　　　　　　　　不做声,
我们的王后? 你来讲。

Hermione I had thought, sir, to have held my peace until
You had drawn oaths from him not to stay. You, sir,
Charge him too coldly. Tell him you are sure
All in Bohemia's well: this satisfaction
The by-gone day proclaimed: say this to him,
He's beat from his best ward.
Leontes   Well said, Hermione.
Hermione To tell he longs to see his son were, strong:
But let him say so then, and let him go;
But let him swear so, and he shall not stay,
We'll thwack him hence with distaffs. —
[*To* Polixenes]
Yet of your royal presence I'll adventure
The borrow of a week. When at Bohemia
You take my lord, I'll give him my commission
To let him there a month behind the gest
Prefix'd for's parting: — yet, good deed, Leontes,
I love thee not a jar of the clock behind
What lady she her lord. — You'll stay?
Polixenes   No, madam.
Hermione Nay, but you will?
Polixenes   I may not, verily.
Hermione *Verily*!
You put me off with limber vows; but I,
Though you would seek to unsphere the stars with oaths,
Should yet say *Sir, no going*. Verily,
You shall not go; a lady's verily is
As potent as a lord's. Will go yet?
Force me to keep you as a prisoner,
Not like a guest: so you shall pay your fees
When you *depart*, and save your thanks. How say you?

候 妙 霓	我预备,王夫, 保持着沉默,要等你迫得他起誓 不再留,我才来启齿。你啊,王夫, 向他进逼得不够热:告诉他,你确知 波希米亚一切都很好:才昨天, 得到这满意的消息:跟他说这个, 他会从防御中后退。
里杭底斯	说得对,候妙霓。
候 妙 霓	他若说牵挂他儿子,那很有力量: 只要他这么说了,便得让他去; 只要他这么赌了咒,他就决不会 再留,我们等于用纺线杆打他走。 〔对包〕我敢于告借您御驾淹留一星期。 当您挽留我王夫在波希米亚时, 我会同意他晏滞在预定的离别 日期之后一个月;可是,当真说, 里杭底斯,我急于想见你,不比 那一位名门闺秀想见她丈夫, 迟那么钟上的一嘀嗒。您肯待下吧?
包列齐倪思	不成,后嫂。
候 妙 霓	别再说不成,留下了?
包列齐倪思	我委实不能。
候 妙 霓	您委实 用柔弱无力的矢愿延宕答应我; 即令您会用咒誓使得星辰们 打从球体里脱落而出,我还是 要对您说道,"王兄,请莫去。"委实, 您不能就去:一个贵妇说"委实", 跟一位贵人说"委实"一般有力量。 您还要去吗?逼得我将您作囚犯, 而不当贵宾;然后,在您临走时, 您得付"礼金",而毋须道谢。怎么说?

My prisoner or my guest? by your dread *verily*,
One of them you shall be.
Polixenes   Your guest, then, madam:
To be your prisoner should import offending;
Which is for me less easy to commit
Than you to punish.
Hermione   Not your gaoler then,
But your kind hostess. Come, I'll question you
Of my lord's tricks and yours when you were boys.
You were pretty lordings then.
Polixenes   We were, fair queen,
Two lads that thought there was no more behind
But such a day to-morrow as to-day,
And to be boy eternal.
Hermione   Was not my lord the verier wag o' the two?
Polixenes   We were as twinn'd lambs that did frisk i'
    the sun
And bleat the one at th' other. What we chang'd
Was innocence for innocence; we knew not
The doctrine of ill-doing, nor dream'd
That any did. Had we pursu'd that life,
And our weak spirits ne'er been higher rear'd
With stronger blood, we should have answer'd heaven
Boldly *Not guilty*, the imposition clear'd
Hereditary ours.
Hermione   By this we gather
You have tripp'd since.
Polixenes   O, my most sacred lady,
Temptations have since then been born to 's! for
In those unfledg'd days was my wife a girl;
Your precious self had then not cross'd the eyes
Of my young play-fellow.
Hermione   Grace to boot!

囚徒,抑宾客？凭您那可怕的"委实",
两者必居其一。

包列齐倪思 那就当宾客吧,
后嫂：当您的囚徒便表示有冒犯；
那个,由我去犯下比由您来责罚
更其不容易。

候　妙　霓 那我就不是狱吏了,
而是您殷勤的女东道主人。来吧,
我要来问您,我王夫和您孩童时
怎么样调皮；那时节你们已经是
出落得英姿俊爽的王孙王子了。

包列齐倪思 我们当时,后妊娥,是两个小后生,
只以为随后的日子都是同今天
一样的明朝,是永远不长的孩童。

候　妙　霓 两人中,我王夫是否更滑稽逗人乐？

包列齐倪思 我们好像一母双生的小羔羊,
在阳光之中跳跃,相对着咩咩叫：
彼此交换的是一片天真对无邪；
我们没学过做坏事,做梦也未曾
想到有谁会把坏事做。若我们
继续那生涯（而我们柔弱的心神
从未被较强的火性激发起来过）,
我们应能对上天大胆地回答道,
"无罪"；我们祖遗的罪辜一笔勾。

候　妙　霓 您这般说法,我们能推断嗣后
你们摔过跤。

包列齐倪思 啊！高纯的后嫂,
我们随后却中了魔道；只因为
我妻子在那尚未成长的时日里,
还是个闺女；珍异的您,自己也尚未
被我这年轻玩侣的双眸所注目。

候　妙　霓 愿上苍恩赐慈悲将我们来拯救！

Of this make no conclusion, lest you say
Your queen and I are devils: yet, go on;
The offences we have made you do we'll answer;
If you first sinn'd with us, and that with us
You did continue fault, and that you slipp'd not
With any but with us.
Leontes   Is he won yet?
Hermione   He'll stay, my lord.
Leontes   At my request he would not.
Hermione, my dearest, thou never spok'st
To better purpose.
Hermione   Never?
Leontes   Never but once.
Hermione   What! have I twice said well? when was't before?
I pr'ythee tell me; cram 's with praise, and make 's
As fat as tame things: one good deed dying tongueless
Slaughters a thousand waiting upon that.
Our praises are our wages; you may ride 's
With one soft kiss a thousand furlongs ere
With spur we heat an acre. But to the goal: —
My last good deed was to entreat his stay;
What was my first? it has an elder sister,
Or I mistake you: O, would her name were Grace!
But once before I spoke to the purpose — when?
Nay, let me have't; I long.
Leontes   Why, that was when
Three crabbèd months had sour'd themselves to death,
Ere I could make thee open thy white hand

对此且慢下结论,否则您要说
您家的后嫂同我是魔鬼;可是,
讲下去:我们使你们犯下的过误,
我们会负责;若你们先跟我们
犯下了罪辜,且继续还跟我们犯,
没有跟旁人、只同我们出舛错。

里杭底斯	赢得他同意吗?
候妙霓	他答应留下,王夫。
里杭底斯	我请,他不肯。候妙霓,我的至爱的, 你从未说得比如今更好过。
候妙霓	从未?
里杭底斯	只除了一次,从不曾。
候妙霓	什么?我有过 两回说得很好?那次是在何时? 请你告诉我;用夸奖来塞饱我们, 将我们猫狗一般喂养得肥肥的: 一桩好事情不经受赞美,杀死了 后面跟着要来的一千桩。称扬 是我们的酬报:只用轻轻一个吻, 你们能叫我们奔驰百余里, 尽夹踢马刺却不能迫使我们 跑完半里的一半的一半。让我们 言归正传:我最后一桩好事是, 恳请他留下:第一桩可是什么? 它有个姐姐,否则我是误会了你: 啊!我但愿那却能给叫作情深 义重的温雅事。我以前只有过一回 说得很适当:是什么时候?别那样, 告诉我;我急于知道。
里杭底斯	哎也,那是在 三个月焦煎的时日厌塞塞逝去时, 正当你张玉掌与我握双成定,

And clap thyself my love; then didst thou utter
I am yours for ever.
Hermione　　　　　It is Grace indeed.
Why, lo you now, I have spoke to the purpose twice;
The one for ever earn'd a royal husband;
Th' other for some while a friend.
　　　　　　　　　　[*Giving her hand to* Polixenes.]
Leontes　　　　　　[*Aside.*]Too hot, too hot!
To mingle friendship far is mingling bloods.
I have tremor cordis on me;—my heart dances;
But not for joy,—not joy.—This entertainment
May a free face put on; derive a liberty
From heartiness, from bounty, fertile bosom,
And well become the agent: 't may, I grant:
But to be paddling palms and pinching fingers,
As now they are; and making practis'd smiles
As in a looking-glass; and then to sigh, as 'twere
The mort o' the deer: O, that is entertainment
My bosom likes not, nor my brows,—Mamillius,
Art thou my boy?
Mamillius　　　Ay, my good lord.
Leontes　　　　　　　　I' fecks!
Why, that's my bawcock. What! hast smutch'd thy
　　　nose?—
They say it is a copy out of mine. Come, captain,
We must be neat;—not neat, but cleanly, captain:
And yet the steer, the heifer, and the calf,
Are all call'd neat.—Still virginalling
Upon his palm!—How now, you wanton calf!
Art thou my calf?

愿两厢缔义结同心:当时你声言,
"我永远属于你。"

候 妙 霓 那的确义重情深。
哎也,你瞧,有过两次我说得很得体:
第一回永远得到个君王作夫婿,
第二回暂时将个朋友赢到手。

[伸手与包列齐倪思。]

里杭底斯 [旁白]太热了,太热了!
友谊联结得过了火会把血液
也联结。我有心悸病:我的心在跳;
但非为欢欣;不是欢欣。这厚待
也许呈一副天真纯洁的面貌,
从真诚亲切之中,恳挚的善意里,
温渥的心内,取得了无拘无束,
因而变成了媒蘖;这是可能的,
我确信无疑:至于摩挲手掌心,
挤捏着手指,如他们此刻正在玩,
以及彼此相视而微微笑,仿佛
面对着菱花镜;然后一同作叹息,
一似鹿死时那一声嘘气;唉哟!
那样的对待我心里不喜欢,额角
所不爱。曼密留诗,你是我孩子吗?

曼密留诗 是啊,好爸爸。

里杭底斯 当真吗?哎也,果真是
我的好人儿。怎么!鼻子弄脏了?
大家都说那跟我的一模一样。
来吧,小把戏,我们得眉宇明净,
头角峥嵘;不对,眉宇要明净,
头角可不得峥嵘,小把戏:为的是
公牛、母牛、小牛都有角。依旧在
揉弄他的手掌!怎么样,爱耍的小牛!
你是我的小牛吗?

Mamillius   Yes, if you will, my lord.
Leontes Thou want'st a rough pash, and the shoots that I have,
To be full like me:—yet they say we are
Almost as like as eggs; women say so,
That will say anything: but were they false
As o'er-dy'd blacks, as wind, as waters,—false
As dice are to be wish'd by one that fixes
No bourn 'twixt his and mine; yet were it true
To say this boy were like me.—Come, sir page,
Look on me with your welkin eye: sweet villain!
Most dear'st! my collop!—Can thy dam?—may't be?
Affection! thy intention stabs the centre:
Thou dost make possible things not so held,
Communicat'st with dreams;—how can this be?—
With what's unreal thou co-active art,
And fellow'st nothing: then 'tis very credent
Thou mayst co-join with something; and thou dost,—
And that beyond commission; and I find it,—
And that to the infection of my brains
And hardening of my brows.
Polixenes   What means Sicilia?
Hermione He something seems unsettled.
Polixenes   How! my lord!
What cheer? How is't with you, best brother?
Hermione   You look
As if you held a brow of much distraction:
Are you mov'd, my lord?
Leontes   No, in good earnest. —

曼密留诗	是的,你若高兴,
	爸爸。
里杭底斯	你得有我这蓬松的顶盖
	和上面的杈叉,才能完全跟我像:
	可是人家说我们跟两个鸡子儿
	一般;那是娘儿们恁说的,她们
	什么都说得出:但她们变化无常,
	像黑布涂上了颜色,像风,像水,
	诡谲得像那把他自己的和我的钱
	不分界限的人儿所心愿的骰子般
	变幻不测,可是如果说这孩子
	跟我像,却不错。来吧,书僮爵士,
	将你那天蓝眼睛睃着我:小捣蛋!
	最最心爱的!我的心肝宝贝儿!
	你妈会那样吗?——这事可能吗?——爱好啊!
	你热切的激发把衷心戳了一刀:
	人们认为不可能的事情你使它
	变得有可能,你跟魂梦通来往;——
	这怎么可能?——你跟虚幻相协作,
	与空虚成双作对:那么,你跟
	有些个东西相联结是极可信了;
	而你果然那么样,超越了权限,
	我且已见到,于是我头脑发昏,
	前额麻木。
包列齐倪思	西西利亚在想什么?
候妙霓	他似乎有点不自在。
包列齐倪思	怎样,王兄?
	你觉得怎样?好吗,王兄?
候妙霓	你看来
	好像在蹙额颦眉,心里极不安:
	有什么烦恼事,王夫?
里杭底斯	没有,说实话。

How sometimes nature will betray its folly,
Its tenderness, and make itself a pastime
To harder bosoms! Looking on the lines
Of my boy's face, methoughts I did recoil
Twenty-three years; and saw myself unbreech'd,
In my green velvet coat; my dagger muzzled,
Lest it should bite its master, and so prove,
As ornaments oft do, too dangerous.
How like, methought, I then was to this kernel,
This squash, this gentleman. — Mine honest friend,
Will you take eggs for money?
Mamillius No, my lord, I'll fight.
Leontes You will? Why, happy man be 's dole! — My brother,
Are you so fond of your young prince as we
Do seem to be of ours?
Polixenes If at home, sir,
He's all my exercise, my mirth, my matter:
Now my sworn friend, and then mine enemy;
My parasite, my soldier, statesman, all:
He makes a July's day short as December;
And with his varying childness cures in me
Thoughts that would thick my blood.
Leontes So stands this squire
Offic'd with me. We two will walk, my lord,
And leave you to your graver steps. — Hermione,
How thou lov'st us show in our brother's welcome;
Let what is dear in Sicily be cheap:
Next to thyself and my young rover, he's
Apparent to my heart.
Hermione If you would seek us,

　　　　　　　一个人有时多么会把他的愚蠢,
　　　　　　　那柔和恺悌的温情,暴露出来,
　　　　　　　供冷酷的旁人作嬉笑之资!望着
　　　　　　　我孩子的相貌,我想我退回到了
　　　　　　　二十三年前,见自己穿着短裤,
　　　　　　　上身是绿丝绒大衣,短剑在鞘里,
　　　　　　　唯恐它要咬主人,像一切装饰品
　　　　　　　那样,往往会变得太危险:我想来,
　　　　　　　那时节我多么像这小果仁儿,
　　　　　　　这嫩豌豆荚,这仁兄。我可敬的朋友,
　　　　　　　有人欺骗你,你将怎样对付他?
曼密留诗　　不行,爸爸,我跟他打架。
里杭底斯　　　　　　　　你会打?
　　　　　　　哎也,祝愿他一生都幸福!王兄,
　　　　　　　您也这么爱您的年轻王子吗,
　　　　　　　跟我们一样?
包列齐倪思　　　　　若是在家里,王兄,
　　　　　　　他是我经常的事务,欢笑之因,
　　　　　　　一本正经的主儿,一会儿是刎颈交,
　　　　　　　一会儿变成了仇人;是我的清客,
　　　　　　　兵丁,冢宰,这一切都兼而有之:
　　　　　　　他叫一个七月天短得像冬日,
　　　　　　　将他那变化多端的孩子劲儿,
　　　　　　　医好我会使血液凝滞的忧思。
里杭底斯　　这相好跟我之间便这样。我们
　　　　　　　父子俩将走开,王兄,离您去徜徉
　　　　　　　自在。候妙霓,对我们王兄的欢迎里,
　　　　　　　表示你怎样爱我们:我们西西利
　　　　　　　宝岛的珍奇要丝毫不吝地付与,
　　　　　　　除了你自己和我这小捣蛋,他是
　　　　　　　最在我心坎上的人。
候妙霓　　　　　　　你要找我们,

We are yours i' the garden. Shall 's attend you there?
Leontes To your own bents dispose you; you'll be found,
Be you beneath the sky. [*Aside.*] I am angling now,
Though you perceive me not how I give line.
Go to, go to!
How she holds up the neb, the bill to him!
And arms her with the boldness of a wife
To her allowing husband!
        [*Exeunt* Polixenes, Hermione, *and* Attendants.]
            Gone already!
Inch-thick, knee-deep, o'er head and ears a fork'd one! —
Go, play, boy, play; — thy mother plays, and I
Play too; but so disgrac'd a part, whose issue
Will hiss me to my grave; contempt and clamour
Will be my knell. — Go, play, boy, play. — There have been,
Or I am much deceiv'd, cuckolds ere now;
And many a man there is, even at this present,
Now while I speak this, holds his wife by the arm
That little thinks she has been sluic'd in his absence,
And his pond fish'd by his next neighbour, by
Sir Smile, his neighbour; nay, there's comfort in't,
Whiles other men have gates, and those gates open'd,
As mine, against their will; should all despair
That hath revolted wives, the tenth of mankind
Would hang themselves. Physic for't there's none;
It is a bawdy planet, that will strike
Where 'tis predominant; and 'tis powerful, think it,
From east, west, north, and south; be it concluded,

可到花园里去寻:我们在那里
等你吧?

里杭底斯 你们爱怎样,随你们的便:
只要在青天下面,总能找得到。——
[旁白]我此刻在垂钓,虽然你们不见我
在如何宽放着纶丝。妙事,妙事!
瞧吧,她怎样在引颈伸喙挨着他!
像个妻子一般地大胆,面向着
听任她抚摩的丈夫!

　　　　　　[包列齐倪思、候妙霓与从人等同下。
　　　　　　已经走了!
有寸把来粗,满头满脑生着角!
去玩,孩子,去玩吧;你妈在玩儿,
我也在玩儿,不过玩得太丢脸,
那结果会嘘我进坟墓:鄙蔑和喧噪
将是我的丧钟。去玩,孩子,去玩吧。
以前已有过老婆偷汉的丈夫,
否则我这话大大错误了;而现在,
就在此刻,正当我说话的时分,
好些个丈夫抓着他妻子的胳膊,
没想到当他不在时,闸门曾打开,
水流涌进来汩没他妻子,他家
池塘里被紧邻微笑爵士垂钓过:
不光我,旁人也有门,跟我的一样,
违着他们的意愿被人家打开来——
这里边还有点安慰。如果丈夫们
妻子不贞洁都悲观绝望,人类
有十分之一要上吊。没有药来救;
这是颗主淫猥的星宿,有它当顶,
就会将祸殃下降到人间;我忖来
它的威力强,从东西南北四面来:
总之,没东西能够替血肉之躯

No barricado for a belly: know't;
It will let in and out the enemy
With bag and baggage. Many thousand of us
Have the disease, and feel't not. — How now, boy!
Mamillius I am like you, they say.
Leontes   Why, that's some comfort. —
What! Camillo there?
Camillo Ay, my good lord.
Leontes Go play, Mamillius; thou'rt an honest man. —
                              [*Exit* Mamillius.]
Camillo, this great sir will yet stay longer.
Camillo You had much ado to make his anchor hold:
When you cast out, it still came home.
Leontes   Didst note it?
Camillo He would not stay at your petitions; made
His business more material.
Leontes   Didst perceive it? —
[*Aside.*] They're here with me already; whispering,
    rounding,
Sicilia is a so-forth. 'Tis far gone
When I shall gust it last. — How came't, Camillo,
That he did stay?
Camillo   At the good queen's entreaty.
Leontes At the queen's be't: *good* should be pertinent;
But so it is, it is not. Was this taken
By any understanding pate but thine?
For thy conceit is soaking, will draw in
More than the common blocks: — not noted, is't,
But of the finer natures? by some severals
Of head-piece extraordinary? lower messes

　　　　　　　当防寨:我知道;人的身躯血肉
　　　　　　　会给那祸殃带同着灾危困厄
　　　　　　　进进出出无阻拦。我们好几千人
　　　　　　　都害着这毛病,可是自己不知道。
　　　　　　　孩子,怎么了?
曼密留诗　　　　　　　他们说我跟你一个样。
里杭底斯　哎也,那倒是有一点安慰。什么?
　　　　　　　喀米罗在那里?
喀　米　罗　　　　　　是哟,我的好主公。
里杭底斯　去玩,曼密留诗;你是个有荣誉的人。

　　　　　　　　　　　　　　　　　[曼密留诗下。
　　　　　　　喀米罗,这位大君子还要待下去。
喀　米　罗　您把他的锚抛定倒费了手续:
　　　　　　　您把它抛出去,它没有带住又回来了。
里杭底斯　你注意到了这个吗?
喀　米　罗　　　　　　您请,他不留;
　　　　　　　认为他乡邦的事务更重要。
里杭底斯　　　　　　　　　你见到?
　　　　　　　[旁白]他们已经在做这鬼样来嘲弄我,
　　　　　　　窃窃耳语道,"西西利亚乃是个——"
　　　　　　　如此这般。事态已经很严重了,
　　　　　　　最后我才发现它。怎么会,喀米罗,
　　　　　　　他肯留下来?
喀　米　罗　　　　　好王后娘娘请了他。
里杭底斯　王后娘娘请了他,不错:那"好"字
　　　　　　　该用得适当;但碰巧并不如此。
　　　　　　　这可是除了你,另有其他的明眼人
　　　　　　　也这般了解? 因为你机灵敏捷;
　　　　　　　瞧到的比普通木头脑袋要多:
　　　　　　　没人能见到,是不是,只除了聪明
　　　　　　　伶俐人? 只几个脑瓜卓越超群的?
　　　　　　　地位差一点的人也许对这事情

Perchance are to this business purblind? say.
Camillo Business, my lord! I think most understand
Bohemia stays here longer.
Leontes   Ha!
Camillo   Stays here longer.
Leontes Ay, but why?
Camillo To satisfy your highness, and the entreaties
Of our most gracious mistress.
Leontes   *Satisfy*
Th' entreaties of your mistress! — *satisfy*! —
Let that suffice. I have trusted thee, Camillo,
With all the nearest things to my heart, as well
My chamber-councils, wherein, priest-like, thou
Hast cleans'd my bosom; I from thee departed
Thy penitent reform'd: but we have been
Deceiv'd in thy integrity, deceiv'd
In that which seems so.
Camillo   Be it forbid, my lord!
Leontes To bide upon't, — thou art not honest; or,
If thou inclin'st that way, thou art a coward,
Which hoxes honesty behind, restraining
From course requir'd; or else thou must be counted
A servant grafted in my serious trust,
And therein negligent; or else a fool
That seest a game play'd home, the rich stake drawn,
And tak'st it all for jest.
Camillo   My gracious lord,
I may be negligent, foolish, and fearful;
In every one of these no man is free,
But that his negligence, his folly, fear,
Among the infinite doings of the world,
Sometime puts forth: in your affairs, my lord,
If ever I were wilful-negligent,
It was my folly; if industriously

              完全看不到？假定说。
喀 米 罗   事情,吾主!
              我想多数人了解到波希米亚王
              还要待下去。
里杭底斯   嘻!
喀 米 罗   还是要待下去。
里杭底斯   是的,可是为什么?
喀 米 罗   为满足御驾,和我们最尊贵的椒房
              娘娘的恳请。
里杭底斯   满足你娘娘的恳请!
              满足!算了吧。我信托给了你,喀米罗,
              我最贴心的一切事,和我的私虑,
              在这些事情上头,跟牧师一般,
              你曾经涤荡过我这胸怀;我向你
              告别时,便是你已然悛改的悔罪者;
              但我们对你的忠诚无疵蒙了骗,
              对你的外貌受了欺。
喀 米 罗   吾主,天不容!
里杭底斯   再来说一遍,你对我不诚实;或者,
              你若有那样的倾向,便是个懦夫,
              从背后切断诚实的腿筋,使它
              不得向前行;若不然,你便给当作
              是个我完全推心置腹的从者,
              而却淡漠不关心;或者被当作
              是个大傻瓜,见一场认真的赌赛,
              一大笔注子已到手,却把它当玩笑。
喀 米 罗   尊崇的吾主,我也许疏虞、拙笨、
              懦怯;没有人对这些能完全不犯,
              总有些他的疏误、愚拙和畏葸,
              从世上无数的行止间显露出来。
              在您的事务中,吾主,假使我曾经
              故意怠慢过,那就是我的愚蠢;

I play'd the fool, it was my negligence,
Not weighing well the end; if ever fearful
To do a thing, where I the issue doubted,
Whereof the execution did cry out
Against the non-performance, 'twas a fear
Which oft affects the wisest: these, my lord,
Are such allow'd infirmities that honesty
Is never free of. But, beseech your grace,
Be plainer with me; let me know my trespass
By its own visage: if I then deny it,
'Tis none of mine.
Leontes   Have not you seen, Camillo, —
But that's past doubt: you have, or your eye-glass
Is thicker than a cuckold's horn, — or heard, —
For, to a vision so apparent, rumour
Cannot be mute, — or thought, — for cogitation
Resides not in that man that does not think it, —
My wife is slippery? If thou wilt confess, —
Or else be impudently negative,
To have nor eyes nor ears nor thought, — then say
My wife's a hobby-horse; deserves a name
As rank as any flax-wench that puts to
Before her troth-plight: say't and justify't.
Camillo   I would not be a stander-by to hear
My sovereign mistress clouded so, without
My present vengeance taken: 'shrew my heart,
You never spoke what did become you less
Than this; which to reiterate were sin
As deep as that, though true.
Leontes   Is whispering nothing?

　　　　　　　　我若殷勤去傻干,那是我的疏忽,
　　　　　　　　没有好好考虑过如何去达到
　　　　　　　　那结局;我假使曾害怕去做某件事,
　　　　　　　　因为怀疑到后果,后来做它时
　　　　　　　　却证明原来不该做,那样的胆怯
　　　　　　　　乃是智者所常有的;这些,吾主,
　　　　　　　　是可以承认的缺点,乃光荣之辈
　　　　　　　　所决计难免的。但是,求吾主宸聪,
　　　　　　　　请对我坦率些;容我知道我自己
　　　　　　　　罪戾的真面目;您说了我若否认它,
　　　　　　　　它就不是我的了。
里杭底斯　　　　　　　　你没有看见吗,
　　　　　　　　喀米罗,——但那是毫无疑问的;你见到,
　　　　　　　　除非你那双瞳仁比老婆偷汉
　　　　　　　　丈夫的角觖还黯昧不明,——或听到,——
　　　　　　　　因为对这样显而易见的事情,
　　　　　　　　传闻不会去缄默,——或想到,——因为
　　　　　　　　不想这事的那人头脑里没思想,——
　　　　　　　　我妻子不贞吗?你若肯承认事实,——
　　　　　　　　否则便得不知羞耻地去否认
　　　　　　　　你有眼睛或耳朵或思想,——便得说
　　　　　　　　我妻子是个荡妇;她该有个丑名
　　　　　　　　跟那还没有订婚就和人不清
　　　　　　　　不白的织麻姑娘一样臭:讲出来,
　　　　　　　　证实我这话。
喀　米　罗　　　　　　　　我不会做个旁观者,
　　　　　　　　听到明君的后妃如此被云翳,
　　　　　　　　而不立即去报复:当真说,您讲话
　　　　　　　　从没有比这个跟您更加不相称;
　　　　　　　　去重复您这话便是去违犯罪过
　　　　　　　　跟您所谴咎的一般深,假定它真的话。
里杭底斯　窃窃的耳语难道不算一回事?

Is leaning cheek to cheek? is meeting noses?
Kissing with inside lip? Stopping the career
Of laughter with a sigh? — a note infallible
Of breaking honesty; — horsing foot on foot?
Skulking in corners? wishing clocks more swift;
Hours, minutes; noon, midnight? and all eyes
Blind with the pin and web but theirs, theirs only,
That would unseen be wicked? — is this nothing?
Why, then the world and all that's in't is nothing;
The covering sky is nothing; Bohemia nothing;
My is nothing; nor nothing have these nothings,
If this be nothing.
Camillo   Good my lord, be cur'd
Of this diseas'd opinion, and betimes;
For 'tis most dangerous.
Leontes   Say it be, 'tis true.
Camillo No, no, my lord.
Leontes   It is; you lie, you lie:
I say thou liest, Camillo, and I hate thee;
Pronounce thee a gross lout, a mindless slave;
Or else a hovering temporizer, that
Canst with thine eyes at once see good and evil,
Inclining to them both. — Were my wife's liver
Infected as her life, she would not live
The running of one glass.
Camillo   Who does infect her?
Leontes Why, he that wears her like her medal, hanging
About his neck, Bohemia: who — if I
Had servants true about me, that bare eyes

脸靠着脸儿,鼻子碰鼻子,都不算?
用嘴唇内膜来亲吻也不算?欢笑
竞赛中停下来,来声叹息又如何?——
贞操破裂的毫无疑问的凭证,——
骑马般脚碰在脚上怎么样?躲到
角落里?愿意钟上的时间快些走?
愿钟点,分钟,中午,子夜都快过?
愿人家眼睛都长白内障,只除了
他们自己的,以便去作恶没人见?
这些都不算一回事?那么,这整个
世界同其中的一切也都全不算;
上面覆盖的青天也不算一回事;
波希米亚也不算;我妻子也不算;
若是这个也不算,一切空,万事空。

喀米罗 尊崇的吾主,请舍弃这违和的见解,
而且请及时;因为它非常危险。

里杭底斯 我的话是真的,你说的确如此吧。

喀米罗 不对,不对,吾主。

里杭底斯 是对的;你撒谎,
撒谎:我说你撒谎,喀米罗,我恨你;
宣称你自己是个愚蠢的乡下佬,
是个呆木的伧夫,再不然便是个
踌躇不决、应顺时势的骑墙派,
眼睛望出来不分甚好歹,倾向好
也倾向于坏:若是我妻子的肝
和她的生命一样也染得有污毒,
她不得活过一沙漏那么久。

喀米罗 是谁
把她染污了?

里杭底斯 哎也,那家伙佩戴她
像挂在他颈上的她的像牌一般,
是波希米亚:我左右若是有忠仆,

To see alike mine honour as their profits,
Their own particular thrifts,—they would do that
Which should undo more doing: ay, and thou,
His cupbearer,—whom I from meaner form
Have bench'd and rear'd to worship; who mayst see,
Plainly as heaven sees earth and earth sees heaven,
How I am galled,—mightst bespice a cup,
To give mine enemy a lasting wink;
Which draught to me were cordial.

Camillo Sir, my lord,
I could do this; and that with no rash potion,
But with a ling'ring dram, that should not work
Maliciously like poison: but I cannot
Believe this crack to be in my dread mistress,
So sovereignly being honourable.
I have lov'd thee,—

Leontes Make that thy question, and go rot!
Dost think I am so muddy, so unsettled,
To appoint myself in this vexation; sully
The purity and whiteness of my sheets,—
Which to preserve is sleep; which being spotted
Is goads, thorns, nettles, tails of wasps;
Give scandal to the blood o' the prince, my son,—
Who I do think is mine, and love as mine,—
Without ripe moving to't?—Would I do this?
Could man so blench?

Camillo I must believe you, sir:
I do; and will fetch off Bohemia for't;
Provided that, when he's remov'd, your highness
Will take again your queen as yours at first,
Even for your son's sake; and thereby for sealing

　　　　　　各各生得有眼睛能望见他们
　　　　　　本身的利益，也能顾到我的荣誉，
　　　　　　他们会做件事扑灭那丑行的重演：
　　　　　　不错，而你，他的引觞者，——我把你
　　　　　　从低贱的位置上已经擢升到尊荣，
　　　　　　你可以分明看到，如天之见地，
　　　　　　如地之见天，我怎样激愤而恼怒，——
　　　　　　你可以在他杯中加香料一撮，
　　　　　　给我的仇家一次持久的长闭目；
　　　　　　那个一干杯将使我何等兴奋。

喀　米　罗　君王，吾主，我可以奉命，而那却
　　　　　　不用急性的剂量，只须使一服
　　　　　　文火徐煎的恶药，它将不像那
　　　　　　凶暴的烈毒；可是我不能听信
　　　　　　我肃敬的坤仪有此罅隙，她懿范
　　　　　　煌煌，这么样卓越。我爱主心切，——

里杭底斯　　谈那个做什么，滚蛋！你以为我是
　　　　　　这么样激动，这么样昏乱，竟自己
　　　　　　去找这烦恼；去污染我枕席的清白，
　　　　　　那洁净保存着使我有安眠，玷污了
　　　　　　是刺棒、荆棘、荨麻、胡蜂的尾巴？
　　　　　　没充分理由，兀自将污辱加给
　　　　　　储君我儿的血统吗？他，我相信
　　　　　　是我儿，且当作自己的亲生来抚爱，
　　　　　　我会做这个吗？人能这般自甘
　　　　　　误入歧途吗？

喀　米　罗　　　　　　　我不能不信您，吾主：
　　　　　　我信了；且将为此把波希米亚
　　　　　　解决掉；不过他倘使被铡除以后，
　　　　　　您将只是为太子殿下的缘故，
　　　　　　依然对中宫王后要爱好如初；
　　　　　　那样便能封闭住胜朝所相熟

The injury of tongues in courts and kingdoms
Known and allied to yours.
Leontes   Thou dost advise me
Even so as I mine own course have set down:
I'll give no blemish to her honour, none.
Camillo   My lord,
Go then; and with a countenance as clear
As friendship wears at feasts, keep with Bohemia
And with your queen: I am his cupbearer.
If from me he have wholesome beverage,
Account me not your servant.
Leontes   This is all:
Do't, and thou hast the one-half of my heart;
Do't not, thou splitt'st thine own.
Camillo   I'll do't, my lord.
Leontes   I will seem friendly, as thou hast advis'd me.
                                                  [*Exit.*]

Camillo   O miserable lady!—But, for me,
What case stand I in? I must be the poisoner
Of good Polixenes: and my ground to do't
Is the obedience to a master; one
Who, in rebellion with himself, will have
All that are his so too.—To do this deed,
Promotion follows: if I could find example
Of thousands that had struck anointed kings
And flourish'd after, I'd not do't; but since
Nor brass, nor stone, nor parchment, bears not one,
Let villainy itself forswear't. I must
Forsake the court: to do't, or no, is certain
To me a break-neck. Happy star reign now!
Here comes Bohemia.
                     [*Enter* Polixenes.]

且有关宫廷上、王国里饶舌之患。
里杭底斯 你这番进言正跟我自己所已定
将采取的行止相符:我将不玷污
她的声名,我决不。
喀 米 罗 吾主,请去吧;
以宴会时节笑对宾朋的容颜
对着波希米亚,也对着您王后。
我为他奉觞;他从我手里如果有
俾益健康的酒浆,莫把我当作
您的臣仆。
里杭底斯 总说一句话:做了它,
你就占有了我半颗心儿;不做,
你将裂开了你的。
喀 米 罗 我会做,吾主。
里杭底斯 我将显得亲和,如你所劝说的。 [下。
喀 米 罗 啊,好悲惨的娘娘!但是我自己
可站在怎样的地位?我得毒死
有德的包列齐倪思;而我去这样做,
原因是为了要服从一个主子;
一位君王,反叛着自己,要求他
自己的臣民也都对他去反叛。
做了这件事马上可升迁。我假使
能找到成千的先例,把曾被香油
涂首的君王杀死的凶手们嗣后
都腾达飞黄,我也决不做;但既然
从未有铜碑,也从无石刻,也从无
羊皮,铸镌铭记得有一个成例,
就让邪恶本身也发誓不去做。
我定得离开这朝廷:做它,或不做,
对我都是件危险事。让福星高照!
波希米亚已到来。

[包列齐倪思上。

Polixenes   This is strange! methinks
My favour here begins to warp. Not speak? —
Good-day, Camillo.
Camillo   Hail, most royal sir!
Polixenes What is the news i' the court?
Camillo   None rare, my lord.
Polixenes The king hath on him such a countenance
As he had lost some province, and a region
Lov'd as he loves himself; even now I met him
With customary compliment; when he,
Wafting his eyes to the contrary, and falling
A lip of much contempt, speeds from me;
So leaves me to consider what is breeding
That changes thus his manners.
Camillo I dare not know, my lord.
Polixenes How! *dare not*! do not. Do you know, and dare not
Be intelligent to me? 'Tis thereabouts;
For, to yourself, what you do know, you must,
And cannot say, you dare not. Good Camillo,
Your chang'd complexions are to me a mirror
Which shows me mine chang'd too; for I must be
A party in this alteration, finding
Myself thus alter'd with't.
Camillo   There is a sickness
Which puts some of us in distemper; but
I cannot name the disease; and it is caught
Of you that yet are well.
Polixenes   How! caught of me!
Make me not sighted like the basilisk:
I have look'd on thousands who have sped the better

包列齐倪思　　　　　　　　这真奇怪了:
看来我在此受欢迎开始在萎缩。
不做声?——你好,喀米罗。

喀 米 罗　　　　　　　　　　　祝福运昌隆,
至尊的宾王!

包列齐倪思　　　　朝廷上有什么消息?

喀 米 罗　没甚么出奇的新闻,宾王。

包列齐倪思　　　　　　　　　　王兄
脸上满都是秋霜,仿如他失去了
某个省,他自己心爱的一大片地区:
只刚才我和他相见,致惯常的问候,
谁知他转眼望他方,嘴唇一撇
表鄙蔑,急匆匆舍我而去,留我
去筹思发生了什么事端,致使他
丰仪举止如此变。

喀 米 罗　　　　　　　我不敢知道,宾王。

包列齐倪思　怎么!不敢?不知道?你是知道了,
而不敢对我明言吗?是那个意思:
因为,对于你自己,你所知道的
你一定知道,你可不能说你不敢。
喀米罗贤卿,你面容变色对我
是一面镜子,那显示我也变了色;
因为我一定跟这变动有关系,
见到自己也跟着一起有变动。

喀 米 罗　有一种疾病使我们有些人精神
不宁;可是我讲不出那叫什么病,
而这是因您所传染上的,然而您
却还无恙。

包列齐倪思　　　　　　怎么!是因我所传染?
莫以为我有蛇怪般放毒的眼睛:
我曾经目注过的人成千上万,
他们因给我望见而格外顺遂,

By my regard, but kill'd none so. Camillo, —
As you are certainly a gentleman, thereto
Clerk-like, experienc'd, which no less adorns
Our gentry than our parents' noble names,
In whose success we are gentle, — I beseech you,
If you know aught which does behove my knowledge
Thereof to be inform'd, imprison't not
In ignorant concealment.

Camillo   I may not answer.

Polixenes   A sickness caught of me, and yet I well!
I must be answer'd. — Dost thou hear, Camillo,
I conjure thee, by all the parts of man
Which honour does acknowledge, — whereof the least
Is not this suit of mine, — that thou declare
What incidency thou dost guess of harm
Is creeping toward me; how far off, how near;
Which way to be prevented, if to be;
If not, how best to bear it.

Camillo   Sir, I will tell you;
Since I am charg'd in honour, and by him
That I think honourable: therefore mark my counsel,
Which must be ev'n as swiftly follow'd as
I mean to utter it, or both yourself and me
Cry *lost*, and so goodnight!

Polixenes   On, good Camillo.

Camillo   I am appointed him to murder you.

Polixenes   By whom, Camillo?

Camillo   By the king.

Polixenes   For what?

Camillo   He thinks, nay, with all confidence he swears,
As he had seen't or been an instrument

　　　　　　　却从无经我一看而杀死的。喀米罗，——
　　　　　　　既然你定必是位士君子，又加
　　　　　　　学士般博闻多见，这学养修能
　　　　　　　对于我们的品位添光彩，不减如
　　　　　　　我们父母所传给的高名，我们
　　　　　　　因继承他们而身居贵胄，——我请你，
　　　　　　　如果你知道什么事有利于我
　　　　　　　所闻见而得知，请莫把它闭锁着，
　　　　　　　隐藏于声言不知中。
喀 米 罗　　　　　　　　　　我不便回答。
包列齐倪思　一场病是因我传染的，而我却无恙！
　　　　　　　你务必要回答。听到没有，喀米罗；
　　　　　　　我向你恳请，凭荣誉所承认、一个人
　　　　　　　所能有的一切高义，——我这请求
　　　　　　　可不是其中最微不足道的，——请你
　　　　　　　明告我，你猜想有什么临头祸害
　　　　　　　正在向着我迫近；有多远，多近；
　　　　　　　怎样去防避，假如能防避的话；
　　　　　　　若不能避免，如何去尽量忍受。
喀 米 罗　　宾王，我来告诉您；既然我被他
　　　　　　　以荣誉相责，而我想他又是荣誉的。
　　　　　　　所以，请听我的劝告，这个您得
　　　　　　　立刻就去做，正如我马上要来说，
　　　　　　　否则您与我便得叫"完了"，跟着
　　　　　　　就完事大吉！
包列齐倪思　　　　　　　　讲下去，喀米罗贤卿。
喀 米 罗　　我被指派来凶杀您。
包列齐倪思　　　　　　　　谁派的，喀米罗？
喀 米 罗　　王上。
包列齐倪思　　　　为什么？
喀 米 罗　　　　　　　　他以为，不是，他完全
　　　　　　　自信且发誓，仿佛他亲眼见到过，

To vice you to't, that you have touch'd his queen
Forbiddenly.
Polixenes   O, then my best blood turn
To an infected jelly, and my name
Be yok'd with his that did betray the best!
Turn then my freshest reputation to
A savour that may strike the dullest nostril
Where I arrive, and my approach be shunn'd,
Nay, hated too, worse than the great'st infection
That e'er was heard or read!
Camillo   Swear his thought over
By each particular star in heaven and
By all their influences, you may as well
Forbid the sea for to obey the moon
As, or by oath remove, or counsel shake
The fabric of his folly, whose foundation
Is pil'd upon his faith, and will continue
The standing of his body.
Polixenes   How should this grow?
Camillo   I know not: but I am sure 'tis safer to
Avoid what's grown than question how 'tis born.
If, therefore you dare trust my honesty, —
That lies enclosèd in this trunk, which you
Shall bear along impawn'd, — away to-night.
Your followers I will whisper to the business;
And will, by twos and threes, at several posterns,
Clear them o' the city: for myself, I'll put
My fortunes to your service, which are here
By this discovery lost. Be not uncertain;
For, by the honour of my parents, I
Have utter'd truth: which if you seek to prove,

或者他自己还是个机关把您
扭捩到如此，说您非法地碰了
他王后。
包列齐倪思　　　　　啊，那样时让我的血液
中毒而凝结成冻，让我的名字
跟那出卖至善者的关联在一起！
那样时让我的芳名变恶臭，我行踪
所至，即令最迟钝的鼻子也嗅到；
而我的到来将遭到远避，还不止，
还要被痛恨，更甚于人们所听说
或读到的最大的瘟疫！
喀　米　罗　　　　　　　　您可凭天上
每一颗星辰和它们所有的气数
来发誓，以期制服他的想法，那好比
在禁止海洋去服从月亮，如果您
想用起誓去消除，或劝告去动摇，
他那座愚蠢之宫的建筑，那基础
乃奠在他信念之上，且将继续
存在着，只要他一朝身躯还存在。
包列齐倪思　这是怎样产生的？
喀　米　罗　　　　　　　那我可不知道：
可是我确信去避免已成的要比
去询问它如何产生来得安全。
若因此您敢信任我胸中的诚实，
可将我带去作人质，今夜就走！
您的从者们我会轻声关照好
去从事，把他们两两三三放出
不同的城墙侧门外。至于我自己，
我将把区区命运供侍奉，那在此
一待事情明白就完了。莫犹豫；
因为，凭我父母的荣名，我说的
是真话，这个，您若想证实，我却

I dare not stand by; nor shall you be safer
Than one condemn'd by the king's own mouth, thereon
His execution sworn.
Polixenes   I do believe thee;
I saw his heart in his face. Give me thy hand;
Be pilot to me, and thy places shall
Still neighbour mine. My ships are ready, and
My people did expect my hence departure
Two days ago. — This jealousy
Is for a precious creature: as she's rare,
Must it be great; and, as his person's mighty,
Must it be violent; and as he does conceive
He is dishonour'd by a man which ever
Profess'd to him, why, his revenges must
In that be made more bitter. Fear o'ershades me;
Good expedition be my friend, and comfort
The gracious queen, part of this theme, but nothing
Of his ill-ta'en suspicion! Come, Camillo;
I will respect thee as a father, if
Thou bear'st my life off hence: let us avoid.
Camillo   It is in mine authority to command
The keys of all the posterns: please your highness
To take the urgent hour: come, sir, away.

[Exeunt.]

	不敢来帮同；您将不会比王上 矢口亲判死罪的人犯较安全。
包列齐倪思	我相信你的话：我见他心思露在 他脸上。把手伸给我：为我当艄公， 你前途地位将永远跟我相邻接。 我的船舶已有备，船上人指望我 两天前就离开。这嫉妒是为一位 宝贵的人儿：她既然珍奇绝妙， 那妒忌必然厉害，而他既然是 权位极君王，那忌妒定必猛烈， 且他既然以为他被那对于他 永矢情义的友人将荣名玷辱， 哎也，他在那上头的报复一定是 因而更加要严酷。恐惧阴翳着我： 愿我的速即离去能对我朋友般 有利，又能安慰那温馨的王后， 他想到我时不能不想到她，但她 还没有成为他无稽的怀疑的对象！ 来啊，喀米罗；你若能拯救我性命 离开这里，我将尊你如父亲： 让我们就走。
喀 米 罗	管所有边门上的钥匙， 是在我职权范围之内：请君主 趁紧急就行吧。来吧，明君，去来！

〔同下。

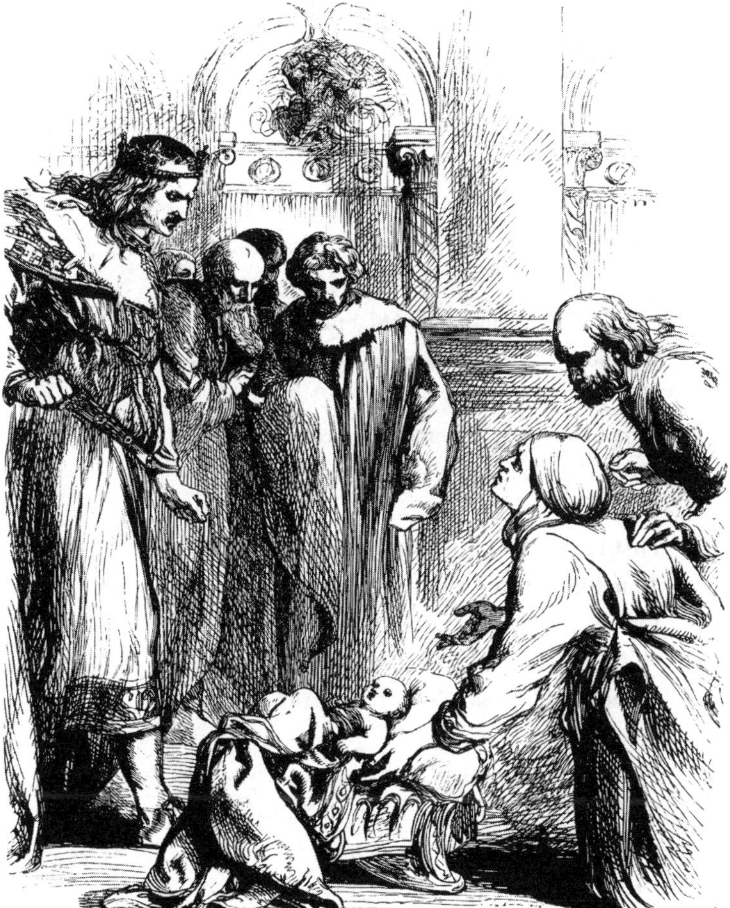

ACT II.

SCENE I. Sicilia. A Room in *the Palace*.

[*Enter* Hermione, Mamillius, *and* Ladies.]
Hermione　Take the boy to you; he so troubles me,
'Tis past enduring.
First Lady　　　　Come, my gracious lord,
Shall I be your playfellow?
Mamillius　　　　　　　No, I'll none of you.
First Lady　Why, my sweet lord?
Mamillius　You'll kiss me hard, and speak to me as if
I were a baby still. —[*To* Second Lady.] I love you better.
Second Lady　And why so, my lord?
Mamillius　　　　　　　　Not for because
Your brows are blacker; yet black brows, they say,
Become some women best; so that there be not
Too much hair there, but in a semicircle
Or a half-moon made with a pen.
Second Lady　　　　　Who taught you this?
Mamillius　I learn'd it out of women's faces. —Pray now,
What colour are your eyebrows?

第 二 幕

第 一 景

[西西利亚。王宫一室]
[候妙霓、曼密留诗与贵妇数人上。

候 妙 霓 你们把孩子来领去;他这么跟我
找麻烦,叫人受不了。
贵 妇 甲 来吧,小殿下,
我和你一起玩好吗?
曼 密 留 诗 不,不跟你玩。
贵 妇 甲 为什么,好殿下?
曼 密 留 诗 你会死劲吻我的脸儿,且跟我
说话时还当我是个娃娃。我乐意
跟你在一起。
贵 妇 乙 为什么,小殿下?
曼 密 留 诗 不是
因为你的眉毛要黑一些;不过
黑眉毛,他们说,跟有些女人很合适,
只要那里毛长得不太密,而是
长成半圆形,或用笔画成半月形。
贵 妇 乙 谁教你这个的?
曼 密 留 诗 我是从女人脸上
学来的。请问,你眉毛是什么颜色?

First Lady   Blue, my lord.
Mamillius   Nay, that's a mock: I have seen a lady's nose
That has been blue, but not her eyebrows.
First Lady   Hark ye:
The queen your mother rounds apace. We shall
Present our services to a fine new prince
One of these days; and then you'd wanton with us,
If we would have you.
Second Lady   She is spread of late
Into a goodly bulk: good time encounter her!
Hermione   What wisdom stirs amongst you? Come,
    sir, now
I am for you again: pray you sit by us,
And tell 's a tale.
Mamillius   Merry or sad shall 't be?
Hermione   As merry as you will.
Mamillius   A sad tale's best for winter. I have one
Of sprites and goblins.
Hermione   Let's have that, good sir.
Come on, sit down; — come on, and do your best
To fright me with your sprites: you're powerful at it.
Mamillius   There was a man, —
Hermione   Nay, come, sit down: then on.
Mamillius   Dwelt by a churchyard: — I will tell it softly;
Yond crickets shall not hear it.
Hermione   Come on then,
And give 't me in mine ear.
    [*Enter* Leontes, Antigonus, Lords, *and others.*]
Leontes   Was he met there? his train? Camillo with him?
First Lord   Behind the tuft of pines I met them; never
Saw I men scour so on their way: I ey'd them

贵　妇　甲	青的,小殿下。
曼密留诗	不对,那是在开玩笑:
	我见过有个夫人的鼻子是青的,
	但是她眉毛不青。
贵　妇　乙	你且听我说;
	王后你妈妈肚子快大了:我们
	过不久就要侍候位新的王子了;
	那时节你才要跟我们玩呢,假使
	我们肯和你玩的话。
贵　妇　甲	她最近腰身
	宽大了好多:祝贺她喜事来临!
候　妙　霓	你们在逗什么巧?过来,小王爷,
	现在我好跟你在一起了:听我说,
	坐在我身旁,讲个故事来听吧。
曼密留诗	故事要快乐的,悲伤的?
候　妙　霓	越快乐越好。
曼密留诗	悲伤的故事冬天讲最好。我有个
	说幽灵鬼怪的。
候　妙　霓	我们就听它吧,好王爷。
	来吧,坐下了:来吧,把你的幽灵
	尽量来吓我;做那个你很能干。
曼密留诗	从前有个人,——
候　妙　霓	别那样,来,坐下来说。
曼密留诗	住在礼拜堂墓园旁。我要轻声些;
	不给那里的蟋蟀们听到。
候　妙　霓	那来吧,
	凑到我耳朵边讲。
	〔里杭底斯、安铁冈纳施、贵人数人与其他人等上。〕
里杭底斯	那里你碰到他的吗?他的随从们?
	喀米罗和他一起?
贵　人　甲	在一丛松树后
	我碰到他们:我从未见人急匆匆

Even to their ships.
Leontes　　　　　How bles'd am I
In my just censure, in my true opinion! —
Alack, for lesser knowledge! — How accurs'd
In being so blest! — There may be in the cup
A spider steep'd, and one may drink, depart,
And yet partake no venom; for his knowledge
Is not infected; but if one present
The abhorr'd ingredient to his eye, make known
How he hath drunk, he cracks his gorge, his sides,
With violent hefts; — I have drunk, and seen the spider.
Camillo was his help in this, his pander: —
There is a plot against my life, my crown;
All's true that is mistrusted: — that false villain
Whom I employ'd, was pre-employ'd by him:
He has discover'd my design, and I
Remain a pinch'd thing; yea, a very trick
For them to play at will. — How came the posterns
So easily open?
First Lord　By his great authority;
Which often hath no less prevail'd than so,
On your command.
Leontes　　　　　I know't too well. — [*To* Hermione]
Give me the boy: — I am glad you did not nurse him:
Though he does bear some signs of me, yet you
Have too much blood in him.
Hermione　　　　　　What is this? sport?
Leontes　Bear the boy hence; he shall not come about her;
Away with him! — and let her sport herself
With that she's big with; — for 'tis Polixences

|里杭底斯| 走得那么快:我目送他们上了船。
我多好运气,判断得正确,说得对!
唉哟,我但愿没有知道得这么多!
这样的幸运,多么该诅咒! 盅子里
也许浸得有一只蜘蛛,一个人
可以喝下去,就走开,不会中毒,
因为他灵明和心智没有受害;
但假使有人把那恶心的成分
给他看,叫他知道如何喝下的,
他会起强烈的哕逆,把喉咙、食管、
胃囊全呕破,连同胸腔都炸裂。
我是喝了那樽中酒,见了那蜘蛛。
喀米罗是他的帮手,他的淫媒:
对我这生命,这王冠,有个奸谋;
我所怀疑的都对:那骗人的坏蛋
我用他,他却早已先被他所雇:
他把我的计划对他泄露了,而我却
变成了个大笑话;是的,变作个
他们随意嬉耍的玩意儿。怎么会
边门这样容易开?

|贵 人 甲| 凭他的大权,
那可一向就和得到您谕旨时
同样有效。

|里杭底斯| 这个我完全明白。
[向候妙霓]把孩子给我:我高兴你没喂他奶:
虽然他跟我有点像,可是他身体里
你血液太多了。

|候 妙 霓| 这是什么? 开玩笑?

|里杭底斯| 把孩子领走;莫叫他走近她身边;
把他带走!——[曼密留诗被引走。]
让她去跟她自己那
肚子里的玩;因为是包列齐倪思

Has made thee swell thus.

Hermione   But I'd say he had not,
And I'll be sworn you would believe my saying,
Howe'er you learn the nayward.

Leontes   You, my lords,
Look on her, mark her well; be but about
To say, *she is a goodly lady* and
The justice of your hearts will thereto add,
'Tis pity she's not honest, honourable:
Praise her but for this her without-door form, —
Which, on my faith, deserves high speech, — and straight
The shrug, the *hum* or *ha*, — these petty brands
That calumny doth use: — O, I am out,
That mercy does; for calumny will sear
Virtue itself: — these shrugs, these *hum's*, and *ha's*,
When you have said *she's goodly*, come between,
Ere you can say *she's honest*: but be it known,
From him that has most cause to grieve it should be,
She's an adultress!

Hermione   Should a villain say so,
The most replenish'd villain in the world,
He were as much more villain: you, my lord,
Do but mistake.

Leontes   You have mistook, my lady,
Polixenes for Leontes: O thou thing,
Which I'll not call a creature of thy place,
Lest barbarism, making me the precedent,
Should a like language use to all degrees,
And mannerly distinguishment leave out
Betwixt the prince and beggar! — I have said,

|候　妙　霓|　　　　　　　　可是我得说他没有，
而我敢起誓你要相信我这话，
不论你怎样否认我。
|里杭底斯|　　　　　　　　　　诸位，列卿们，
望着她，仔细端详她；只等你们
正要说，"她是位美貌的娘娘"，马上
你们心里的正义会加上这样一句，
"可惜她不贞静贤淑，不值得敬重"：
只要对她这外表有所称扬时，——
这话，说实话，还值得称赞，——立刻
肩膀一耸，一声"哼"，一声"哈"，这些个
诽谤所使的这些丑标志，——啊，
我错了！——我是说怜悯所使的，因为
诽谤把标志只加在美德身上：
这些耸肩膀，"哼"与"哈"，当你们刚好
说过"她美貌"之后，还没有说到
"她贞静贤淑"之前，会加到中间来。
但是你们得知道，那最有原因
伤心的人要宣称，这该是这样的，
她是个通奸的淫妇。
|候　妙　霓|　　　　　　　　　若是个坏蛋
(世界上最坏到绝点的坏蛋)这样说，
他便成了个双重的那样的坏蛋：
你只是弄错了，王夫。
|里杭底斯|　　　　　　　　是你弄错了，
娘娘，把包列齐倪思当里杭底斯。
啊，你这东西！你这样高的地位，
我不来称你作东西，怕的是粗野
将我当先例，会用同样的语气
对一切品位，而在公侯与乞丐间
不作有礼貌的区分：我已经说过，

She's an adultress; I have said with whom:
More, she's a traitor; and Camillo is
A federary with her; and one that knows
What she should shame to know herself
But with her most vile principal, that she's
A bed-swerver, even as bad as those
That vulgars give boldest titles; ay, and privy
To this their late escape.
Hermione　　　　　No, by my life,
Privy to none of this. How will this grieve you,
When you shall come to clearer knowledge, that
You thus have publish'd me! Gentle my lord,
You scarce can right me throughly then, to say
You did mistake.
Leontes　　　　No; if I mistake
In those foundations which I build upon,
The centre is not big enough to bear
A school-boy's top. — Away with her to prison!
He who shall speak for her is afar off guilty
But that he speaks.
Hermione　　　　　There's some ill planet reigns:
I must be patient till the heavens look
With an aspéct more favourable. — Good my lords,
I am not prone to weeping, as our sex
Commonly are; the want of which vain dew
Perchance shall dry your pities; but I have
That honourable grief lodg'd here, which burns
Worse than tears drown: beseech you all, my lords,
With thoughts so qualified as your charities
Shall best instruct you, measure me; — and so
The king's will be perform'd!
Leontes　[*To the* Guard.]Shall I be heard?
Hermione　Who is't that goes with me? — Beseech your
　　　　highness
My women may be with me; for, you see,

　　　　　　她是个通奸的妇人；我说过跟谁：
　　　　　　她又加是个叛逆者，喀米罗和她
　　　　　　同谋，他知道她自己也羞知的勾当，
　　　　　　除非跟她最卑鄙的主谋者一同知，
　　　　　　那就是她是个践踏婚誓的妇人，
　　　　　　恶劣得世人把那最可耻的称号
　　　　　　相呼的那些个滥贱一般无二；
　　　　　　哎也，她预先知道他们要逃走。
候　妙　霓　不，凭我的生命，我不知这件事。
　　　　　　你这般当众辱骂我，待你将来
　　　　　　把真相弄明时，你会多么悲伤！
　　　　　　亲爱的王夫，那时节你就是声言
　　　　　　你过去错了，也不能完全对得起我。
里杭底斯　不会；假使我凭借的根据有错，
　　　　　　这大地，这宇宙中心，便会连一只
　　　　　　学童的陀螺都容不下。送她进监狱！
　　　　　　谁替她说话，不论怎样不相干，
　　　　　　也就有了罪，哪怕他只稍稍求情。
候　妙　霓　有什么恶星宿当头：我得耐心些，
　　　　　　等天宇朗照得较为吉祥时再说。
　　　　　　列位贵卿们，我不会轻易哭泣，
　　　　　　像我们女性通常的那样；缺少了
　　　　　　易流的眼泪许会使你们的怜悯
　　　　　　干涸；可是在我这里头藏得有
　　　　　　光荣的悲痛，它燃烧比眼泪的浸淫
　　　　　　远较难受。请你们各位，贵卿们，
　　　　　　以仁爱所最能教导你们的想法
　　　　　　来对我作判断；然后，将王上的决意
　　　　　　来加以执行！
里杭底斯　［向众卫士］你们听到命令吗？
候　妙　霓　谁跟我一同去？请得王上恩准，
　　　　　　我的伴娘们或能陪着我；因为，

My plight requires it.—Do not weep, good fools;
There is no cause: when you shall know your mistress
Has deserv'd prison, then abound in tears
As I come out: this action I now go on
Is for my better grace.—Adieu, my lord:
I never wish'd to see you sorry; now
I trust I shall.—My women, come; you have leave.
Leontes Go, do our bidding; hence!
[*Exeunt* Queen, guarded; *with* Ladies.]
First Lord Beseech your highness, call the queen again.
Antigonus Be certain what you do, sir, lest your justice
Prove violence, in the which three great ones suffer,
Yourself, your queen, your son.
First Lord   For her, my lord,—
I dare my life lay down,—and will do't, sir,
Please you to accept it,—that the queen is spotless
I' the eyes of heaven and to you; I mean
In this which you accuse her.
Antigonus   If it prove
She's otherwise, I'll keep my stables where
I lodge my wife; I'll go in couples with her;
Than when I feel and see her no further trust her;
For every inch of woman in the world,
Ay, every dram of woman's flesh, is false,
If she be.
Leontes Hold your peaces.
First Lord   Good my lord,—
Antigonus It is for you we speak, not for ourselves:

|||你见到我这处境需要这么样。
不要哭,好傻子们;并没有理由:
将来我出来的时候,你们若知道
你们的娘娘该进牢狱,到那时
才涕泪交流吧:我如今遇这讼凶
倒是会有利于我的沐受天恩。
再会,王夫:我从未愿望过你伤心;
现在我相信我却将如此。来吧,
我的伴娘们;你们已得到允许。
里杭底斯	去,执行命令去:就离开这里!
	〔王后被押解,伴娘数人随后,同下。
贵人甲	求吾王开恩,将王后召回来吧。
安铁冈纳施	请先行确定您要做什么事,王上,
否则您这场审判会变成强暴:
在这案子里人尊位贵的有三位
受损伤,您自己、您王后,以及储君。
贵人甲	关于她,吾主,我敢将我的生命
作注子,而且就押下,王上,请您
接受它,——王后对于您,在上苍照鉴下,
是清纯无疵的:我说的乃是关于
您对她所下的指控。
安铁冈纳施	假使能判明
她不是这样,我妻子所居的住宅
我要改辟为马厩;我须得和她
同进出以便监视;不觉她在身旁
或不见她时不再信任她;因为,
她假使不贞,这世上的女人每一寸,
哎也,她们的一丁点儿的皮肉
也都是不贞的。
里杭底斯	你们都住口!
贵人甲	好主上,——
安铁冈纳施	我们是为您而说的,不是为自己。

You are abus'd, and by some putter-on
That will be damn'd for't: would I knew the villain,
I would land-damn him. Be she honour-flaw'd, —
I have three daughters; the eldest is eleven;
The second and the third, nine and some five;
If this prove true, they'll pay for't. By mine honour,
I'll geld 'em all: fourteen they shall not see,
To bring false generations: they are co-heirs;
And I had rather glib myself than they
Should not produce fair issue.
Leontes   Cease; no more.
You smell this business with a sense as cold
As is a dead man's nose: but I do see't and feel't
As you feel doing thus; and see withal
The instruments that feel.
Antigonus   If it be so,
We need no grave to bury honesty;
There's not a grain of it the face to sweeten
Of the whole dungy earth.
Leontes   What! Lack I credit?
First Lord   I had rather you did lack than I, my lord,
Upon this ground: and more it would content me
To have her honour true than your suspicion;
Be blam'd for't how you might.
Leontes   Why, what need we
Commune with you of this, but rather follow
Our forceful instigation? Our prerogative
Calls not your counsels; but our natural goodness
Imparts this; which, if you, — or stupified

您蒙受欺骗,那挑拨的奸人自会
被打入地狱;我但愿知道那恶棍,
我要当众揭发他。若她的贞洁
给玷污的话,——我生得有三个女儿;
大的十一岁,第二、第三是九岁
和五岁不到;假使这话是当真,
她们将受罚来谢罪:凭我的荣誉,
我把她们都阉割掉;不叫她们
长到十四岁,去生杂种的后代:
她们是我的平分的继承人;而我,
宁愿我自己给去势,也不愿她们
不孳生子息。

里杭底斯　　　　　　住口!莫往下说了。
你感觉这件事像个死人用鼻子
嗅觉到什么;但是我见到和感到
好似你现在感到这么样,且看见
我这感觉的器官。

安铁冈纳施　　　　　　如果是这样,
我们毋须有香冢来瘞埋贞洁了:
再没有清贞的种子来使这整片
肮脏秽臭的泥污地面芬芳了。

里杭底斯　什么?我不能听信于你们?

贵　人　甲　　　　　　　主上,
在这件事上,我宁愿您缺乏自信,
不愿我缺乏;更能使我满足的是,
她的贞洁是真的,您猜疑得不对,
不管您将怎么样受责备。

里杭底斯　　　　　　　　哎也,
我们何用跟你们谈这个,只须
随我们自己有力的驱策去行事?
我们大权在握,本毋须征求意见,
因我们天性和蔼,故谈起了这个;

Or seeming so in skill, — cannot or will not
Relish a truth, like us, inform yourselves
We need no more of your advice: the matter,
The loss, the gain, the ord'ring on't, is all
Properly ours.
Antigonus And I wish, my liege,
You had only in your silent judgment tried it,
Without more overture.
Leontes   How could that be?
Either thou art most ignorant by age,
Or thou wert born a fool. Camillo's flight,
Added to their familiarity, —
Which was as gross as ever touch'd conjecture,
That lack'd sight only, nought for approbation,
But only seeing, all other circumstances
Made up to th' deed, — doth push on this proceeding.
Yet, for a greater confirmation, —
For, in an act of this importance, 'twere
Most piteous to be wild, — I have despatch'd in post
To sacred Delphos, to Apollo's temple,
Cleomenes and Dion, whom you know
Of stuff'd sufficiency: now, from the oracle
They will bring all, whose spiritual counsel had,
Shall stop or spur me. Have I done well?
First Lord Well done, my lord, —
Leontes Though I am satisfied, and need no more
Than what I know, yet shall the oracle
Give rest to the minds of others such as he
Whose ignorant credulity will not
Come up to th' truth: so have we thought it good

　　　　　　如果你们，——或者是愚蠢，或者是
　　　　　　假装如此，——不能或不愿似我们，
　　　　　　爱真情实况，可以跟你们自己说，
　　　　　　我们并不再需要你们的谆劝：
　　　　　　这桩事，它的得与失，怎样去处理，
　　　　　　全是我们自己的事。
安铁冈纳施　　　　　　　　我但愿，主君，
　　　　　　您在静默的独白明察中将它
　　　　　　来观照，不事多显露。
里杭底斯　　　　　　　　　　那怎么能够？
　　　　　　你若非因年老而变得异常无知，
　　　　　　定是生成了个冥顽不灵之徒。
　　　　　　他们的亲昵（那是尚未亲眼
　　　　　　目睹的猜疑所曾接触的最分明
　　　　　　不过的事，它不差证据，仅仅还
　　　　　　没给人看见，其他的一切情况
　　　　　　都指向这件事），加上喀米罗的逃跑，
　　　　　　迫使人走上这条路；可是，为求得
　　　　　　更大的证据，——因为，遇到这样件
　　　　　　重大事，鲁莽会造成悲惨的结局，——
　　　　　　我已派克廖弥尼司和第盎两人，
　　　　　　你们都知道他们完全有能力，
　　　　　　前往神圣的台尔福，阿波罗的圣庙，
　　　　　　去求取灵谕。如今，从那神殿上，
　　　　　　他们将带回一切；那神灵的启示
　　　　　　一来到，将会止住或策励我前进。
　　　　　　我做得对吗？
贵　人　甲　　　　　　　您做得很对，主上。
里杭底斯　纵然我已经满足，不需要比我所
　　　　　　知道的更多些证据，但神谕会叫
　　　　　　有些人头脑安静些，比如他，坚持着
　　　　　　迟钝的轻信，不愿去接近真实。

From our free person she should be confin'd;
Lest that the treachery of the two fled hence
Be left her to perform. Come, follow us;
We are to speak in public; for this business
Will raise us all.
Antigonus [*Aside.*]To laughter, as I take it,
If the good truth were known. [*Exeunt.*]

SCENE II. *The outer Room of a Prison.*

[*Enter* Paulina *and* Attendants.]

Paulina The keeper of the prison, — call to him;
Let him have knowledge who I am.
[*Exit an* Attendant.]
Good lady!
No court in Europe is too good for thee;
What dost thou then in prison?
[*Re-enter* Attendant, *with* the Gaoler]
Now, good sir,
You know me, do you not?
Gaoler For a worthy lady,
And one who much I honour.
Paulina Pray you, then,
Conduct me to the queen.
Gaoler I may not, madam;
To the contrary I have express commandment.
Paulina Here's ado,
To lock up honesty and honour from
The access of gentle visitors! Is't lawful, pray you,
To see her women? any of them? Emilia?
Gaoler So please you, madam,

所以我们想，她应被禁闭起来，
千万不能让她随心所欲地
接近我，以免那两个逃亡者的奸谋
留给她来实施。来吧，跟着我们：
我们要当众去说话；因为这件事
会振奋我们大家。

安铁冈纳施　　　　　　　[旁白]去哗笑，据我想，
若是真情实事被大家所知道。

　　　　　　　　　　　　　　　　　[同下。

第 二 景

[监狱门首]
[宝理娜与侍从数人上。]

宝 理 娜　把牢头禁子叫唤来；让他知道
　　　　　我是谁。——[一侍从下。]
　　　　　　　　　　　好娘娘，欧洲没有个宫廷
　　　　　不配由你去当后妃；那么，你待在
　　　　　监狱里做什么？[侍从同狱卒上。
　　　　　　　　　　　却说，监里的官长，
　　　　　你认得我不认得？

狱　　　卒　　　　　　　　是位贵上夫人，
　　　　　小人在此有礼了。

宝 理 娜　　　　　　　　那么，就请你
　　　　　领我到王后那里去。

狱　　　卒　　　　　　　　我不敢，夫人：
　　　　　小人奉特别命令不叫那么办。

宝 理 娜　这真叫无事添忙，好端端把尊荣
　　　　　和贞淑锁起来，不让优娴的来客
　　　　　会见到！请问，见她的伴娘可以吗？
　　　　　她们不拘哪一个？爱米丽亚？

狱　　　卒　要请您，夫人，

To put apart these your attendants, I
Shall bring Emilia forth.
Paulina　　　　　　　I pray now, call her.
Withdraw yourselves.　　　　　[*Exeunt* Attendants.]
Gaoler　　　　　And, madam,
I must be present at your conference.
Paulina　Well, be't so, pr'ythee.　　　[*Exit* Gaoler.]
Here's such ado to make no stain a stain
As passes colouring.
　　　　　　　[*Re-enter* Gaoler, *with* Emilia.]
　　　　　　　　Dear gentlewoman,
How fares our gracious lady?
Emilia　As well as one so great and so forlorn
May hold together: on her frights and griefs, —
Which never tender lady hath borne greater, —
She is, something before her time, deliver'd.
Paulina　A boy?
Emilia　　　　A daughter; and a goodly babe,
Lusty, and like to live: the queen receives
Much comfort in't; says *My poor prisoner,
I am as innocent as you.*
Paulina　　　　　　I dare be sworn; —
These dangerous unsafe lunes i' the king, beshrew them!
He must be told on't, and he shall: the office
Becomes a woman best; I'll take't upon me;
If I prove honey-mouth'd, let my tongue blister;
And never to my red-look'd anger be
The trumpet any more. — Pray you, Emilia,
Commend my best obedience to the queen;
If she dares trust me with her little babe,
I'll show't the king, and undertake to be
Her advocate to th' loud'st. We do not know

　　　　　　　摒退了左右的侍从,我将去带领
　　　　　　　爱米丽亚到外面来。
宝　理　娜　　　　　　　　请你去叫她。
　　　　　　　你们且退出去。　　　　　　　〔众侍从下。
狱　　　卒　　　　　　　还有,夫人,小人
　　　　　　　得在你们谈话时在一旁待着。
宝　理　娜　好吧,就这样,请你。　　　　〔狱卒下。
　　　　　　　这真叫无事添忙,把没有玷污
　　　　　　　硬当作玷污,弄得染色也染不掉。
　　　　　　　　　　〔狱卒引爱米丽亚上。
　　　　　　　亲爱的大娘娘,我们娘娘可好?
爱米丽亚　尽到恁般尊贵又恁般苦恼的
　　　　　　　所能受得了。因受了惊恐和悲伤,——
　　　　　　　娇贵的娘娘从没遭受到更凶的,——
　　　　　　　她还不怎么达月就早产下来了。
宝　理　娜　是个男孩?
爱米丽亚　　　　　　是个姑娘;这娃娃
　　　　　　　长得又美又壮健,会活的模样;
　　　　　　　娘娘就打这里头得好些安慰;
　　　　　　　她说道,"我的可怜的囚犯,我跟你
　　　　　　　一般无罪。"
宝　理　娜　　　　　　我敢于起誓:王上
　　　　　　　这些危险的癫狂爆发,真糟糕!
　　　　　　　他一定得给禀报,他将被禀报:
　　　　　　　这任务女人做最好;由我来担负。
　　　　　　　假如我甜嘴蜜舌,让我这舌头
　　　　　　　起水泡,再也别替我赤红的愤怒
　　　　　　　作传声的号子。劳您驾,爱米丽亚,
　　　　　　　请代我向娘娘致敬:她若是敢把
　　　　　　　她那小娃儿信托给我,我将会
　　　　　　　抱给王上去瞧去,还要承担起
　　　　　　　为了她提高嗓子作辩护。我不知

How he may soften at the sight o' the child:
The silence often of pure innocence
Persuades, when speaking fails.
Emilia   Most worthy madam,
Your honour and your goodness is so evident,
That your free undertaking cannot miss
A thriving issue: there is no lady living
So meet for this great errand. Please your ladyship
To visit the next room, I'll presently
Acquaint the queen of your most noble offer;
Who but to-day hammer'd of this design,
But durst not tempt a minister of honour,
Lest she should be denied.
Paulina   Tell her, Emilia,
I'll use that tongue I have: if wit flow from it
As boldness from my bosom, let't not be doubted
I shall do good.
Emilia   Now be you bless'd for it!
I'll to the queen: please you come something nearer.
Gaoler Madam, if 't please the queen to send the babe,
I know not what I shall incur to pass it,
Having no warrant.
Paulina You need not fear it, sir:
This child was prisoner to the womb, and is,
By law and process of great nature thence
Freed and enfranchis'd: not a party to
The anger of the king, nor guilty of,
If any be, the trespass of the queen.
Gaoler I do believe it.
Paulina Do not you fear: upon mine honour, I
Will stand betwixt you and danger.

                              [*Exeunt.*]

　　　　　　见到这孩子他会要怎样软下来：
　　　　　　往往纯洁天真的沉默能打动，
　　　　　　当劝说不生功效时。
爱米丽亚　　　　　　　　　　　最高贵的夫人，
　　　　　　您的品位和仁德是恁般分明，
　　　　　　您这下慷慨的仗义不会没有
　　　　　　好结果：这世上没有第二位贵夫人
　　　　　　更适于去负这重大的使命。请夫人
　　　　　　且到这房间里头来，我立即向娘娘
　　　　　　去禀明您这出色的建议，只今天
　　　　　　她才想出了这计划，但不敢去请
　　　　　　品位高贵的代行人，怕人家不肯。
宝理娜　　　告诉她，爱米丽亚，我自会使用我
　　　　　　这喉舌：若机敏从它那里出来，
　　　　　　像勇敢打我胸中出来一个样，
　　　　　　可尽管放心我将会办得好。
爱米丽亚　　　　　　　　　　　　祝贺
　　　　　　天赐您后福无穷！我就去报娘娘。
　　　　　　请您，来近些。
狱　卒　　　　　　　　　　　夫人，若王后乐意
　　　　　　把孩子送出来，我不知让她通过
　　　　　　会叫我受什么处分，未经过令准。
宝理娜　　　你不用害怕，狱官：这孩子原来是
　　　　　　她母亲肚里的囚犯，如今经法律
　　　　　　和伟大造化的事态进行，而获得
　　　　　　释放和自由；她不遭君王恼怒，
　　　　　　也不犯王后——假使她犯下的话——
　　　　　　所犯的罪行。
狱　卒　　　　　　　　　　小人相信您这话。
宝理娜　　　你不用害怕：凭我的荣誉，我站在
　　　　　　你和危险之间。

〔同下。

SCENE III. *A Room in the Palace.*

[*Enter* Leontes, Antigonus, Lords,
and other Attendants.]

Leontes   Nor night nor day no rest: it is but weakness
To bear the matter thus,—mere weakness. If
The cause were not in being,—part o' the cause,
She the adultress; for the harlot king
Is quite beyond mine arm, out of the blank
And level of my brain, plot-proof; but she
I can hook to me:—say that she were gone,
Given to the fire, a moiety of my rest
Might come to me again.—Who's there?
First Attendant   My lord?
Leontes   How does the boy?
First Attendant   He took good rest to-night;
'Tis hop'd his sickness is discharg'd.
Leontes   To see his nobleness!
Conceiving the dishonour of his mother,
He straight declin'd, droop'd, took it deeply,
Fasten'd and fix'd the shame on't in himself,
Threw off his spirit, his appetite, his sleep,
And downright languish'd.—Leave me solely:—go,
See how he fares.—
[*Exit* First Attendant.]
         Fie, fie! no thought of him;
The very thought of my revenges that way
Recoil upon me: in himself too mighty,
And in his parties, his alliance,—let him be,
Until a time may serve: for present vengeance,
Take it on her. Camillo and Polixenes

第 三 景

[官中一室]
[里杭底斯、安铁冈纳施、贵人数人、侍从数人上。

里杭底斯 夜晚没有,白天也没有安宁;
这样去挨受这事情,只能是软弱,
仅仅的软弱。假使那作奸者没了,——
作奸者之一,她这通奸的淫妇;
因为这淫棍国王我完全奈何他
不得,在我脑筋的箭垛和射程外,
计谋和策略休想伤得他分毫;
但是她,我能钩她来:假定她去了,
送进了火里,我的一部分安宁
也许会回来。谁在那里?

侍 从 甲 [趋前]吾王?
里杭底斯 孩子怎样了?
侍 从 甲 他今夜休息得很好;
希望他的病已经消释。
里杭底斯 看他那
英伟的气概! 想起他母亲的耻辱,
他立即萎靡不振,垂头丧气,
难受到心里,把羞辱揽给他自己,
把精神、胃口、睡眠一古脑全丢掉,
干脆伤心失了志。让我一个人
在这里:去,去看看他现在怎样了。 [侍从甲下。
呸,呸! 不要去想他吧;想起他
我的报复之念就油然而生:
他自己已力量太大,况加上他那些
同盟者,他那些亲朋党羽;由他去,
且等待时机来到:为目下的报复,
可在她身上找出路。包列齐倪思

Laugh at me; make their pastime at my sorrow:
They should not laugh if I could reach them; nor
Shall she within my power.
      [*Enter* Paulina, *with* a Child.]
First Lord   You must not enter.
Paulina Nay, rather, good my lords, be second to me:
Fear you his tyrannous passion more, alas,
Than the queen's life? a gracious innocent soul,
More free than he is jealous.
Antigonus   That's enough.
Second Attendant Madam, he hath not slept tonight;
  commanded
None should come at him.
Paulina   Not so hot, good sir;
I come to bring him sleep. 'Tis such as you, —
That creep like shadows by him, and do sigh
At each his needless heavings, — such as you
Nourish the cause of his awaking: I
Do come, with words as med'cinal as true,
Honest as either, to purge him of that humour
That presses him from sleep.
Leontes   What noise there, ho?
Paulina No noise, my lord; but needful conference
About some gossips for your highness.
Leontes   How! —
Away with that audacious lady! — Antigonus,
I charg'd thee that she should not come about me:
I knew she would.
Antigonus I told her so, my lord,
On your displeasure's peril, and on mine,
She should not visit you.

与喀米罗在对我哂笑;把我的悲哀
作他们的消遣:我若能抓到他们,
他们便不会哗笑,她在我权力内,
可休想能笑乐。
〔宝理娜抱婴孩上。

贵　人　甲　　　　　　　你不得进去。
宝　理　娜　　　　　　　　　　　不,
列位大人们,倒要请你们帮我忙:
你们更怕他暴戾的激情吗,唉哟,
却不怕王后没有命?一个天真
圣洁的灵魂,满怀的清纯无辜,
跟他那嫉妒的想法更渺不相干。
安铁冈纳施　莫再多说了。
侍　从　乙　　　　　　　夫人,王上今晚上
没睡觉;谕令不让谁来惊动他。
宝　理　娜　别这么激动,请你;我带睡眠来
给他。你就是这样,像影子一般
在他身边爬,他叹声不必叹的长息
你也跟着叹,你就是这样添了他
睡不着的原因:我带来的话儿既有
药性且又真,再加上诚实,能替他
排除那硬叫他不得睡眠的怪想。
里杭底斯　那是什么闹声,喂呀?
宝　理　娜　　　　　　　　　吾王,
不是闹声;只是些必要的谈话,
是商量给你请谁行洗礼的事情。
里杭底斯　怎么的!叫那大胆的夫人出去。
安铁冈纳施,我关照过你不叫她
挨近我:我知道她会。
安铁冈纳施　　　　　　　我告诉过她,
王上,说不许她来,否则会甘冒
您的恼怒,和我的。

Leontes　　　　　　What, canst not rule her?
Paulina　From all dishonesty he can: in this, —
Unless he take the course that you have done,
Commit me for committing honour, — trust it,
He shall not rule me.
Antigonus　　　　　La you now, you hear
When she will take the rein, I let her run;
But she'll not stumble.
Paulina　　　　　Good my liege, I come, —
And, I beseech you, hear me, who professes
Myself your loyal servant, your physician,
Your most obedient counsellor: yet that dares
Less appear so, in comforting your evils,
Than such as most seem yours: — I say I come
From your good queen.
Leontes　　　　　*Good queen*!
Paulina　　　　　　　Good queen, my lord,
Good queen: I say, good queen;
And would by combat make her good, so were I
A man, the worst about you.
Leontes　　　　　　Force her hence!
Paulina　Let him that makes but trifles of his eyes
First hand me: on mine own accord I'll off;
But first I'll do my errand — The good queen,
For she is good, hath brought you forth a daughter;
Here 'tis; commends it to your blessing.
　　　　　　　　　　　[*Laying down the* child.]
Leontes　　　　　　　　Out!
A mankind witch! Hence with her, out o' door:
A most intelligencing bawd!
Paulina　　　　　　　Not so:
I am as ignorant in that as you

里杭底斯　　　　　　　　　什么？管不住她？
宝　理　娜　用卑鄙的手段，他能够；在这件事上，
　　　　　　（除非他采用您所使的手段，把我
　　　　　　关进了监牢，因为我品行贞洁，）
　　　　　　请相信我这话，他可管我不了。
安铁冈纳施　您瞧，如今！您听吧；当她要走她
　　　　　　自己的路时，我让她去跑；可是
　　　　　　她不会失足。
宝　理　娜　　　　　　我的好主君，我到来，
　　　　　　而且请您听我说，我自认是您
　　　　　　忠诚的臣仆，您的太医，您最最
　　　　　　崇敬的上言人，可是我敢在助长您
　　　　　　缺失时，显得比那些最像您忠仆的，
　　　　　　不那么顺从：我说，我来自您那位
　　　　　　贞德的王后。
里杭底斯　　　　　　贞德的王后！
宝　理　娜　　　　　　　　　是的，
　　　　　　贞德的王后，王上，贞德的王后；
　　　　　　我说，是贞德的王后；我若是个男子，
　　　　　　我会以决斗去证明她贞德，即令我
　　　　　　在您左右最胆怯。
里杭底斯　　　　　　　拉她走。
宝　理　娜　　　　　　　　　谁轻视
　　　　　　自己的眼睛，让他来拉我：我自己
　　　　　　会走；但我得先把差使来办好。
　　　　　　贞德的王后，因为她确是贞德的，
　　　　　　为您生了个姑娘：在这里；把她
　　　　　　送给您去为她祝福。　　　　　〔将婴孩放下。
里杭底斯　　出去！母老虎似的巫婆！赶她走，
　　　　　　轰她出门外：专作淫媒的龟鸨！
宝　理　娜　不是那样；您那样称呼我，我跟您
　　　　　　同样不在行，而且规矩得跟您

In so entitling me; and no less honest
Than you are mad; which is enough, I'll warrant,
As this world goes, to pass for honest.
Leontes   Traitors!
Will you not push her out? Give her the bastard: —
Thou dotard! [*To* Antigonus] Thou art woman-tir'd, un-
    roosted
By thy Dame Partlet here: — take up the bastard;
Take't up, I say; give't to thy crone.
Paulina   For ever
Unvenerable be thy hands, if thou
Tak'st up the princess by that forced baseness
Which he has put upon't!
Leontes   He dreads his wife.
Paulina   So I would you did; then 'twere past all doubt
You'd call your children yours.
Leontes   A nest of traitors?
Antigonus   I am none, by this good light.
Paulina   Nor I; nor any,
But one that's here; and that's himself: for he
The sacred honour of himself, his queen's,
His hopeful son's, his babe's, betrays to slander,
Whose sting is sharper than the sword's; and will not, —
For, as the case now stands, it is a curse
He cannot be compell'd to't, — once remove
The root of his opinion, which is rotten
As ever oak or stone was sound.
Leontes   A callat

恼怒得一般厉害；这么样老实，
我敢担保，按如今这世界来说，
是足够叫做老实的了。

里杭底斯　　　　　　　　逆贼们！
你们不推她出去吗？把这小杂种
交给她。[向安铁冈纳施]
　　　　　　你这老糊涂！怕老婆的班头，
你见你老婆巴忒兰在此，吓坏了。
抱起那杂种；抱起来，我说；把她
给你的老太婆。

宝　理　娜　　　　　　你若听了他强加
给她的杂种这贱名，把公主抱起来，
你这两只手将永远卑鄙！

里杭底斯　　　　　　　　　他怕他
妻子。

宝　理　娜　　我但愿您也怕；那就没疑问，
您会认可孩子们是自己的了。

里杭底斯　你们全都是逆贼！
安铁冈纳施　　　　　　　　我可不是，
凭这好天光。

宝　理　娜　　　　　　我也不是；别的人
也不是，这里只除了一个，那便是
他自己；他把他自己神圣的荣誉，
王后的，他前途远大的儿子的，他这
娃娃的，都出卖给了诽谤，它的刺
比剑尖还锋利；而且他不会，——因为，
按情势来说，他不能被迫去做，
这真该诅咒，——他一次也不会排除
他那看法的根柢，那真腐烂得
不像样，正如橡树或石头永远
健壮。

里杭底斯　　　　　一个长舌的娼妇，她最近

Of boundless tongue, who late hath beat her husband,
And now baits me!—This brat is none of mine;
It is the issue of Polixenes:
Hence with it! and together with the dam,
Commit them to the fire.

Paulina   It is yours!
And, might we lay the old proverb to your charge,
So like you 'tis the worse.—Behold, my lords,
Although the print be little, the whole matter
And copy of the father,—eye, nose, lip,
The trick of his frown, his forehead; nay, the valley,
The pretty dimples of his chin and cheek; his smiles;
The very mould and frame of hand, nail, finger:—
And thou, good goddess Nature, which hast made it
So like to him that got it, if thou hast
The ordering of the mind too, 'mongst all colours
No yellow in't, lest she suspect, as he does,
Her children not her husband's!

Leontes   A gross hag!
And, losel, thou art worthy to be hang'd
That wilt not stay her tongue.

Antigonus   Hang all the husbands
That cannot do that feat, you'll leave yourself
Hardly one subject.

Leontes   Once more, take her hence.

Paulina   A most unworthy and unnatural lord
Can do no more.

Leontes   I'll have thee burn'd.

Paulina   I care not.
It is an heretic that makes the fire,
Not she which burns in't. I'll not call you tyrant

打了她丈夫,如今又来煎逼我!
这小鬼不是我的;是包列齐倪思
所生:滚她的;跟她娘一起,把她们
扔进火里去!

宝 理 娜　　　　　　她是你生的;如果
我们把这老格言应用到您身上,
"这么像你,真是糟。"你们瞧,大人们,
虽然这版子是小的,她整个内容
和复印的式样是她父亲的;眼睛、
鼻子、嘴唇、皱眉时的相貌、额角,
还不止,更有这颐上颊上的酒涡,
美得很,她的笑脸,还有手、指甲、
手指的形状和骨骼:至于你,好造化
女神,你把她做得这么样像她爸,
若是你也安排她的心,可莫要
给予她猜忌的性格;否则她也会
疑心,跟他一个样,她生的儿女
不是她丈夫的亲生。

里杭底斯　　　　　　粗鄙的丑八怪!
还有,你这胆小鬼,你配给绞死,
不叫她闭嘴。

安铁冈纳施　　　　　建不了那功绩的丈夫,
把他们全都绞死了,您将几乎
一个子民都不剩。

里杭底斯　　　　　　我再说一遍,
拉她走。

宝 理 娜　　　　一个最没出息、最不近
人情的昏君做不出什么别的来。
里杭底斯　我来把你上火刑。
宝 理 娜　　　　　　我不放在心上:
引火燃烧的是个邪教徒,并非那
被焚的人。我不来叫你作暴君;

But this most cruel usage of your queen, —
Not able to produce more accusation
Than your own weak-hing'd fancy, — something savours
Of tyranny, and will ignoble make you,
Yea, scandalous to the world.

Leontes On your allegiance,
Out of the chamber with her! Were I a tyrant,
Where were her life? She durst not call me so,
If she did know me one. Away with her!

Paulina I pray you, do not push me; I'll be gone. —
Look to your babe, my lord; 'tis yours: Jove send her
A better guiding spirit! — What needs these hands?
You that are thus so tender o'er his follies,
Will never do him good, not one of you.
So, so: — farewell; we are gone.

[*Exit.*]

Leontes Thou, traitor, hast set on thy wife to this.
My child? — away with't. — even thou, that hast
A heart so tender o'er it, take it hence,
And see it instantly consum'd with fire;
Even thou, and none but thou. Take it up straight:
Within this hour bring me word 'tis done, —
And by good testimony, — or I'll seize thy life,
With what thou else call'st thine. If thou refuse,
And wilt encounter with my wrath, say so;
The bastard-brains with these my proper hands
Shall I dash out. Go, take it to the fire;
For thou set'st on thy wife.

Antigonus I did not, sir:
These lords, my noble fellows, if they please,
Can clear me in't.

Lords We can: — my royal liege,

但你对你王后的这非常的虐待,——
除了你自己根据薄弱的幻想外,
拿不出更多的罪状,——有暴虐的味道
会使你可鄙,岂止如此,对世人
声名狼藉。

里杭底斯 以你们的忠诚来相责,
将她赶出这卧房! 我若是个暴君,
她性命在哪里? 倘使她知道我是,
便不敢这样称呼我。把她赶走!

宝 理 娜 请你们莫来推我;我自己会出去。
看顾着你这娃娃,王上;她是你
亲生的:愿天神派个较好的使者,
来将她指引! 你们又何必动手?
你们对他的愚蠢这么样奉命,
决不会对他有好处,不会有的。
就这样,这样;再会了;我们去了。　　　　[下。

里杭底斯 你这逆贼,你指使你妻子干这个。
我的孩子! 滚她的! ——就要你,你的心
对她这么知痛痒,把她从这里
拿走,用心马上取火来把她烧:
就要你,不要旁人烧。立刻抱出去:
限你一小时,回来要报说已办好,——
还得有好证见,——否则就要你的命,
连同你其他的一切。你假使拒绝,
而且想跟我的忿怒作对,尽管说;
这杂种的脑浆我用自己这双手
会叫它迸裂。去,送她进火里去;
是你指使你妻子的。

安铁冈纳施 我没有,王上:
这几位大臣,我高贵的同侪,他们
若高兴,能替我来作证。

众 贵 人 我们能,主君,

He is not guilty of her coming hither.

Leontes You're liars all.

First Lord Beseech your highness, give us better credit:
We have always truly serv'd you; and beseech
So to esteem of us: and on our knees we beg, —
As recompense of our dear services,
Past and to come, — that you do change this purpose,
Which, being so horrible, so bloody, must
Lead on to some foul issue: we all kneel.

Leontes I am a feather for each wind that blows: —
Shall I live on, to see this bastard kneel
And call me father? better burn it now,
Than curse it then. But, be it; let it live: —
It shall not neither. — [*To* Antigonus.] You, sir, come you hither:
You that have been so tenderly officious
With Lady Margery, your midwife, there,
To save this bastard's life, — for 'tis a bastard,
So sure as this beard's grey, — what will you adventure
To save this brat's life?

Antigonus   Anything, my lord,
That my ability may undergo,
And nobleness impose: at least, thus much;
I'll pawn the little blood which I have left
To save the innocent: — anything possible.

Leontes It shall be possible. Swear by this sword
Thou wilt perform my bidding.

Antigonus   I will, my lord.

Leontes Mark, and perform it, — seest thou? for the fail
Of any point in't shall not only be

		她到此,罪辜不在他。
里杭底斯		你们全撒谎。
贵 人 甲	求请吾王要多多相信我们些:
	我们一向很真心为王驾奔走,
	恳请要垂念我们的忠诚;我们
	跪着请,作为对我们过去和将来
	恳挚的忠勤的恩赐,王上要变更
	这意思,这是这么样骇人听闻,
	这么样残忍,一定会造成恶果。
	我们都跪下。
里杭底斯		我是随风飘的羽毛。
	我可要活着,眼见这野种跪下来
	叫我父亲?与其到将来诅咒她,
	不如现在烧了好。可是,就这样;
	让她活就是:她也不一定就会活。——
	[向安铁冈纳施]你,阁下,这里来;你曾经和你那
	接生婆令阃贵夫人,怎般怜爱地
	喜欢管闲事,要救这野种的性命,——
	因为这是个野杂种,正像这胡须
	颜色是花白的,毫无可疑,——你敢做
	什么事,去救这小鬼的性命?
安铁冈纳施		任何事,
	吾王,只要我做得到,宽仁责我做:
	至少这么多:我将把还有的一点点
	血液作赌注,来救这天真的婴孩:
	任何事,只要可能。
里杭底斯		事情是可能的。
	凭这柄剑起个誓,说你将遵命而行。
安铁冈纳施	我遵命,王上。
里杭底斯		听着,要去做,——你注意!——
	这里边任何一点你不做,不仅

Death to thyself, but to thy lewd-tongu'd wife,
Whom for this time we pardon. We enjoin thee,
As thou art liegeman to us, that thou carry
This female bastard hence; and that thou bear it
To some remote and desert place, quite out
Of our dominions; and that there thou leave it,
Without more mercy, to it own protection
And favour of the climate. As by strange fortune
It came to us, I do in justice charge thee,
On thy soul's peril and thy body's torture,
That thou commend it strangely to some place
Where chance may nurse or end it. Take it up.
Antigonus I swear to do this, though a present death
Had been more merciful. — Come on, poor babe:
Some powerful spirit instruct the kites and ravens
To be thy nurses! Wolves and bears, they say,
Casting their savageness aside, have done
Like offices of pity. — Sir, be prosperous
In more than this deed does require! — and blessing,
Against this cruelty, fight on thy side,
Poor thing, condemn'd to loss!

[*Exit with the* child.]

Leontes   No, I'll not rear
Another's issue.   [*Enter* a Attendant.]
Second Attendant   Please your highness, posts
From those you sent to the oracle are come
An hour since: Cleomenes and Dion,
Being well arriv'd from Delphos, are both landed,
Hasting to the court.
First Lord   So please you, sir, their speed
Hath been beyond account.
Leontes   Twenty-three days
They have been absent: 'tis good speed; foretells
The great Apollo suddenly will have
The truth of this appear. Prepare you, lords;

你自己,你那长舌妇也准会丧命,
我们今番姑且饶了她。我命你,
作为我们的家臣,要把这女杂种
带起走,送到遥远荒僻的、远离
我们这邦疆的他方去,抛她在那里,
不再受顾惜,让她自己去卫护,
听凭天时的恩厚。因为她的来
是由于异常的运气,我秉着公平
命令你,你灵魂冒着险,身体负危难,
把她送到远处去,那里偶然事
许给她哺乳,或把她了结。抱起来。

安铁冈纳施 我誓必将去这么做,虽然立即死
会比这仁慈些。来吧,可怜的娃儿:
让什么威显的神灵感应鸢鸟与
渡乌,去做你的奶娘!狼和熊,据说,
把凶残放在一边,也曾经做过
同样的哀怜善举。吾王,祝福您
比这桩好事所应受的更加幸运!
而天赐的弘恩帮你奋战这凶残,
可怜的东西,被判要遭受抛弃! 〔抱婴孩下。

里杭底斯 不行;我不来养旁人的孩子。
〔侍从上。

侍　从　乙 　　　　　　禀王上,
您派往灵坛的使节所遣返的报差
一小时之前已经到:克廖弥尼司
和第盎,已从台尔福安然归返,
都已经上岸,正在迅速到宫里来。

贵　人　甲 可向您告慰,王上,他们的迅捷
超出了估计。

里杭底斯 　　　　他们去了二十三天:
赶得快;预示伟大的阿波罗立即
要这事的真相显露。预备好,列卿;

Summon a session, that we may arraign
Our most disloyal lady; for, as she hath
Been publicly accus'd, so shall she have
A just and open trial. While she lives,
My heart will be a burden to me. Leave me;
And think upon my bidding.

[*Exeunt.*]

召集公庭法谳,我们好对我们
最不忠贞的御妻提出指控状;
因为,她既已被公开宣布了罪行,
她应有公平与公开的鞠审。她活着,
我的心对我将是个负担。离开我,
去计划布置我的命令。　　　　　〔同下。

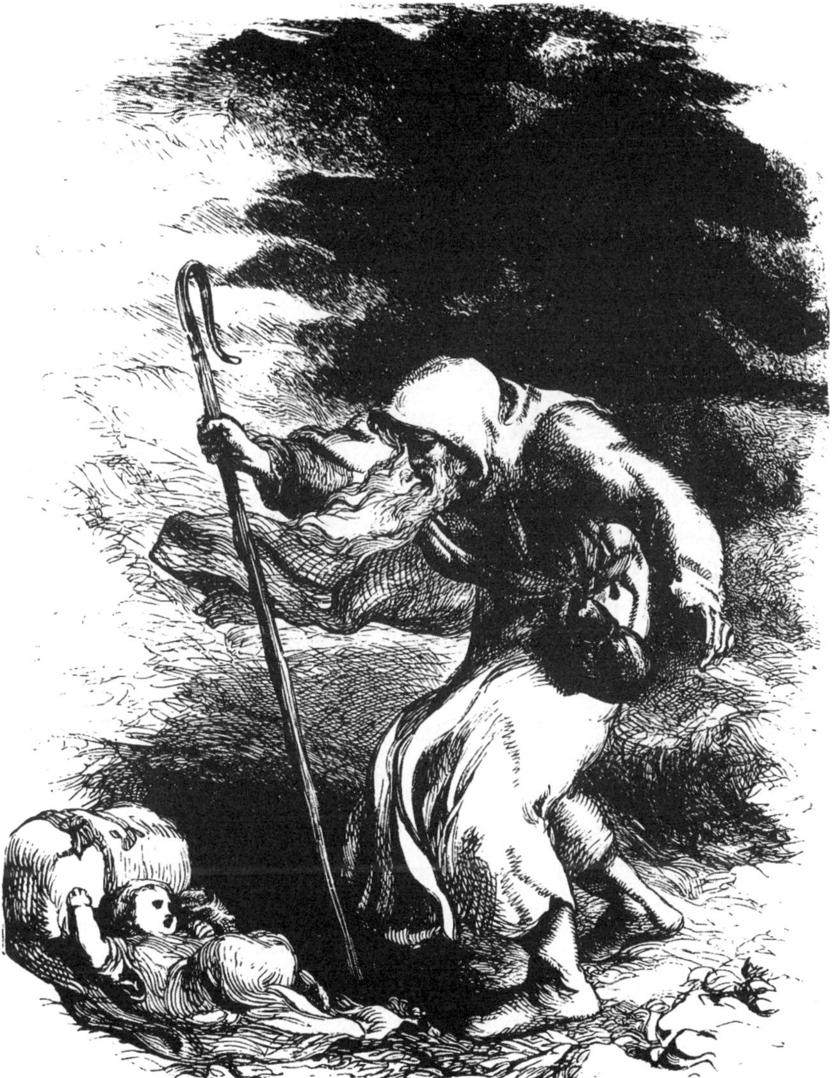

ACT III.

SCENE I. Sicilia. *A Street in some Town.*

[*Enter* Cleomenes *and* Dion.]

Cleomenes   The climate's delicate; the air most sweet;
Fertile the isle; the temple much surpassing
The common praise it bears.
Dion   I shall report,
For most it caught me, the celestial habits, —
Methinks I so should term them, — and the reverence
Of the grave wearers. O, the sacrifice!
How ceremonious, solemn, and unearthly,
It was i' the offering!
Cleomenes   But of all, the burst
And the ear-deaf'ning voice o' the oracle,
Kin to Jove's thunder, so surprised my sense
That I was nothing.
Dion   If the event o' the journey
Prove as successful to the queen, — O, be't so! —
As it hath been to us rare, pleasant, speedy,
The time is worth the use on't.

第 三 幕

第 一 景

［西西利亚一城镇］
［克廖弥尼司与第盎上。］

克廖弥尼司 那气候好宜人,空气无比的清新,
岛上的地土肥沃,那神庙远超过
它所负广大的赞誉。

第　盎 　　　　　　我会要禀报,
因为它吸引我,那些神圣的衣装,——
我想来我应当这样称呼它们,——
以及它们庄严的穿戴者的崇宏
之象。啊,那牺牲的献祭!供奉时
又多么仪礼端庄,肃敬,与超尘
而绝俗!

克廖弥尼司 　　　　但驾乎一切之上,宣灵谕
震耳欲聋的巨吼声,如同天神
弘雷之霹雳,那么样震惊我心神,
我感到渺小得如同无物。

第　盎 　　　　　　　倘使
这旅程的结局能对于王后有幸,——
啊,但愿它这样!——如旅程对我们
显见得这般神奇、愉快与迅速,
花在这上头的时间就未曾白费。

Cleomenes Great Apollo
Turn all to th' best! These proclamations,
So forcing faults upon Hermione,
I little like.
Dion   The violent carriage of it
Will clear or end the business: when the oracle, —
Thus by Apollo's great divine seal'd up, —
Shall the contents discover, something rare
Even then will rush to knowledge. — Go, — fresh horses; —
[*To* Attendat]And gracious be the issue!   [*Exeunt.*]

SCENE II. *A Court of Justice.*

[*Enter* Leontes, Lords, *and Officers.*]
Leontes   This sessions, — to our great grief we pronounce, —
Even pushes 'gainst our heart; — the party tried,
The daughter of a king, our wife; and one
Of us too much belov'd. Let us be clear'd
Of being tyrannous, since we so openly
Proceed in justice; which shall have due course,
Even to the guilt or the purgation. —
Produce the prisoner.
Officer   It is his highness' pleasure that the queen
Appear in person here in court. —
Silence!
[*Enter* Hermione *guarded*; Paulina, *and* Ladies *attending.*]
Leontes   Read the indictment.
Officer   [*Reads.*] Hermione, queen to the worthy Leontes, king of Sicilia, thou art here accused and arraigned of high treason, in committing adultery with Polixenes, king of Bohemia; and conspiring with Camillo to take away the life of our sovereign

克廖弥尼司	但愿伟大的阿波罗化一切为祥和！ 这些公告把罪名硬加在候妙霓 身上，我可不喜欢。
第　　盎	把事情区处得 这么样暴烈，将会使真相见分晓， 或把它定论：当这灵谕（这般 经由阿波罗的长老密封在此）， 过天把内容显示出来时，那时节 当会有什么奇妙事忽然暴露。—— 〔向一侍从〕去：换新马！祝愿有欢快的结局！ 　　　　　　　　　　　　　　　〔同下。

第 二 景

〔公堂〕
〔里杭底斯、贵人数人、公吏数人上。

里杭底斯	这公庭法谳，我们非常伤心地 宣布，简直穿刺到我们心头： 受审的当事者是位君王的女儿， 我们的妻子，最为我们所心爱。 让我们洗去暴虐的名声，既然 我们这般公开地来进行庭审， 这会要循序进行，一直到定罪 或释放。将罪犯提来。
公　　吏	吾王御旨命王后亲自来到庭。 肃静！ 　　　　〔候妙霓被解上；宝理娜与伴娘数人随侍。
里杭底斯	宣读起诉状。
公　　吏	〔读状〕"候妙霓，西西利亚王盛德的里杭底斯的王后，你在此被控犯谋反叛逆罪，具体的罪行是与波希米亚王包列齐倪思通奸，以及和喀米罗同谋企图

lord the king, thy royal husband: the pretence whereof being by circumstances partly laid open, thou, Hermione, contrary to the faith and allegiance of true subject, didst counsel and aid them, for their better safety, to fly away by night.

Hermione   Since what I am to say must be but that
Which contradicts my accusation, and
The testimony on my part no other
But what comes from myself, it shall scarce boot me
To say *Not guilty*: mine integrity,
Being counted falsehood, shall, as I express it,
Be so receiv'd. But thus, — if powers divine
Behold our human actions, — as they do, —
I doubt not, then, but innocence shall make
False accusation blush, and tyranny
Tremble at patience. — You, my lord, best know, —
Who least will seem to do so, — my past life
Hath been as continent, as chaste, as true,
As I am now unhappy: which is more
Than history can pattern, though devis'd
And play'd to take spectators; for behold me, —
A fellow of the royal bed, which owe
A moiety of the throne, a great king's daughter,
The mother to a hopeful prince, — here standing
To prate and talk for life and honour 'fore
Who please to come and hear. For life, I prize it
As I weigh grief, which I would spare: for honour,
'Tis a derivative from me to mine,
And only that I stand for. I appeal
To your own conscience, sir, before Polixenes
Came to your court, how I was in your grace,
How merited to be so; since he came,
With what encounter so uncurrent I

行弑我们的主君王上你的王夫；这罪行的逆谋因被形势泄露了一部分，所以你，候妙霓，背弃了忠贞的臣民的忠义与信誓，怂恿且帮助他们，为安全计，黄夜逃遁。"

候 妙 霓 我所要申辩的既然不能不反驳
那对我的指控，而我一方的证辞
又只能出自我本人，由我说"无罪"
可说已不中用：我的清纯无辜
既被当作了欺骗，它定将，我要说，
被认为如此。但这样：倘上界神灵
能望见我们人间的行动，——他们会，——
我毫不怀疑，无辜必将使诬指
脸红，使暴虐见容忍而颤抖。你啊，
王上，很知道，——但显得一无所知，——
我过去的生活多清纯、贞洁、精真，
正如我如今多不幸；这不幸，历史
举不出相似的先例，而现在却被
筹谋戏弄得供哗众取闹之用。
瞧我，往日御床上的侍侣，曾占有
宸座的半边，一位大君主的女儿，
一个前程无限大的王子的娘亲，
站在这里，在任何愿来听的人们
面前，喋喋不休地求生命，争清誉。
因为生命如今对于我不外乎
伤心，我甘愿轻易地将它舍弃：
至于清贞，我把它遗给子女们，
我对它不能含糊。我向你的良心
申诉，王上：在包列齐倪思来到你
宫中以前，我怎样得你的眷顾，
如何受之而无愧；自从他来后，
我有过什么样言谈举措，逸出了
礼让所允许的寻常交接的限度，

Have strain'd to appear thus: if one jot beyond
The bound of honour, or in act or will
That way inclining, harden'd be the hearts
Of all that hear me, and my near'st of kin
Cry *fie* upon my grave!
Leontes I ne'er heard yet
That any of these bolder vices wanted
Less impudence to gainsay what they did
Than to perform it first.
Hermione That's true enough;
Though 'tis a saying, sir, not due to me.
Leontes You will not own it.
Hermione More than mistress of
Which comes to me in name of fault, I must not
At all acknowledge. For Polixenes, —
With whom I am accus'd, — I do confess
I lov'd him, as in honour he requir'd;
With such a kind of love as might become
A lady like me; with a love even such,
So and no other, as yourself commanded:
Which not to have done, I think had been in me
Both disobedience and ingratitude
To you and toward your friend; whose love had spoke,
Ever since it could speak, from an infant, freely,
That it was yours. Now for conspiracy,
I know not how it tastes; though it be dish'd
For me to try how: all I know of it
Is that Camillo was an honest man;
And why he left your court, the gods themselves,
Wotting no more than I, are ignorant.
Leontes You knew of his departure, as you know
What you have underta'en to do in 's absence.
Hermione Sir,
You speak a language that I understand not:

　　　　　　　以致理应被当众指控为罪犯；
　　　　　　　倘使我丝毫超越了清贞的制限，
　　　　　　　在行动，或在意向上倾向到那边，
　　　　　　　让所有耳闻者的心对我变铁石，
　　　　　　　让我的亲人们在我墓上叱"可鄙"！
里杭底斯　我从未听说过任何无耻的恶徒
　　　　　　　脸皮有那么厚，会用成倍的无耻
　　　　　　　去否认当初所犯的罪行。
候妙霓　　　　　　　　　你这话
　　　　　　　很不错；但跟我，王上，却毫不相关。
里杭底斯　你不肯承认。
候妙霓　　　　　说我曾经违犯过
　　　　　　　超越了被认是我的过失的非行，
　　　　　　　我决不承认。关于包列齐倪思，——
　　　　　　　我和他一同被控，我承认我爱他
　　　　　　　以这样一种爱，它符合我这身份，
　　　　　　　也符合他所须的尊敬；这样的爱，
　　　　　　　只此而无他，正是你自己所命令，
　　　　　　　不奉命，我想，在我当会是对你
　　　　　　　和对你的朋友，等于抗命和负义，
　　　　　　　他对你的爱，从他能说话就开始，
　　　　　　　自婴孩时起，已对你充分表白过。
　　　　　　　至于，你说到阴谋叛逆，我不知
　　　　　　　那是什么样味道，虽然它如今
　　　　　　　盛在盘盂中要我尝滋味：对这事，
　　　　　　　尽我所知的来说，喀米罗是个
　　　　　　　诚实人；为什么他要离去你朝廷，
　　　　　　　天神们，知道得不比我多，也未知。
里杭底斯　你知道他离去，正如你也知道
　　　　　　　他不在此间时节，你预备做什么。
候妙霓　　王上，
　　　　　　　你说的语言我不懂：我这生命

My life stands in the level of your dreams,
Which I'll lay down.

Leontes   Your actions are my dreams;
You had a bastard by Polixenes,
And I but dream'd it: — as you were past all shame, —
Those of your fact are so, — so past all truth:
Which to deny concerns more than avails; for as
Thy brat hath been cast out, like to itself,
No father owning it, — which is, indeed,
More criminal in thee than it, — so thou
Shalt feel our justice; in whose easiest passage
Look for no less than death.

Hermione   Sir, spare your threats:
The bug which you would fright me with, I seek.
To me can life be no commodity:
The crown and comfort of my life, your favour,
I do give lost; for I do feel it gone,
But know not how it went: my second joy,
And first-fruits of my body, from his presence
I am barr'd, like one infectious: my third comfort,
Starr'd most unluckily, is from my breast, —
The innocent milk in its most innocent mouth, —
Hal'd out to murder: myself on every post
Proclaim'd a strumpet; with immodest hatred
The child-bed privilege denied, which 'longs
To women of all fashion; lastly, hurried
Here to this place, i' the open air, before
I have got strength of limit. Now, my liege,
Tell me what blessings I have here alive,
That I should fear to die. Therefore proceed.

|||是在你幻想的射程之内，我将它
放弃。

里杭底斯 你自己的行动是我的幻想：
你跟包列齐倪思生了个野女儿，
而我不过在梦中见到她。你既然
浑不知羞耻，——你们有这般行径的
都如此，——所以你浑不知说句真话：
否认实事更为你所关心，但对你
没好处；正像你那野女儿给丢掉，
如她命运所应得，没父亲去认她，——
这件事，当真，是你，不是她，犯着罪，——
所以你定将身受我们的法律
裁制，在它那最宽和的进程之内，
不必去指望比死较轻微的惩罚。

候妙霓 王上，你这些恐吓，省了吧：你这
用来吓唬我的东西，我正要找它。
对于我，生命已没有一点安乐：
我此生欢乐之极致，你的爱宠，
我认为已丧失；我觉得它已消逝，
是怎样去的，则不知。我第二件乐事，
是我头生的孩子，我被禁跟他
相见，像是有恶疠。我第三件乐事，
她命运最孽蹙，她无比天真的嘴里
还含着天真的奶汁，从我这胸头
给拉走，且横遭凶杀：至于我自己，
在每根布告桩柱上被宣布为娼妓：
属于各色妇女的分娩后的权利，
因遭逢过度的痛恨而被剥夺：
最后，在我体力能恢复前，露天下，
被仓皇赶到此间来。现在，主君，
请告我，我活在人间有什么幸福，
会害怕去死？所以，请进行就是。

But yet hear this; mistake me not;—no life,—
I prize it not a straw,—but for mine honour
(Which I would free), if I shall be condemn'd
Upon surmises—all proofs sleeping else,
But what your jealousies awake—I tell you
'Tis rigour, and not law.—Your honours all,
I do refer me to the oracle:
Apollo be my judge!

First Lord　　　　This your request
Is altogether just: therefore, bring forth,
And in Apollo's name, his oracle:

　　　　　　　　　　[*Exeunt certain* Officers.]

Hermione　The Emperor of Russia was my father;
O that he were alive, and here beholding
His daughter's trial! that he did but see
The flatness of my misery; yet with eyes
Of pity, not revenge!

[*Re-enter* Officers, *with* Cleomenes *and* Dion.]

Officer　You here shall swear upon this sword of justice,
That you, Cleomenes and Dion, have
Been both at Delphos, and from thence have brought
This seal'd-up oracle, by the hand deliver'd
Of great Apollo's priest; and that since then,
You have not dar'd to break the holy seal,
Nor read the secrets in't.

Cleomenes, Dion　　　　All this we swear.

Leontes　Break up the seals and read.

Officer　[*Reads.*] *Hermione is chaste ; Polixenes bla-
　　meless ; Camillo a true subject ; Leontes a jealous
　　tyrant ; his innocent babe truly begotten ; and the
　　king shall live without an heir , if that which is*

但还请听这个；莫误会我的意思；
不是生命，我重视它不及一根草：——
但为我的荣誉，那个，我要它无罪；
假使我将被判罪，只根据猜疑，
所有的证据都睡去，只有你的嫉妒
所催醒的为凭，我告诉你说，这是
淫威，并不是法律。列位贵人们，
我向神谕提申诉：阿波罗大神
为我宣判！

贵　人　甲　　　　　这请求完全合情理：
因此上，以阿波罗之名，宣布神谕。

〔公吏数人下。

候　妙　霓　俄罗斯大皇帝是我的父亲：啊！
但愿他还活在人间，到此来看他
女儿受审讯；但愿他只要能见到
我这极度的悲惨；而且以怜悯，
不要以报复的心情和眼光来看！

〔公吏数人引克廖弥尼司与第盎上。

公　　　吏　你们两人将按着这公审的法剑
宣誓，说你们，克廖弥尼司与第盎，
都曾到过台尔福，从那里带回来
这通密缄的灵谕，伟大的阿波罗
座前的祭司所亲手授与，而且
你们不曾敢开启这神封，没读过
内中的秘密。

克廖弥尼司〕　　　　　对于这一切我们都
第　　盎〕
宣誓。

里杭底斯　　　打开了封缄，宣读。
公　　　吏　〔宣读〕"候妙霓贞洁；包列齐倪思无辜；喀米罗是个
忠实的臣民；里杭底斯是个嫉妒的暴君；他纯洁的
婴儿是他的亲生；国王将没有胤嗣，倘若失掉的没

lost be not found.

Lords Now blessed be the great Apollo!
Hermione   Praised!
Leontes Hast thou read truth?
Officer   Ay, my lord; even so
As it is here set down.
Leontes There is no truth at all i' the oracle:
The sessions shall proceed: this is mere falsehood!
          [*Enter a* Servant *hastily.*]
Servant My lord the king, the king!
Leontes   What is the business?
Servant O sir, I shall be hated to report it:
The prince your son, with mere conceit and fear
Of the queen's speed, is gone.
Leontes   How! gone?
Servant   Is dead.
Leontes Apollo's angry; and the heavens themselves
Do strike at my injustice. How now there!
                         [Hermione *faints.*]
Paulina This news is mortal to the queen: — Look down
And see what death is doing.
Leontes   Take her hence:
Her heart is but o'ercharg'd; she will recover. —
I have too much believ'd mine own suspicion: —
Beseech you tenderly apply to her
Some remedies for life. —
                    [*Exeunt* Paulina *and* Ladies *with*
                              Hermione.]
                         Apollo, pardon
My great profaneness 'gainst thine oracle! —
I'll reconcile me to Polixenes;

有去寻得。"
众　贵　人　　伟大的阿波罗,我们赞颂他光荣!
候　妙　霓　　赞颂!
里杭底斯　　　你当真读了灵谕吗?
公　　吏　　　　　　　　　　当真,
　　　　　　吾王;读的正是在这里写下的。
里杭底斯　　这灵谕所讲并非真话:这庭审
　　　　　　将继续进行:这完全是一派胡言。
　　　　　　　　　［仆从上。
仆　　从　　君王吾主,禀王上!
里杭底斯　　　　　　　　　有什么事情?
仆　　从　　啊,王上! 我禀报这消息将遭到
　　　　　　痛恨:您的王储小殿下,只为了
　　　　　　思念母后的命运,为了她担惊,
　　　　　　是去了。
里杭底斯　　　　　怎样? 去了?
仆　　从　　　　　　　　　　是死了。
里杭底斯　　　　　　　　　　　　　阿波罗
　　　　　　在发怒;天神们对我的不公在行施
　　　　　　打击。　　　　　　　　［候妙霓昏厥。］
　　　　　　　　　什么事,那边?
宝　理　娜　　　　　　　　这消息对王后
　　　　　　夺了她的命:——望下边;瞧吧,死神
　　　　　　多凶残。
里杭底斯　　　　　　抬她走:她的心只是承载
　　　　　　过了度;她还会苏醒:我太相信了
　　　　　　我自己的猜疑;请你对她温和地
　　　　　　施用些救生的药剂。——
　　　　　　　　　［宝理娜与伴娘数人舁候妙霓下。
　　　　　　　　　　　阿波罗,要请
　　　　　　原谅我对你灵谕的莫大亵渎!
　　　　　　我要跟包列齐倪思言归于好,

New woo my queen; recall the good Camillo—
Whom I proclaim a man of truth, of mercy;
For, being transported by my jealousies
To bloody thoughts and to revenge, I chose
Camillo for the minister to poison
My friend Polixenes: which had been done,
But that the good mind of Camillo tardied
My swift command, though I with death and with
Reward did threaten and encourage him,
Not doing it and being done: he, most humane,
And fill'd with honour, to my kingly guest
Unclasp'd my practice; quit his fortunes here,
Which you knew great; and to the certain hazard
Of all incertainties himself commended,
No richer than his honour: — how he glisters
Thorough my rust! And how his piety
Does my deeds make the blacker!
                    [*Re-enter* Paulina.]
Paulina   Woe the while!
O, cut my lace, lest my heart, cracking it,
Break too!
First Lord What fit is this, good lady?
Paulina What studied torments, tyrant, hast for me?
What wheels? racks? fires? what flaying? boiling
In leads or oils? what old or newer torture
Must I receive, whose every word deserves
To taste of thy most worst? Thy tyranny
Together working with thy jealousies, —
Fancies too weak for boys, too green and idle

向我的王后重复求情，召回那
良善的喀米罗，我此刻正式宣称，
他是个忠贞仁爱的好人；由于
被我疯狂的嫉妒所疾卷而去，
一心想流血报复，我选中喀米罗
作我的爪牙，要毒死包列齐倪思：
这事若非喀米罗的好心延缓了
我急疾的命令，早已经大错铸成；
虽然他做与不做，我用死、用酬报
威胁利诱他：可是他，仁善异常
而又富于光荣感，对我的宾王
显露出我的权谋策略，捐弃了
他在此间的、你知道很大的财产，
宁使他自己肯定冒一切的风险，
只除荣誉外别无财富：便这般，
他如何透过我的黄锈，闪耀青光！
而他的美德，怎样使我的行径
显得更黯黑！

〔宝理娜上。

宝理娜 　　　　　惨痛，唉哟，恶时辰！
啊，拉断这衣绳，否则啊，我的心，
迸断它，会把它自己一同迸破！

贵人甲 这是什么激情在爆发，好夫人？

宝理娜 你有什么计谋好的酷刑啊，凶王，
来镇我？什么刑轮？脱肢架？火焚？
什么剥皮与抽筋？油镬里煎熬，
流铅中沸滚？我得受什么旧有
或翻新的荼毒，如今我这每句话
都该挨受你的惨虐？你的凶暴，
跟你那忌妒配合着相成而作恶，
这忌妒，嗳呀，这些幻想，太愚蠢，
男孩子决不会有，太幼稚荒谬，

For girls of nine, — O, think what they have done,
And then run mad indeed, — stark mad! for all
Thy by-gone fooleries were but spices of it.
That thou betray'dst Polixenes, 'twas nothing;
That did but show thee, of a fool, inconstant,
And damnable ingrateful; nor was't much
Thou wouldst have poison'd good Camillo's honour,
To have him kill a king; poor trespasses, —
More monstrous standing by: whereof I reckon
The casting forth to crows thy baby daughter,
To be or none or little, though a devil
Would have shed water out of fire ere done't;
Nor is't directly laid to thee, the death
Of the young prince, whose honourable thoughts, —
Thoughts high for one so tender, — cleft the heart
That could conceive a gross and foolish sire
Blemish'd his gracious dam: this is not, — no,
Laid to thy answer: but the last, — O lords,
When I have said, cry *Woe*! — the queen, the queen,
The sweetest, dearest creature's dead; and vengeance for't
Not dropp'd down yet.
First Lord   The higher powers forbid!
Paulina   I say she's dead: I'll swear't. If word nor oath
Prevail not, go and see: if you can bring
Tincture, or lustre, in her lip, her eye,
Heat outwardly or breath within, I'll serve you

满九岁的女孩也不可能有,啊!
去想吧,它们闯下了什么祸根,
然后去发疯,去暴乱癫狂去吧;
因为你过去所干的傻事,相形下,
都不过是些须微末。你图谋坑害
包列齐倪思,那不算什么,仅仅
显示出你是个傻瓜,喜怒无常,
把敌友恩仇来个大混账;你企图
毒害喀米罗的清操美誉,要他
去杀死一位君王,也不算了不起;
这些罪辜都还是不足道,远较
骇人的却还有:其中我把你抛弃
女儿孩婴给老鸦去喂养,还当作
不算一回事;虽然纵令是魔鬼,
下得这样的辣手前,燃烧的眼睛
也会先流泪:年轻的王子的死,
这件事也不能要你直接去负责,
他那可敬的思想,——年纪恁稚幼,
思想恁高超,——坼裂了那颗童心,
当它想到了鄙野愚蠢的严亲
竟会污辱他尊仰的慈母:这不要,
不,叫你来认账:但是那最后的,——
啊,大人们!等我说过后,你们
都得叫"惨痛"!——王后,王后,最可爱
最可亲的人儿已经死,而上天的报应
还未曾降落。

贵 人 甲   上界的神灵们不让!
宝 理 娜 我说她已死;我发誓:如果说话
咒誓都没用,你们自己可去看:
若是你们能使她的嘴唇回红,
或眼睛再亮,身上有暖意,或内里
有气息,我将侍奉你们好似我

  As I would do the gods. —But, O thou tyrant!
Do not repent these things; for they are heavier
Than all thy woes can stir; therefore betake thee
To nothing but despair. A thousand knees
Ten thousand years together, naked, fasting,
Upon a barren mountain, and still winter
In storm perpetual, could not move the gods
To look that way thou wert.
Leontes   Go on, go on:
Thou canst not speak too much; I have deserv'd
All tongues to talk their bitterest!
First Lord   Say no more:
Howe'er the business goes, you have made fault
I' the boldness of your speech.
Paulina   I am sorry for't:
All faults I make, when I shall come to know them,
I do repent. Alas, I have show'd too much
The rashness of a woman: he is touch'd
To th' noble heart—What's gone and what's past help,
Should be past grief: do not receive affliction
At my petition; I beseech you, rather
Let me be punish'd, that have minded you
Of what you should forget. Now, good my liege,
Sir, royal sir, forgive a foolish woman:
The love I bore your queen, —lo, fool again! —
I'll speak of her no more, nor of your children;
I'll not remember you of my own lord,
Who is lost too: take your patience to you,
And I'll say nothing.
Leontes   Thou didst speak but well,

侍奉上界的天神们。可是你,啊,
你这暴君!你莫为这些事悔恨,
因为它们太沉重,你所有的悲痛
休想动弹得它们分毫;因此上,
只能预备去绝望,只此而无他。
一千次长跪,一万个年头,无休
无止,赤着身,饿着斋,在光石山头,
永远是隆冬,风雪横飞没尽期,
也不能促使天神们怜悯,使他们
移动目光向你望。

里 杭 底 斯　　　　　说下去,说吧;
不可能说得太多:我应受一切人
最苛刻的谴责。

贵 人 甲　　　　　不要再说了:不管
事情怎么样,你出言过于放肆,
对君王有违犯。

宝 理 娜　　　　　我为此感到抱歉:
我所犯一切过误,当知道它们时,
我都懊悔。唉呀!我过于呈露出
一个女人的鲁莽:他高贵的心情
感动了。过去的事情没法补救的,
应当不再去悲伤:别生受痛苦,
我请求;我恳愿您对我加以责罚,
是我提醒了您理应忘记的事情。
如今,我的好主君,君王我主啊,
请您宽恕一个傻女子:我对您
王后的心爱,——瞧,我又在发傻了!——
我将不再讲起她,和您的孩子们;
我将不叫您记起我自己的夫君,
他也已完了:保持您心地的平静,
我将不再说什么。

里 杭 底 斯　　　　　你说得却很对,

When most the truth; which I receive much better
Than to be pitied of thee. Pr'ythee, bring me
To the dead bodies of my queen and son:
One grave shall be for both; upon them shall
The causes of their death appear, unto
Our shame perpetual. Once a day I'll visit
The chapel where they lie; and tears shed there
Shall be my recreation: so long as nature
Will bear up with this exercise, so long
I daily vow to use it. — Come, and lead me
To these sorrows.

[*Exeunt.*]

SCENE III. Bohemia. *A desert Country near the Sea.*

[*Enter* Antigonus *with the* Child, *and* a Mariner.]

Antigonus　　Thou art perfect, then, our ship hath touch'd upon
The deserts of Bohemia?

Mariner　　　　　　Ay, my lord; and fear
We have landed in ill time: the skies look grimly,
And threaten present blusters. In my conscience,
The heavens with that we have in hand are angry,
And frown upon 's.

Antigonus　Their sacred wills be done! — Go, get aboard;
Look to thy bark: I'll not be long before
I call upon thee.

Mariner　Make your best haste; and go not
Too far i' the land: 'tis like to be loud weather;
Besides, this place is famous for the creatures
Of prey that keep upon't.

Antigonus　　　　　Go thou away:
I'll follow instantly.

Mariner　　　　I am glad at heart

尽是些真话,我听来要比你可怜我
有劲得好多。请你和我到我王后
和儿子的尸体那里:他们将葬在
同一个墓中:墓上将竖起碑铭,
把他们的死因敷陈,我的耻辱
将永志不渝。他们长眠的小教堂
我一天去瞻望一次,我在那厢
流的泪将会恢复我心神的健康:
只要我身体能支持这个礼拜,
我起誓我每天习常要去。来吧,
领我去茹悲饮痛。　　　　　　　　　　　　　　　　［同下。

第　三　景

［波希米亚。近海之荒野］
　　［安铁冈纳施抱婴孩。与一水手上。

安铁冈纳施　那么,你完全有把握,我们的船
是挨着波希米亚的荒野靠的岸?
水　　手　是啊,老爷;还担心俺们的拢岸
时候不大好:天公颜色多吓人,
马上要有大风暴。凭俺良心讲,
老天爷对俺们手上的娃儿在生气,
跟俺们在皱眉。
安铁冈纳施　　　　　　　愿天意能得完成!
你去,回船上;小心着你的船儿:
我不久就回来跟你打话。
水　　手　　　　　　　　　请尽快,
不要往里边走得过远了:这天气
像是要有大风暴;而且,这地方
闻名有呆在它地头的毒虫野兽。
安铁冈纳施　你去:我马上跟着来。
水　　手　　　　　　　我衷心乐意

To be so rid o' th' business.

[Exit.]

Antigonus Come, poor babe: —
I have heard (but not believ'd) the spirits of the dead
May walk again: if such thing be, thy mother
Appear'd to me last night; for ne'er was dream
So like a waking. To me comes a creature,
Sometimes her head on one side, some another:
I never saw a vessel of like sorrow,
So fill'd and so becoming: in pure white robes,
Like very sanctity, she did approach
My cabin where I lay: thrice bow'd before me;
And, gasping to begin some speech, her eyes
Became two spouts: the fury spent, anon
Did this break from her: *Good Antigonus,*
Since fate, against thy better disposition,
Hath made thy person for the thrower-out
Of my poor babe, according to thine oath, —
Places remote enough are in Bohemia,
There weep, and leave it crying; and, for the babe
Is counted lost for ever, Perdita
I pr'ythee call't. For this ungentle business,
Put on thee by my lord, thou ne'er shalt see
Thy wife Paulina more: so, with shrieks,
She melted into air. Affrighted much,
I did in time collect myself; and thought
This was so, and no slumber. Dreams are toys;
Yet, for this once, yea, superstitiously,
I will be squar'd by this. I do believe
Hermione hath suffer'd death, and that
Apollo would, this being indeed the issue

这样了结这件事。 [下。

安铁冈纳施 　　　　可怜的娃儿,
来吧:我听说,但不信,死人的鬼魂
会到世上来:若是真的话,你妈
昨夜对我显了灵,因为从没有
做梦像这般跟醒时一模一样。
朝我来了个人儿,她有时把头
侧向这一边,有时侧向那一边;
我从未见那个泪人儿这么悲哀,
这么样热泪盈眶,泣涕涟涟痛:
她一身缟素的长袍,好清真圣洁,
行近我躺着的船舱,向我三鞠躬,
喘息着正要开言,她两眼变成
一双水龙头:那火性过后,她立即
这样开言:"亲爱的安铁冈纳施,
既然命运,违反着你的好情性,
根据你发的誓,叫你做了扔掉
我可怜的娃儿的人,在波希米亚
有的是遥远的地方,那里你可以
前去,把这哭着的孩子丢下来;
并且,因为这娃儿是当作永远
没有的了,我请你叫它哀笛达:
为了这件不仁的勾当,我夫君
加在你身上,你将永远不再见
你的妻子宝理娜":她说到这里,
几声尖锐的绝叫,驀地不见了。
惊骇得厉害,我渐渐恢复了平静,
心想果真有这事,并不是梦寐。
梦境是虚幻事;可是这一遭,是啊,
我要迷信一下子,作这般想法。
我信候妙霓已经丧生;而按照
阿波罗的神意,这姑娘确是国王

Of King Polixenes, it should here be laid,
Either for life or death, upon the earth
Of its right father. Blossom, speed thee well!
                    [*Laying down the* child.]
There lie; and there thy character: there these;
                    [*Laying down a bundle.*]
Which may if fortune please, both breed thee, pretty,
And still rest thine. — The storm begins: — poor wretch,
That for thy mother's fault art thus expos'd
To loss and what may follow! — Weep I cannot,
But my heart bleeds: and most accurs'd am I
To be by oath enjoin'd to this. — Farewell!
The day frowns more and more: — thou'rt like to have
A lullaby too rough: — I never saw
The heavens so dim by day. A savage clamour! —
Well may I get aboard! — This is the chase:
I am gone for ever.
                    [*Exit, pursued by a bear.*]
              [*Enter an old* Shepherd.]

Shepherd I would there were no age between ten and three-and-twenty, or that youth would sleep out the rest; for there is nothing in the between but getting wenches with child, wronging the anciently, stealing, fighting. — Hark you now! Would any but these boiled brains of nineteen and two-and-twenty hunt this weather? They have scared away two of my best sheep, which I fear the wolf will sooner find than the master: if anywhere I have them, 'tis by the seaside, browsing of ivy. — Good luck, an't be thy will! what have we here? [*Taking up the child.*] Mercy on's, a bairn: A very pretty bairn! A boy or a child, I wonder? A pretty one; a very pretty one: sure, some scape: though I am not bookish, yet I can read waiting-gentlewoman in the scape. This has

包列齐倪思所生,她应当被抛在
这地方,随她去活或去死,在她
生身父亲的土地上。小花朵,祝你
幸运! 〔置婴孩于地。〕
　　躺在那里;那是你的身份:
那里是这些; 〔置包裹于地。〕
　　你运气好的话,这些
可能帮着叫有人哺养你,小宝贝,
而还是归你所有。风暴打来了:
可怜的小东西!为了你妈的过错,
你要这般身受到抛弃,和所有
跟着来的一切后果。哭泣我不能,
可是我的心在殷殷作痛,我又且
痛苦到极点,起了誓不能不做
这件事。再会!天色越来越黝暗:
你许会有支太粗暴的催眠曲子。
我从未见过白天这么暗。野兽
在号叫!但愿我安全回到船上!
是只给赶打的野兽:我这可完了。

〔下,被一大熊所追逐。〕
〔牧羊人上。〕

牧　羊　人　我但愿十岁跟二十三岁中间没什么年岁,或者年轻人把那段时光一觉睡掉;因为在那些年头干不出什么事情来,只除了叫女人生小孩,跟老年人过不去,偷东西,打架。此刻你且听!这样的天气除了十九、二十二岁热昏了头的家伙以外,还有谁打猎?他们把我两头最好的羊吓跑了;我恐怕狼倒要比主人先找到它们;我若在哪里找得到它们的话,准是在海边,在吃常春藤。好运道,假使天意要如此!这是什么?〔抱起婴孩〕天可怜见,是个娃娃;好漂亮一个娃娃!是个小子还是个姑娘,我倒奇怪?美,美得很;准是什么罪过:我虽然没有学问,可瞧得出是贵户人家的伴娘

been some stair-work, some trunk-work, some behind-door-work; they were warmer that got this than the poor thing is here. I'll take it up for pity: yet I'll tarry till my son comes; he hallaed but even now. — Whoa, ho hoa! [*Enter* Clown.]

Clown   Hilloa, loa!

Shepherd   What, art so near? If thou'lt see a thing to talk on when thou art dead and rotten, come hither. What ail'st thou, man?

Clown   I have seen two such sights, by sea and by land! — but I am not to say it is a sea, for it is now the sky: betwixt the firmament and it, you cannot thrust a bodkin's point.

Shepherd   Why, boy, how is it?

Clown   I would you did but see how it chafes, how it rages, how it takes up the shore! But that's not to the point. O, the most piteous cry of the poor souls! sometimes to see 'em, and not to see 'em; now the ship boring the moon with her mainmast, and anon swallowed with yest and froth, as you'd thrust a cork into a hogshead. And then for the land service, — to see how the bear tore out his shoulder-bone; how he cried to me for help, and said his name was Antigonus, a nobleman. — But to make an end of the ship, — to see how the sea flap-dragon'd it: — but first, how the poor souls roared, and the sea mocked them; — and how the poor gentleman roared, and the bear mocked him, — both roaring louder than the sea or weather.

Shepherd   Name of mercy! when was this, boy?

Clown   Now, now; I have not winked since I saw these sights: the men are not yet cold under water, nor the bear half dined on the gentleman; he's at it now.

Shepherd   Would I had been by to have helped the old man!

Clown   I would you had been by the ship-side, to have helped her: there your charity would have

犯的罪过。这是什么楼梯上的活儿,什么箱子上的活儿,什么门背后的活儿;他们生她出来的可比这可怜东西在这儿要暖和呢。可怜她,我要把她抱起来;可是我且待一下,等我儿子来;刚才只一会儿,他还在叫应我呢。喂哟,喂,哟嗨!

〔小丑上。

小　　　丑　嗨哟,嗨!

牧 羊 人　什么?你来得怎近了?你若是想看件东西,好给你去唠叨个没完,直讲到你死掉,烂掉,到这儿来。有什么难受,人儿?

小　　　丑　在海边,在岸上,我看见了两桩这样的怪事!可是我不说这是海,因为那是天:在天跟那东西之间,你插不下一个钻子尖。

牧 羊 人　哎也,孩子,怎么回事?

小　　　丑　但愿你只要看到它怎样发怒,它怎样狂暴,它怎样冲打岸滩边!但那可不是我的话头。啊!那些可怜的人儿叫得多惨;一会儿看到他们,一会儿不见;这下子那船儿把它的主桅戳穿月亮,跟着就叫泡沫飞白吞了下去,仿佛你把个软木瓶塞扔进只大酒桶里似的。再来说岸上的营生:眼看着那只大熊怎样把他的肩膀骨拉出来;他怎样对我叫救命,又说他名叫安铁冈纳施,是个贵人。可是,来讲完那条船怎么样:眼看着海水怎样吞了它下去:可是,首先那些可怜的人儿怎样呼号着,而海浪嘲笑他们;还有那可怜的贵人怎样呼号着,而那头大熊嘲笑他,他们两下子吼叫得比海浪、比风暴还响。

牧 羊 人　天可怜见!这是什么时候,孩子?

小　　　丑　现在,现在;我看到这些景象以后还没霎过眼呢:那些个人儿在水底下还没冷,那大熊也还没把那贵人吃上半顿饭:它现在还在吃。

牧 羊 人　但愿我在近边,好救那老人家一命!

小　　　丑　我但愿你在那条船儿近边,才好救它:那里你的善心

lacked footing.

Shepherd Heavy matters, heavy matters! But look thee here, boy. Now bless thyself: thou mettest with things dying, I with things new-born. Here's a sight for thee; look thee, a bearing-cloth for a squire's child! Look thee here; take up, take up, boy; open't. So, let's see:—it was told me I should be rich by the fairies: this is some changeling: — open't. What's within, boy?

Clown You're a made old man; if the sins of your youth are forgiven you, you're well to live. Gold! all gold!

Shepherd This is fairy-gold, boy, and 'twill prove so: up with it, keep it close: home, home, the next way! We are lucky, boy: and to be so still requires nothing but secrecy— Let my sheep go: — come, good boy, the next way home.

Clown Go you the next way with your findings. I'll go see if the bear be gone from the gentleman, and how much he hath eaten: they are never curst but when they are hungry: if there be any of him left, I'll bury it.

Shepherd That's a good deed. If thou mayest discern by that which is left of him what he is, fetch me to the sight of him.

Clown Marry, will I; and you shall help to put him i' the ground.

Shepherd 'Tis a lucky day, boy; and we'll do good deeds on't.

[*Exeunt.*]

可没地方立脚。

牧 羊 人　惨事！惨事！但你瞧这里,孩子。如今要恭喜你自己:你碰见的是死去的东西,我碰见的是新生的东西。这儿给你看件好东西;你瞧,一个乡绅人家的孩子穿的抱衣！你瞧这里:抱起来,抱起来,孩子;把它打开。就这样,我们来看:人家告诉我,我要靠神仙们发财:这是什么仙家的掉包娃儿。——把它打开。里面是什么东西,孩子?

小　　　丑　你是个发了财的老头儿:你年轻时节的罪辜若是叫饶恕了你的话,你是会有好日子过了。黄金！全是黄金！

牧 羊 人　这是仙家赏的黄金,孩儿,事情将会见得当真如此:抱起来,小心守护着它:回家,回家,走下一条路。我们运气好,孩子;要永远这么着,用不到别的,只要保守秘密就是了。我的羊儿,让它们去吧。来,好孩子,打下一条路回家去。

小　　　丑　你带着找到的东西走下一条路去。我要去看那大熊可离开了那贵人没有,它吃掉了多少:它们从不伤人,除非饿狠了。若是他还有给吃剩的部分,我去埋了它。

牧 羊 人　那是件好事。你若见到有什么他给吃残的部分还认得出他来,领我去认认他的模样。

小　　　丑　凭圣处女,我准会;你定得帮着把他埋进地里去。

牧 羊 人　这日子运道好,孩儿,我们今儿要做点好事。

〔同下。

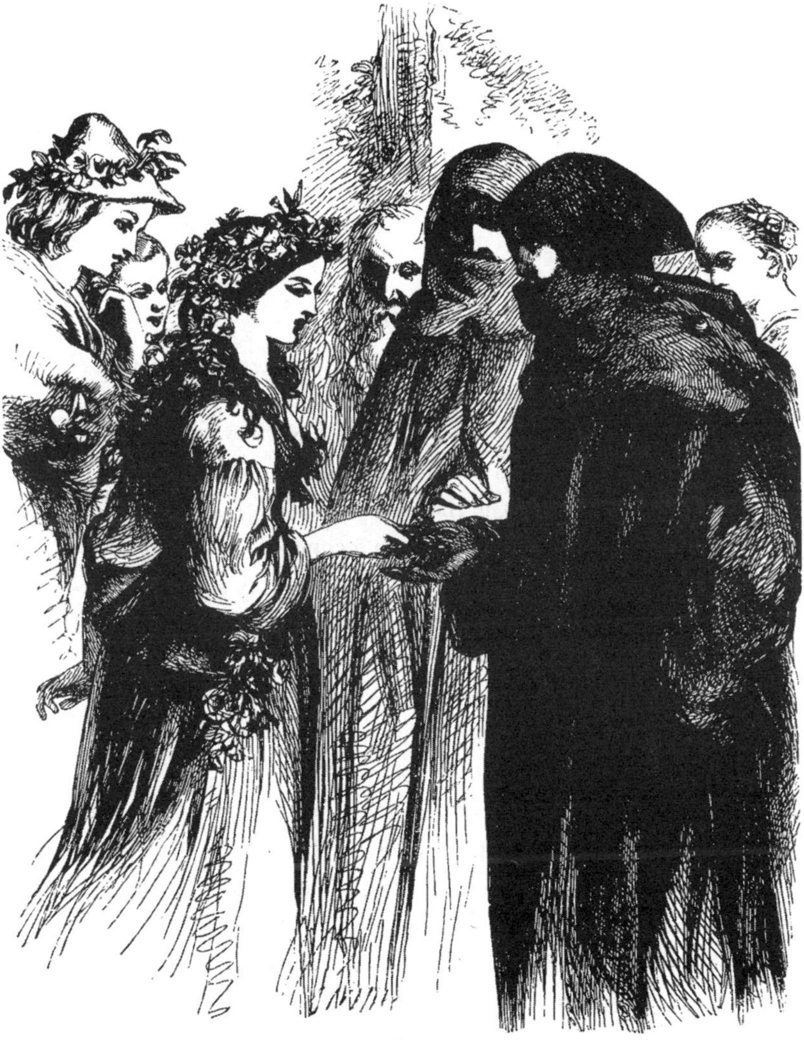

ACT IV.

SCENE I.

[*Enter* Time, *as Chorus.*]

Time   I, — that please some, try all; both joy and terror
Of good and bad; that make and unfold error, —
Now take upon me, in the name of Time,
To use my wings. Impute it not a crime
To me or my swift passage, that I slide
O'er sixteen years, and leave the growth untried
Of that wide gap, since it is in my power
To o'erthrow law, and in one self-born hour
To plant and o'erwhelm custom. Let me pass
The same I am, ere ancient'st order was
Or what is now received: I witness to
The times that brought them in; so shall I do
To the freshest things now reigning, and make stale
The glistering of this present, as my tale
Now seems to it. Your patience this allowing,
I turn my glass, and give my scene such growing
As you had slept between. Leontes leaving
The effects of his fond jealousies, so grieving

第 四 幕

第 一 景

[“时间”老人,作为歌舞者,上。

"时间"老人 我叫有些人高兴,把大家来考验,
好人和坏人见了我都会开欢颜,
又会生恐惧,错误由我生,又可以
由我来暴露,如今我用我的名义,
展翅作长飞。莫以为我疾疾飞翔,
一溜就过了十六年,不让那漫长
岁月里的生发滋长引起人注意,
是一桩罪过;因为我有的是权力
去推翻规律,又能在同一小时中
将习俗树立了起来又摧毁一空。
让我跟往常一样,那时候还没有
最古老的秩序,也无近今的时兽;
我曾亲见到它们被采纳;且将要
看到目前最新鲜的事情有朝
一日从此刻的光辉变成为腐臭,
正如这故事和它相形下已陈旧。
在诸君宽许之下,我来把沙钟
倒过来,使我搬演的戏文里遭逢
列位睡眠时所发生的事故。暂且把
里杭底斯——愚蠢的妒忌使他

That he shuts up himself; imagine me,
Gentle spectators, that I now may be
In fair Bohemia; and remember well,
I mention'd a son o' the king's, which Florizel
I now name to you; and with speed so pace
To speak of Perdita, now grown in grace
Equal with wondering: what of her ensues,
I list not prophesy; but let Time's news
Be known when 'tis brought forth: — a shepherd's daugh-
    ter,
And what to her adheres, which follows after,
Is the argument of Time. Of this allow,
If ever you have spent time worse ere now;
If never, yet that *Time* himself doth say
He wishes earnestly you never may.

                                                     [*Exit.*]

伤心得幽居而独处——在旁抛一抛，
想象我，亲爱的观众，此刻已经到
明媚的波希米亚来；并且请记住，
我说有位叫弗洛律采尔的王储；
我还要急急说起衰笛达，她如今
已长得窈窕淑美，一见使人惊：
她将怎么样我不想在这里预言；
等我有消息到来时再来搬演。
一个牧羊人的女儿，和跟她身份
相适合的一些后事，是我的话因。
请诸君准我把情节来这般推移，
若你们曾看过比这还要坏的戏；
若不曾看过，我"时间"得对列位说，
我切愿你们眼福再不会这么薄。　　　　〔下。

SCENE II. Bohemia. *A Room in the palace of* Polixenes.

[*Enter* Polixenes *and* Camillo.]

Polixenes I pray thee, good Camillo, be no more importunate: 'tis a sickness denying thee anything; a death to grant this.

Camillo It is fifteen years since I saw my country; though I have for the most part been aired abroad, I desire to lay my bones there. Besides, the penitent king, my master, hath sent for me; to whose feeling sorrows I might be some allay, or I o'erween to think so, — which is another spur to my departure.

Polixenes As thou lovest me, Camillo, wipe not out the rest of thy services by leaving me now: the need I have of thee, thine own goodness hath made; better not to have had thee than thus to want thee; thou, having made me businesses which none without thee can sufficiently manage, must either stay to execute them thyself, or take away with thee the very services thou hast done; which if I have not enough considered, — as too much I cannot, — to be more thankful to thee shall be my study; and my profit therein the heaping friendships. Of that fatal country Sicilia, pr'ythee, speak no more; whose very naming punishes me with the remembrance of that penitent, as thou call'st him, and reconciled king,

第 二 景

[波希米亚。包列齐倪思宫中一室]
[包列齐倪思与喀米罗上。]

包列齐倪思 我请你,好喀米罗,莫再执意要求了:任何事不答应你,都使我难受;答应你吧,简直是要命。

喀 米 罗 我离开宗邦到现在已十五年了:虽然我大部分时间在外邦生活,但我愿意把骨头埋在家乡。而况那后悔的君王,我的故主,还在找我回去;我也许能把他由衷的悲伤减少些许,这是激发我离开的另一个原因,除非我把自己估计得太高。

包列齐倪思 既然你爱我,喀米罗,现在离开我就是抹掉你以往对我的所有的勤劳。你自己对我这么好,已经使我少你不得:与其要这样失掉你,倒不如当初不曾有你。你替我办了旁人不经你协助所不能充分办妥的事,你便得待下来亲自把它们推行出去,若不然你就得把已经做下的勤劳也一起带走;你这些辛勤若是我过去酬谢得不够,——事实上我是不可能酬谢得充分的,——我将会想方设法如何来对你表示更多的谢意,而这么做对我自己也有好处,友谊会产生友谊。关于那个凶煞之邦西西利亚,请你莫再提起了,说到它我就会受刑罚似的回忆起那个如你所称

my brother; whose loss of his most precious queen and children are even now to be afresh lamented. Say to me, when sawest thou the Prince Florizel, my son? Kings are no less unhappy, their issue not being gracious, than they are in losing them when they have approved their virtues.

Camillo Sir, it is three days since I saw the prince. What his happier affairs may be, are to me unknown; but I have missingly noted he is of late much retired from court, and is less frequent to his princely exercises than formerly he hath appeared.

Polixenes I have considered so much, Camillo, and with some care; so far that I have eyes under my service which look upon his removedness; from whom I have this intelligence, — that he is seldom from the house of a most homely shepherd, — a man, they say, that from very nothing, and beyond the imagination of his neighbours, is grown into an unspeakable estate.

Camillo I have heard, sir, of such a man, who hath a daughter of most rare note: the report of her is extended more than can be thought to begin from such a cottage.

Polixenes That's likewise part of my intelligence: but, I fear, the angle that plucks our son thither. Thou shalt accompany us to the place; where we will, not appearing what we are, have some question with the shepherd; from whose simplicity I think it not uneasy to get the cause of my son's resort thither. Pr'ythee, be my present partner in this business, and lay aside the thoughts of Sicilia.

Camillo I willingly obey your command.

Polixenes My best Camillo! — We must disguise ourselves. [*Exeunt.*]

SCENE III. *A Road near the* Shepherd's *cottage.*

[*Enter* Autolycus, *singing.*]

Autolycus When daffodils begin to peer, —

呼的、已悔悟并跟我们重新和好了的王兄；他丧失他那最宝贵的王后和儿女，一提起就会叫我们伤心。告诉我，你什么时候见的储君吾儿弗洛律采尔？君王们看见儿女不肖，或德行高超而又失掉他们，同样地不幸。

喀 米 罗　　王上，我见到王储还在三天以前。他高兴去做什么事，我不知道；可是我想念着他而注意到，他近来不常在宫里，而且不像以前那样经常练习符合他储君身份的功夫。

包列齐倪思　　我也注意到这些，喀米罗，而且用了心；以至叫手下人看顾着，他为何如此形影萧疏；我得来的消息是，他踪迹不离一个极简朴的牧羊人家里；那个人，他们说，本来一无所有，而且出于他的邻居们意料之外，近来可变得暴富起来了。

喀 米 罗　　我听到过这样个人，王上，他有个了不起的女儿：她的声名传扬得那么四远皆知，人们都想不到会出自这样个茅舍人家。

包列齐倪思　　那也是我收到的消息里的一点；可是，我担心，把我们的儿子钓去的是那只鱼钩。你要陪伴我们到那地方去；那里，我们将不露我们的形相，跟那牧羊人谈些话；从他的愚蠢里，我想要得知我儿子为何时常去，不会有困难。请你和我一同去做这件事，把西西利亚的念头放过一边吧。

喀 米 罗　　我愿意遵从尊命。
包列齐倪思　　我顶好的喀米罗！——我们得化了装去。

〔同下。

第 三 景

〔牧羊人茅舍附近一行道〕
〔奥托力革厮歌唱着上。

奥托力革厮　　"水仙花的朵儿开始在显眼，

With, hey! the doxy over the dale, —
Why, then comes in the sweet o' the year:
  For the red blood reigns in the winter's pale.

The white sheet bleaching on the hedge, —
  With, hey! the sweet birds, O, how they sing! —
Doth set my pugging tooth on edge;
  For a quart of ale is a dish for a king.

The lark, that tirra-lirra chants, —
  With, hey! with, hey! the thrush and the jay, —
Are summer songs for me and my aunts,
  While we lie tumbling in the hay.

I have serv'd Prince Florizel, and in my time wore three-pile; but now I am out of service:

But shall I go mourn for that, my dear?
  The pale moon shines by night:
And when I wander here and there,
  I then do most go right.

If tinkers may have leave to live,
  And bear the sow-skin budget,
Then my account I well may give
  And in the stocks avouch it.

My traffic is sheets; when the kite builds, look to lesser linen. My father named me Autolycus; who being, as I am, littered under Mercury, was likewise a snapper-up of unconsidered trifles. With die and drab I purchased this caparison; and my revenue is the

还有那,嗨! 浪姑娘在溪谷里,
哎也,这年头的甜头露了脸;
　　红血关身,叫寒天的白血避。

"漂白的床单儿晾在篱笆上,
　　还有那,嗨! 小鸟儿唱得多美!
把俺的虎牙儿惹得活痒痒;
　　一夸脱老麦酒给国王喝都配。

"听那百灵鸟,得儿儿地尽啭,
　　还有那,嗨! 画眉儿和樫鸟,
夏天唱给浪姑姑听,还有俺,
　　当俺们躺在草堆里相搂抱。"

俺侍候过王太子弗洛律采尔,有个时候穿过三毳天鹅绒;可是现在俺已经不再侍候他了。

"好人儿,俺可要为那事伤心?
　　白苍苍的月亮夜里照得亮;
当俺到处晃,东找找来西寻寻,
　　那时节路走得对头,快进港。

"补锅匠若能到处跑,找活计,
　　背扛着那只猪皮的大口袋,
那俺尽可以讲讲俺的手艺,
　　便戴上脚枷公开说也不碍。"

俺的买卖是床单;鹞鹰做窠时,小心你们的小件衣衫。俺老子叫俺奥托力革斯这名儿;他跟俺一样,是在妙手空空儿老祖师牟陶莱的星宿照耀下生下来的,也是个攫取人家不留神的小东西的好手。托赖骰子和窑姐儿,俺弄到了这身漂亮衣服;俺的经常收

silly-cheat: gallows and knock are too powerful on the highway; beating and hanging are terrors to me; for the life to come, I sleep out the thought of it. — A prize! a prize!

[*Enter* Clown.]

Clown Let me see: — every 'leven wether tods; every tod yields pound and odd shilling; fifteen hundred shorn, what comes the wool to?

Autolycus [*Aside.*] If the springe hold, the cock's mine.

Clown I cannot do't without counters. — Let me see; what am I to buy for our sheep-shearing feast? *Three pound of sugar; five pound of currants; rice* — what will this sister of mine do with rice? But my father hath made her mistress of the feast, and she lays it on. She hath made me four and twenty nosegays for the shearers, — three-man song-men all, and very good ones; but they are most of them means and bases; but one puritan amongst them, and he sings psalms to hornpipes. I must have saffron to colour the warden pies; mace — dates, — none, that's out of my note; *nutmegs, seven; a race or two of ginger,* — but that I may beg; *four pound of prunes, and as many of raisins o' the sun.*

Autolycus [*Grovelling on the ground.*] O that ever I was born!

Clown I' the name of me, —

Autolycus O, help me, help me! Pluck but off these rags; and then, death, death!

Clown Alack, poor soul! thou hast need of more rags to lay on thee, rather than have these off.

Autolycus O sir, the loathsomeness of them offend me more than the stripes I have received, which are mighty ones and millions.

Clown Alas, poor man! a million of beating may come to a great matter.

Autolycus I am robb'd, sir, and beaten; my money and apparel ta'en from me, and these detestable things put upon me.

Clown What, by a horseman or a footman?

入是小偷小摸。害怕上绞架,挨拳打脚踢,俺吃不消大路上的买卖;挨揍,挨绞索,俺骇怕;身后怎么样,俺睡觉把它睡掉,不去想它。中了彩!中了彩!

〔小丑上。

小　　　丑　我来看:每十一头阉公羊好剪二十八磅毛;每捆值一镑几个先令;一千五百头剪下来,那羊毛一共值多少?

奥托力革厮　〔旁白〕若是机关灵的话,这只山鹬是俺的了。

小　　　丑　我没有筹码计算不出来。我来看;为我们的剪毛宴我要买些什么?"三磅白糖;五磅没籽葡萄干;稻米",我这妹子要稻米来做什么?可是我的爸叫她当了这酒筵的女主人,她倒做得挺不坏。她替我扎了二十四把花束给剪毛工,他们都是唱三折曲的,而且唱得很好;可是他们大多数都是唱中音和低音的;他们里边只有一个是清教徒,他唱圣诗跟乡下角笛舞的调子相和。我一定要买些番红花的橙黄来把冬梨饼染上颜色;肉豆蔻、枣椰子,——没有;那不开在我单子上;——豆蔻七颗;一两块姜,——可是那我能向他们讨;——四磅梅子干,日晒的葡萄干也是四磅。

奥托力革厮　啊!俺怎么会生在这世上的啊!　　　　〔匍匐于地。〕

小　　　丑　凭我的名儿!——

奥托力革厮　啊!救救俺,救救俺!只要拉掉这些破烂,然后死,死!

小　　　丑　唉呀,可怜的人儿!你需要再多些破烂加在身上,把这些拉掉不得。

奥托力革厮　啊,小爷!穿着它们起恶心,要比俺挨那鞭子狠狠地抽,抽上几百万下,还难受呢。

小　　　丑　唉呀,可怜的人儿!一百万鞭可已够多的了。

奥托力革厮　俺碰到强盗打劫,小爷,还挨了打;俺的钱和衣服都给抢了去,还把这些可恨的破烂套在俺身上。

小　　　丑　怎么,给骑马的强人还是走路的强人抢的?

Autolycus A footman, sweet sir, a footman.

Clown Indeed, he should be a footman, by the garments he has left with thee: if this be a horseman's coat, it hath seen very hot service. Lend me thy hand, I'll help thee: come, lend me thy hand.
[*Helping him up.*]

Autolycus O, good sir, tenderly, O!

Clown Alas, poor soul!

Autolycus O, good sir, softly, good sir: I fear, sir, my shoulder blade is out.

Clown How now! canst stand?

Autolycus Softly, dear sir! [*Picks his pocket.*] good sir, softly; you ha' done me a charitable office.

Clown Dost lack any money? I have a little money for thee.

Autolycus No, good sweet sir; no, I beseech you, sir: I have a kinsman not past three quarters of a mile hence, unto whom I was going; I shall there have money or anything I want: offer me no money, I pray you; that kills my heart.

Clown What manner of fellow was he that robbed you?

Autolycus A fellow, sir, that I have known to go about with *troll-my-dames*; I knew him once a servant of the prince; I cannot tell, good sir, for which of his virtues it was, but he was certainly whipped out of the court.

Clown His vices, you would say; there's no virtue whipped out of the court: they cherish it, to make it stay there; and yet it will no more but abide.

Autolycus Vices, I would say, sir. I know this man well: he hath been since an ape-bearer; then a process-server, a bailiff; then he compassed a motion of the Prodigal Son, and married a tinker's wife within a mile where my land and living lies; and, having flown over many knavish professions, he settled only in rogue: some call him Autolycus.

Clown Out upon him! prig, for my life, prig: he haunts

奥托力革厮		走路的强人,好小爷,走路的强人。
小	丑	当真,他该是个走路的,从他留给你的衣服上看出来:假使这是个骑马强人的上衣,那是穿得过狠了。把手伸给我,我来搀你起来:来,把手伸给我。[挽之使起。]
奥托力革厮		啊!好小爷,轻轻儿的,啊!
小	丑	唉呀,可怜的人儿!
奥托力革厮		啊!好小爷;轻点儿个,好小爷!俺害怕,小爷,俺的肩胛骨脱出来了。
小	丑	觉得怎样?能站吗?
奥托力革厮		轻点儿个,好小爷;[扒彼之衣袋]好小爷,轻点儿个。您对俺行了件好事。
小	丑	你缺少钱使吧?我来给你点钱。
奥托力革厮		不,好好小爷;不用,俺请您,小爷。俺有个亲戚离这儿不到四分之三英里,俺正要去找他;俺在那儿会有钱,或是俺所要的不管什么东西:莫送钱给俺,俺请你!那刺到俺心里。
小	丑	那打劫你的是个怎样的家伙?
奥托力革厮		一个家伙,小爷,俺知道他是走来走去兜玩"弹穿拱门"的:俺知道他有一阵曾做过王太子的下人。俺说不上,好小爷,是为了他的哪一件美德,可是他准是给从宫里鞭打出来的。
小	丑	为了他的缺德,你是想说;没有美德会给从宫里鞭打出来的:他们宝爱美德,要它待在那儿,可是它待不久就走了。
奥托力革厮		俺要说的正是缺德,小爷。俺跟这人儿很熟:他随后干过猴子出把戏;后来又当过奉公差遣的,做个执行吏;跟着便弄到了手一套"浪子回头"的木偶戏,又娶了个跟俺田地和家业所在相近一英里之内的一个补锅匠的老婆;混过了好些光棍活计之后,他终于安定在当流氓痞子上头:有人叫他奥托力革厮。
小	丑	滚他妈的!是个贼,千真万确,是个贼:他时常混到

wakes, fairs, and bear-baitings.

Autolycus Very true, sir; he, sir, he; that's the rogue that put me into this apparel.

Clown Not a more cowardly rogue in all Bohemia; if you had but looked big and spit at him, he'd have run.

Autolycus I must confess to you, sir, I am no fighter: I am false of heart that way; and that he knew, I warrant him.

Clown How do you now?

Autolycus Sweet sir, much better than I was; I can stand and walk: I will even take my leave of you and pace softly towards my kinsman's.

Clown Shall I bring thee on the way?

Autolycus No, good-faced sir; no, sweet sir.

Clown Then fare thee well: I must go buy spices for our sheep-shearing.

Autolycus Prosper you, sweet sir!

[*Exit* Clown.]

Your purse is not hot enough to purchase your spice. I'll be with you at your sheep-shearing too. If I make not this cheat bring out another, and the shearers prove sheep, let me be unrolled, and my name put in the book of virtue!

[*Sings.*]

> Jog on, jog on, the footpath way,
> And merrily hent the stile-a:
> A merry heart goes all the day,
> Your sad tires in a mile-a.   [*Exit.*]

SCENE IV. A Shepherd's *Cottage*.

[*Enter* Florizel *and* Perdita.]

Florizel These your unusual weeds to each part of you
Do give a life,—no shepherdess, but Flora
Peering in April's front. This your sheep-shearing

	礼拜堂节前守夜,赶集,斗熊的场所去。
奥托力革厮	一点不错,小爷;是他,小爷;就是那流氓把俺套上这衣服的。
小　　丑	全波希米亚没有个更胆怯的流氓:你只要对他高傲无礼,口吐唾沫,他就会逃跑。
奥托力革厮	俺得向您承认,小爷,俺不能打架:俺在那上头胆子小,那个他知道,俺管保他。
小　　丑	你现在觉得怎样?
奥托力革厮	好小爷,比刚才好多了:俺能站能走了。俺甚至要离开您,慢慢走到俺亲戚那儿去。
小　　丑	我要陪你一起走吗?
奥托力革厮	不用,俊小爷;不用,好小爷。
小　　丑	那就祝你好:我得去为我们的剪毛宴买点香料去。

〔下。

奥托力革厮	祝你顺遂,好小爷!你的钱包不够去替你买香料了。你那剪毛宴俺也要跟你在一块。俺若是不能叫这回欺骗生出下一回来,把剪羊毛的人儿变成羊,让俺从花名册上给划掉,把俺这名儿登上道德登记簿上去。
歌:	"快步,快步,走人行的小道,
	欢欢喜喜地跨过那阶梯:
	满心的欢喜耐得整天跑,
	心里悲伤了走不上一英里。"

〔下。

第　四　景

〔牧羊人茅舍前草坪〕
〔弗洛律采尔与哀笛达上。

| 弗洛律采尔 | 你这些不寻常的衣裳使你生气盎然:你不是牧羊女儿,是花神馥乐拉在阳春四月的前驱队里露丰标。你这场剪铰羊毛的庆宴 |

Is as a meeting of the petty gods,
And you the queen on't.
Perdita   Sir, my gracious lord,
To chide at your extremes it not becomes me, —
O, pardon that I name them! — your high self,
The gracious mark o' the land, you have obscur'd
With a swain's wearing; and me, poor lowly maid,
Most goddess-like prank'd up. But that our feasts
In every mess have folly, and the feeders
Digest it with a custom, I should blush
To see you so attir'd; swoon, I think,
To show myself a glass.
Florizel   I bless the time
When my good falcon made her flight across
Thy father's ground.
Perdita   Now Jove afford you cause!
To me the difference forges dread: your greatness
Hath not been us'd to fear. Even now I tremble
To think your father, by some accident,
Should pass this way, as you did. O, the fates!
How would he look to see his work, so noble,
Vilely bound up? What would he say? Or how
Should I, in these my borrow'd flaunts, behold
The sternness of his presence?
Florizel   Apprehend
Nothing but jollity. The gods themselves,
Humbling their deities to love, have taken
The shapes of beasts upon them: Jupiter
Became a bull and bellow'd; the green Neptune

好比是小小天神们一同来聚会，
而你是宴上的女娥王。

哀笛达 　　　　　　　　储君殿下，
由我来责备您这些过度的言谈
不相称：啊！我提到它们，请原谅。
您高贵的自身，这宇内英俊的表率，
您把牧羊子的衣着将它隐盖住，
而我，穷苦微贱的小姑娘，却这样
活像女神般装扮起。我们的庆宴
除非每一只盘盏都盛得有痴愚，
而且吃的人照常把它消灭掉，
我见到您这般穿着不能不脸红，——
您发誓，我想，要使人间的习俗
摔一跤，且叫我面对菱花见龟鉴。

弗洛律采尔 当我的那只幸福的鹞鹰飞过你
父亲的牧地时，我对那时光祝福。

哀笛达 如今，大概是天神叫您这么做！
对于我，您我贵贱不相同形成了
悚惧：您品位高超，不惯于害怕。
就在此刻，我想到您父亲碰巧会
跟您一样到这里来，便不免颤抖。
啊，天上司命运的女神们！您父亲
见到他世子您殿下，原来多高贵，
如今装束得这般低微，他可将
怎么样？他会说什么？而我，穿戴着
这些借来的鲛绡和珠翠，将怎样
面对他颜容的峻厉？

弗洛律采尔 　　　　　　　不用想别的，
只顾感欢乐就是了。天神们也为
恋爱降低过他们为神的身份，
曾采用畜生的形象：天王巨璧特
变成一头牛，哞叫过；碧绿的海龙王

A ram and bleated; and the fire-rob'd god,
Golden Apollo, a poor humble swain,
As I seem now: — their transformations
Were never for a piece of beauty rarer, —
Nor in a way so chaste, since my desires
Run not before mine honour, nor my lusts
Burn hotter than my faith.

Perdita   O, but, sir,
Your resolution cannot hold when 'tis
Oppos'd, as it must be, by the power of the king:
One of these two must be necessities,
Which then will speak, that you must change this purpose,
Or I my life.

Florizel   Thou dearest Perdita,
With these forc'd thoughts, I pr'ythee, darken not
The mirth o' the feast: or I'll be thine, my fair,
Or not my father's; for I cannot be
Mine own, nor anything to any, if
I be not thine: to this I am most constant,
Though destiny say no. Be merry, gentle;
Strangle such thoughts as these with any thing
That you behold the while. Your guests are coming:
Lift up your countenance, as it were the day
Of celebration of that nuptial which
We two have sworn shall come.

Perdita   O lady Fortune,
Stand you auspicious!

Florizel   See, your guests approach:
Address yourself to entertain them sprightly,
And let's be red with mirth.
[*Enter* Shepherd, *with* Polixenes *and* Camillo, *disguised*;
     Clown, Mopsa, Dorcas, with others.]

Shepherd Fie, daughter! When my old wife liv'd, upon

奈泼钧变一头公羊,也曾咩咩叫;
穿火袍的日神阿波罗,金光灿烂,
变成个穷苦的牧羊人,跟我一个样。
他们为之而变化的俏佳人,英姿
绝不更卓绝,或情操能和你比拟,
既然我不让色情赶在我荣誉前,
不准欲火燃烧得比情焰更炽烈。

衷 笛 达 啊!可是,您的那决心准守不住,
殿下,当它被君王的权力反对时,
那一定无疑。这样的两件事,其中
一桩准发生,到时候自然会分晓:
您必得改变那意向,或者我改变
这生涯。

弗洛律采尔 你,最亲爱的衷笛达,请你
莫把这些牵强的思虑使我们
这欢宴郁郁无欢:我或者是你的,
我的丽妹,或者不是我父亲的;
我不是我自己的人,也不为任何人
所有,假使不属于你的话:这一点
我信守不渝,即令命运说不然。
尽情欢乐吧,可爱的;用你眼前
所见的情景把这些思想湮灭掉。
你的宾客们在来了:两颊笑春风,
仿佛这是那新婚庆喜日,那一天
我们曾双双起誓一定要到来。

衷 笛 达 啊,司命运的女神,请施恩嘉惠!
弗洛律采尔 看吧,你的宾客们已纷纷来近;
准备去活泼泼欢娱他们,让我们
红艳艳满脸欢欣。

[牧羊人导乔装的包列齐倪思与喀米罗上;小丑、瑁
泊沙、桃卡丝与余众上。

牧 羊 人 不行,女儿!往日我老妻在世时,

This day she was both pantler, butler, cook;
Both dame and servant; welcom'd all; serv'd all;
Would sing her song and dance her turn; now here
At upper end o' the table, now i' the middle;
On his shoulder, and his; her face o' fire
With labour, and the thing she took to quench it
She would to each one sip. You are retir'd,
As if you were a feasted one, and not
The hostess of the meeting: pray you, bid
These unknown friends to us welcome, for it is
A way to make us better friends, more known.
Come, quench your blushes, and present yourself
That which you are, mistress o' the feast: come on,
And bid us welcome to your sheep-shearing,
As your good flock shall prosper.
Perdita   [*To* Polixenes.] Sir, welcome!
It is my father's will I should take on me
The hostess-ship o' the day: —
[*To* Camillo.]   You're welcome, sir!
Give me those flowers there, Dorcas. —Reverend sirs,
For you there's rosemary and rue; these keep
Seeming and savour all the winter long:
Grace and remembrance be to you both!
And welcome to our shearing!
Polixenes   Shepherdess—
A fair one are you! — well you fit our ages
With flowers of winter.
Perdita   Sir, the year growing ancient, —
Not yet on summer's death nor on the birth
Of trembling winter, — the fairest flowers o' the season
Are our carnations and streak'd gillyvors,

　　　　　　　这一天她管伙食房,供应酒肴,
　　　　　　　又兼当厨子;是主母,又是仆人;
　　　　　　　欢迎大伙儿,侍候他们,轮到她
　　　　　　　还要唱歌和跳舞;一会儿在此,
　　　　　　　在餐桌上首,一会儿又到了中间;
　　　　　　　跟这个跳舞,又跟那个;劳累得
　　　　　　　脸上通红,举杯消乏时还要对
　　　　　　　每一个啜酒祝福。你退在后边,
　　　　　　　倒像个被请的来客,不像女主人:
　　　　　　　请你,对这些不认识的朋友表示
　　　　　　　我们的欢迎;因为这是替我们
　　　　　　　结交得深一点,更加相熟些。来吧,
　　　　　　　莫害臊,做出宴会主妇的样子来:
　　　　　　　来啊,欢迎我们来到你这剪铰
　　　　　　　羊毛的宴会上来,好叫你的羊群
　　　　　　　繁荣昌盛。

裒　笛　达　　[向包列齐倪思]老伯伯,欢迎! 我父亲
　　　　　　　要我当今天的女主人。[向喀米罗]您也欢迎,
　　　　　　　老伯伯。给我那两个花束,桃卡丝。
　　　　　　　两位可敬的老伯伯,这里有两束
　　　　　　　迷迭香和芸香给你们;这些花儿
　　　　　　　一冬天都保持花形美好和花香:
　　　　　　　致你们两位以天恩和忆念,欢迎
　　　　　　　光临我们的剪毛宴!

包列齐倪思　　　　　　　　　牧羊女郎,——
　　　　　　　你是个美人儿,——你把冬天的花儿
　　　　　　　配上我们的年龄很合适。

裒　笛　达　　　　　　　　　　　　　老伯伯,
　　　　　　　这年景渐渐变得老了,不由于
　　　　　　　盛夏的消亡,也无关寒战的隆冬
　　　　　　　已经诞生,这季节里最美的花儿
　　　　　　　是我们的石竹,和那条纹的墙花,

Which some call nature's bastards: of that kind
Our rustic garden's barren; and I care not
To get slips of them.
Polixenes   Wherefore, gentle maiden,
Do you neglect them?
Perdita   For I have heard it said
There is an art which, in their piedness, shares
With great creating nature.
Polixenes   Say there be;
Yet nature is made better by no mean
But nature makes that mean; so, o'er that art
Which you say adds to nature, is an art
That nature makes. You see, sweet maid, we marry
A gentler scion to the wildest stock,
And make conceive a bark of baser kind
By bud of nobler race. This is an art
Which does mend nature, — change it rather; but
The art itself is nature.
Perdita   So it is.
Polixenes   Then make your garden rich in gillyvors,
And do not call them bastards.
Perdita   I'll not put
The dibble in earth to set one slip of them;
No more than were I painted, I would wish
This youth should say, 'twere well, and only therefore
Desire to breed by me. — Here's flowers for you;
Hot lavender, mints, savory, marjoram;
The marigold, that goes to bed with the sun,
And with him rises weeping; these are flowers
Of middle summer, and I think they are given
To men of middle age. You're very welcome!

那有人叫它造化的私生子；那个，
我们乡村的花园里不长，而我也
不想摘些来荐奉。

包列齐倪思 可爱的姑娘，
为什么你瞧不起它们？

哀　笛　达 因为我听说
它们斑斓的五彩一半是手艺
所形成，那人工跟造化平分了秋色。

包列齐倪思 就说有这样的手艺吧；但造化
不能被人工所改进，除非那人工
为造化所创造：因而，那手艺，你说
它对造化能有所增加，它上头
另有造化的手艺来把它创造。
你看到，亲爱的姑娘，我们将一支
比较高贵的嫩枝接入那最最
粗野的树木，使那微贱的树身
长出贵种的新芽：这就是那改进
造化的人工，或许说改变它，可是
那人工本身就是造化。

哀　笛　达 它就是。

包列齐倪思 那么，叫你的花园里多长些墙花，
而且莫再把私生子称呼它们。

哀　笛　达 我不会把小锹插进土里，即令去
栽它们一支；正好比，我若抹上粉，
我不愿这后生对我说，这样很好，
而且只为了这样，愿跟我生孩子。
这里有花给你们；辛芳的薰衣草、
薄荷、夏芳香、牛膝草；和太阳同时
去入睡、也跟太阳一同起身而
哭泣的金盏草：这些是仲夏的花，
我想好把它们给中年人。极欢迎
你们。

Camillo I should leave grazing, were I of your flock,
And only live by gazing.
Perdita   Out, alas!
You'd be so lean that blasts of January
Would blow you through and through. — Now, my fairest
    friend,
I would I had some flowers o' the spring that might
Become your time of day; — and yours, and yours,
That wear upon your virgin branches yet
Your maidenheads growing. — O Proserpina,
For the flowers now, that, frighted, thou lett'st fall
From Dis's waggon! — daffodils,
That come before the swallow dares, and take
The winds of March with beauty; violets dim
But sweeter than the lids of Juno's eyes
Or Cytherea's breath; pale primroses,
That die unmarried ere they can behold
Bright Phoebus in his strength, — a malady
Most incident to maids; bold oxlips, and
The crown-imperial; lilies of all kinds,
The flower-de-luce being one. — O, these I lack,
To make you garlands of; and, my sweet friend,
To strew him o'er and o'er!
Florizel   What, like a corse?
Perdita No; like a bank for love to lie and play on;
Not like a corse; or if, — not to be buried,
But quick, and in mine arms. Come, take your flowers;
Methinks I play as I have seen them do
In Whitsun pastorals: sure, this robe of mine

喀 米 罗	假使我在你羊群里的话, 我会不去吃草,凭眼睛就看个饱。
裒 笛 达	苦啊,唉哟!那您会瘦得恁可怜, 正月的寒飚会把您吹透又吹彻。 现在,我最最俊秀的朋友,但愿我 有些春天的花儿跟你的年华配; 还有你们的,你们的,你们的童贞 正长在你们碧碧清贞的枝桠上: 啊,泊罗漱琵娜!要说起那花儿, 如今,你当时因害怕、从地司车上 所掉,那金黄的水仙,燕子还不敢 冒寒它们已先来,使三月的料峭 寒风一见惊华美;幽静的紫罗兰, 虽素雅,却要比天后朱诺的眼睑 或爱神昔西丽亚的呼息更甜美; 苍白的莲馨花,见到灿烂的日神 斐勃斯光明朗照前,未嫁而先夭, 那是处女们常遭的病恹恹的摧折; 显赫的牛唇花和皇冠似的贝母; 各种百合花,鸢尾是其中之一。 啊!我没有这些个花儿为你们 和我亲爱的朋友来编结花冠, 再把他花雨缤纷地撒得花满身!
弗洛律采尔	什么?像个尸体般?
裒 笛 达	不是,要像个 花堤般好给燕侣莺俦在上面 偃卧和游戏;不像个尸体;或者, 假如像的话,——不是去埋葬,要勃勃 有生气,且在我臂腕中。来吧,拿着 你们的花儿:看来我这般形景 好像他们在降灵节演的牧歌剧 中间的扮演:的确,我这件褒袍

Does change my disposition.
Florizel   What you do
Still betters what is done. When you speak, sweet,
I'd have you do it ever; when you sing,
I'd have you buy and sell so; so give alms;
Pray so; and, for the ordering your affairs,
To sing them too: when you do dance, I wish you
A wave o' the sea, that you might ever do
Nothing but that; move still, still so, and own
No other function: each your doing,
So singular in each particular,
Crowns what you are doing in the present deeds,
That all your acts are queens.
Perdita   O Doricles,
Your praises are too large: but that your youth,
And the true blood which peeps fairly through it,
Do plainly give you out an unstained shepherd,
With wisdom I might fear, my Doricles,
You woo'd me the false way.
Florizel   I think you have
As little skill to fear as I have purpose
To put you to't. But, come; our dance, I pray:
Your hand, my Perdita; so turtles pair
That never mean to part.
Perdita   I'll swear for 'em.
Polixenes This is the prettiest low-born lass that ever
Ran on the green-sward: nothing she does or seems

改变了我的情性。
弗洛律采尔 　　　　　你这才说的,
比刚才更好。当你说话时,心爱的,
我愿你不停地说着;当你歌唱时,
我愿你买卖东西的时候也这样;
也这般施舍;也这般祈祷;而且,
在安排事务时,也把它们一声声
吟唱;当你舞蹈时,我愿你是海上
一个浪,好使你永远那样,不去做
别的;永远滉漾永远漂荡,
不做其他的动作:你每桩行动,
它的每一个细关末节都如此
无双而妙绝,以至恰好使得你
正在着手的那些事登峰而造极,
这就使你做的事桩桩和件件
都成了姬姜。
哀 笛 达 　　　　　啊,陶律葛理斯!
您过于夸奖:但您那轻轻的年岁,
以及您本真纯朴的血流使你
说时脸红红,显得你是个白玉
无瑕的牧羊人;可是用那股聪明
我恐怕,陶律葛理斯,您对我求爱
用得不正路。
弗洛律采尔 　　　　　我想你绝无理由
去恐惧,正如我毫无用意叫你怕。
可是,来吧;我们一起舞,我请你。
将手搀着我,我的哀笛达:雉鸠们
便这般作对成双,永远不相离。
哀 笛 达 我可以替它们起誓。
包列齐倪思 　　　　　这是个曾在
草坪上奔跑的最美的寻常百姓家
姑娘:她这相貌和举止有味道

But smacks of something greater than herself,
Too noble for this place.
Camillo   He tells her something
That makes her blood look out: good sooth, she is
The queen of curds and cream.
Clown   Come on, strike up.
Dorcas Mopsa must be your mistress; marry, garlic,
To mend her kissing with!
Mopsa   Now, in good time!
Clown Not a word, a word; we stand upon our manners. —
Come, strike up.
[*Music. Here a dance Of* Shepherds *and* Shepherdesses.]
Polixenes Pray, good shepherd, what fair swain is this
Which dances with your daughter?
Shepherd They call him Doricles; and boasts himself
To have a worthy feeding; but I have it
Upon his own report, and I believe it:
He looks like sooth. He says he loves my daughter:
I think so too; for never gaz'd the moon
Upon the water as he'll stand, and read,
As 'twere, my daughter's eyes: and, to be plain,
I think there is not half a kiss to choose
Who loves another best.
Polixenes   She dances featly.
Shepherd So she does anything; though I report it,
That should be silent; if young Doricles
Do light upon her, she shall bring him that
Which he not dreams of.
[*Enter a* Servant.]
Servant O master, if you did but hear the pedlar at the door, you would never dance again after a tabor and

	显得比她身份高；对这个所在 太高贵。
喀　米　罗	他对她说了些什么，使她 两颊泛红晕。当真，她是位奶酪 和乳脂的王后。
小　　　丑	来吧，吹打起来。
桃　卡　丝	瑂泊沙一定得做你的舞伴：你吃上 大蒜，凭圣处女，吻起她来格外好。
瑂　泊　沙	你挑中这时候来捣乱！
小　　　丑	不要吵，不要吵：我们要做得礼貌周全。来吧，吹打 起来。　　　　　　　　　　　　　　　　　［乐声起。 　　　　　　　　　　　　　　［众牧羊人与牧羊女起舞。
包列齐倪思	请问，好牧羊老人，这个俊牧人 是什么样人，他在跟你的女儿 一起舞？
牧　羊　人	他们说他叫陶律葛理斯， 他夸口有块值价的牧地；可是我 听他自己说，而且相信他：他看来 的确像那样。他说他爱我女儿： 我也这么想；因为月亮从来不 对着水那么样凝视，像他站在 那里凝注着我那女儿的眼睛； 而且，老实说，要想在他俩亲吻中 分辨出谁更爱谁，不可能。
包列齐倪思	她舞得 很利落。
牧　羊　人	她做什么事都这样，我虽说 那不用张扬。后生的陶律葛理斯 倘使到手了她，她将会带给他 他连做梦也没有梦到的东西。 　　　　　　　　　　　　　　　　　　［仆人上。
仆　　　人	啊，主人！你只要听到了门口那货郎叫卖，你决不再

pipe; no, the bagpipe could not move you: he sings several tunes faster than you'll tell money: he utters them as he had eaten ballads, and all men's ears grew to his tunes.

Clown He could never come better: he shall come in. I love a ballad but even too well, if it be doleful matter merrily set down, or a very pleasant thing indeed and sung lamentably.

Servant He hath songs for man or woman of all sizes; no milliner can so fit his customers with gloves: he has the prettiest love-songs for maids; so without bawdry, which is strange; with such delicate burdens of *'dildos* and' *fadings, jump her and thump her*; and where some stretch-mouth'd rascal would, as it were, mean mischief, and break a foul gap into the matter, he makes the maid to answer *Whoop, do me no harm, good man,*—puts him off, slights him, *with Whoop, do me no harm, good man.*

Polixenes This is a brave fellow.

Clown Believe me, thou talkest of an admirable conceited fellow. Has he any unbraided wares?

Servant He hath ribbons of all the colours i' the rainbow; points, more than all the lawyers in Bohemia can learnedly handle, though they come to him by the gross; inkles, caddisses, cambrics, lawns; why he sings 'em over as they were gods or goddesses; you would think a smock were a she-angel, he so chants to the sleeve-hand and the work about the square on't.

Clown Pr'ythee bring him in; and let him approach singing.

Perdita Forewarn him that he use no scurrilous words in his tunes.

[*Exit* Servant.]

Clown You have of these pedlars that have more in them than you'd think, sister.

Perdita Ay, good brother, or go about to think.

[*Enter* Autolycus, *Singing.*]

		会要跟着小鼓和笛子舞蹈了；不，风笛不能动你的心了。他唱几只调儿比你数钱还快；他唱着它们仿佛他把山歌吃进肚里去了似的，大伙儿的耳朵变得长在他调门上的一般。
小	丑	他来得再好没有了：他该走进里边来：我把一支山歌爱听得甚么似的，若是它把伤心事儿谱得很乐，或者把件真正的乐事唱得很悲伤。
仆	人	他有各种尺码的歌儿唱给男人也唱给女人听；没有个做女人衣帽的裁缝替主顾们缝手套能有他那么顺手：他唱给姑娘们听的情歌再美不能美了；那么一点儿不淫猥，真奇怪；有这么愉快的"底而多"和"我吹小笛"的叠唱，还有"摔倒她和拳打她"；唱到那里有什么脏嘴巴的坏蛋家，仿佛是，起恶意，用丑话插进歌里头来时，他叫那小姑娘回答道，"嘿，别损人，好汉子"；轻蔑他，用这么句话，"嘿，别损人，好汉子，"来对付。
包列齐倪思		这人对妇女颇有礼貌。
小	丑	信我的话，你讲的是个出奇的妙想天开的人。他可有什么不褪色的货吗？
仆	人	他有彩虹里各种颜色的缎带；扣絛他多得比波希米亚所有的律师能讲得头头是道的还要多，即使他们的案子成批地来；毛线带、毛丝带、细白麻纱、上好荨麻布：哎也，他叫唱得仿佛它们是上界的天神或女神似的。您会以为一件女衬衣是位女天使，他把袖口和胸前的花绣唱得那么好听。
小	丑	请你领他进来，让他来时一壁厢走一壁厢唱。
哀笛达		关照他在曲调里别用粗鄙不堪的字句。

〔仆人下。

小	丑	有些小贩，他们有的东西比你所能设想到的要多，妹子。
哀笛达		不错，好阿哥，比你所极力去设想的要多。

〔奥托力革厮上，唱。

Lawn as white as driven snow;
Cypress black as e'er was crow;
Gloves as sweet as damask-roses;
Masks for faces and for noses;
Bugle-bracelet, necklace amber,
Perfume for a lady's chamber;
Golden quoifs and stomachers,
For my lads to give their dears;
Pins and poking-sticks of steel,
What maids lack from head to heel.
Come, buy of me, come; come buy, come buy;
Buy, lads, or else your lasses cry:
Come, buy.

Clown If I were not in love with Mopsa, thou shouldst take no money of me; but being enthralled as I am, it will also be the bondage of certain ribbons and gloves.

Mopsa I was promis'd them against the feast; but they come not too late now.

Dorcas He hath promised you more than that, or there be liars.

Mopsa He hath paid you all he promised you: may be he has paid you more, — which will shame you to give him again.

Clown Is there no manners left among maids? will they wear their plackets where they should bear their faces? Is there not milking-time, when you are going to bed, or kiln-hole, to whistle off these secrets, but you must be tittle-tattling before all our guests? 'tis well they are whispering. Clamour your tongues, and not a word more.

Mopsa I have done. Come, you promised me a tawdry lace, and a pair of sweet gloves.

Clown Have I not told thee how I was cozened by the way, and lost all my money?

Autolycus And indeed, sir, there are cozeners abroad; therefore it behoves men to be wary.

Clown Fear not thou, man; thou shalt lose nothing here.

"苎麻布白得像风飘的雪花；
黑绉绸乌黢漆黑像乌鸦；
手套香喷喷像石竹色蔷薇；
假面用来遮俊鼻子和蛾眉；
黑水钻手镯，琥珀珠项圈，
俏娘娘绣房里使用的香水；
绣金的头巾和花彩的胸衣，
小哥哥好买来送给小阿姨；
别针和烫褶绉颈衣的小钢棍，
姑娘们缺少的，从头顶到脚跟：
都来向我买；都来买，都来买；
不然小阿姨要哭着把你们怪：
都来买。"

小　　　丑　我若是不跟瑁泊沙要好，你便拿不到我的钱；可是我爱上了她，就不能不买点缎带和手套。

瑁　泊　沙　你答应剪毛宴前给我的；可是现在给我还不算太迟。

桃　卡　丝　他答应你的东西还不止那么多，不然的话就有人撒谎。

瑁　泊　沙　他答应你的都已经给了你：也许他给得你太多了，你还给他时会丢你的脸。

小　　　丑　姑娘们之间不讲礼貌吗？她们当着外人，可要把彼此的私事拿出来讲，不顾顾面子吗？是不是没有挤奶的时间，或者在睡觉之前，熬麦芽糖的炉灶前面，去轻轻谈这些秘密，却定要在客人面前来噜嗦？幸亏他们在轻声谈话：停住你们的嘴，莫再讲一句话。

瑁　泊　沙　我说完了。来，你答应我一串圣奥特莱项圈和一副香手套。

小　　　丑　我没有告诉过你吗，我在路上受了骗，把钱都给骗掉了？

奥托力革厮　当真，小爷，外面确是有骗子；所以咱们要小心。

小　　　丑　别害怕，人儿，你在这儿决不会丢东西。

Autolycus I hope so, sir; for I have about me many parcels of charge.
Clown What hast here? ballads?
Mopsa Pray now, buy some: I love a ballad in print a-life; for then we are sure they are true.
Autolycus Here's one to a very doleful tune. How a usurer's wife was brought to bed of twenty money-bags at a burden, and how she long'd to eat adders' heads and toads carbonadoed.
Mopsa Is it true, think you?
Autolycus Very true; and but a month old.
Dorcas Bless me from marrying a usurer!
Autolycus Here's the midwife's name to't, one Mistress Taleporter, and five or six honest wives that were present. Why should I carry lies abroad?
Mopsa Pray you now, buy it.
Clown Come on, lay it by; and let's first see more ballads; we'll buy the other things anon.
Autolycus Here's another ballad, of a fish that appeared upon the coast on Wednesday the fourscore of April, forty thousand fathom above water, and sung this ballad against the hard hearts of maids: it was thought she was a woman, and was turned into a cold fish for she would not exchange flesh with one that loved her. The ballad is very pitiful, and as true.
Dorcas Is it true too, think you?
Autolycus Five justices' hands at it; and witnesses more than my pack will hold.
Clown Lay it by too: another.
Autolycus This is a merry ballad; but a very pretty one.
Mopsa Let's have some merry ones.
Autolycus Why, this is a passing merry one, and goes to the tune of *Two maids wooing a man*. There's scarce a maid westward but she sings it: 'tis in request, I can tell you.
Mopsa We can both sing it: if thou'lt bear a part, thou shalt hear; 'tis in three parts.
Dorcas We had the tune on't a month ago.

奥托力革厮	俺希望这样,小爷;因为俺带着好几包值钱的东西。
小　　丑	你这儿有什么?歌谣?
瑁泊沙	请你买一点:我喜欢印张上的歌曲,当真的,因为那样时我们有把握那歌曲里的事情是真的了。
奥托力革厮	这里有一支,调子很悲苦,讲个放债人的老婆怎样一胎生下了二十只钱袋;还说她只想吃烤炙过的蛇头和癞蛤蟆。
瑁泊沙	你认为是真的吗?
奥托力革厮	真得很,而且事情还只发生了一个月。
桃卡丝	祝福我不要嫁个放债人!
奥托力革厮	这里还有个收生婆的名儿哩,叫做推尔胞特老娘,还有五六个规矩老实的大娘在旁呢。为什么俺要散播人家撒的谎?
瑁泊沙	请你买下了吧。
小　　丑	来吧,放过这个:让我们先多看些歌曲;马上我们再来买其他的东西。
奥托力革厮	这儿还有支歌曲,讲四月十八号礼拜三有条鱼在海边上出现,离水面有四万英呎高,唱这支曲儿说姑娘们心肠太硬不好:做歌曲的相好认为她原来是个女人,只因她不肯跟她的情郎要好而变成了条冷冰冰的鱼。这支歌曲很可怜,而且极真实。
桃卡丝	你想这是真的吗?
奥托力革厮	有五位法官签字证明,证件多得俺这包里装不下。
小　　丑	也把这放开了:再看一支。
奥托力革厮	这是支欢乐的歌曲,可是美得很。
瑁泊沙	我们要有几支欢乐的。
奥托力革厮	哎也,这是支非常欢乐的,跟"两个姑娘追一个郎"同一个调子:打这儿往西几乎没有个姑娘不唱的:大家都要买,俺能告诉你们。
瑁泊沙	我们两个都会唱:若是你会唱一份的话,可以听我们来唱;这是三个人唱的。
桃卡丝	我们一个月前就会了这曲调。

Autolycus I can bear my part; you must know 'tis my occupation; have at it with you.
[*Song.*]

Get you hence, for I must go
Where it fits not you to know.

Dorcas *Whither?*
Mopsa *O, whither?*
Dorcas *Whither?*
Mopsa *It becomes thy oath full well*
Thou to me thy secrets tell.
Dorcas *Me too! Let me go thither.*
Mopsa *Or thou goest to the grange or mill;*
Dorcas *If to either, thou dost ill.*
Autolycus *Neither.*
Dorcas *What, neither?*
Autolycus *Neither.*
Dorcas *Thou hast sworn my love to be;*
Mopsa *Thou hast sworn it more to me;*
Then whither goest? — say, whither?

Clown We'll have this song out anon by ourselves; my father and the gentlemen are in sad talk, and we'll not trouble them. — Come, bring away thy pack after me. — Wenches, I'll buy for you both; — Pedlar, let's have the first choice. — Follow me, girls.
[*Exit with* Dorcas *and* Mopsa.]

Autolycus [*Aside.*] And you shall pay well for 'em.

Will you buy any tape,
Or lace for your cape,
My dainty duck, my dear-a?
Any silk, any thread,
Any toys for your head,
Of the new'st and fin'st, fin'st wear-a?
Come to the pedlar;
Money's a meddler

奥托力革厮　俺能唱俺的一份；你们得知道这是俺的本行：跟你们一起来唱吧。

　　　　　　　　　　　　　［唱］
　　　　　　　"你离开这里，我一定得跑，
　　　　　　　　到哪里可不好给你知道。"
桃　卡　丝　　"去哪里？"
珇　泊　沙　　"啊！去哪里？"
桃　卡　丝　　"去哪里？"
珇　泊　沙　　"你赌的咒怎么一点不记牢，
　　　　　　　你把你的秘密说给我听。"
桃　卡　丝　　"也说给我听；让我去哪里。"
珇　泊　沙　　"或许你去到田庄或磨坊。"
桃　卡　丝　　"不管到哪里，都是去乱撞。"
奥托力革厮　　"哪里也不去。"
桃　卡　丝　　"什么，哪里也不去？"
奥托力革厮　　"哪里也不去。"
桃　卡　丝　　"你已经发誓做我的情人。"
珇　泊　沙　　"你对我起的誓更要亲昵：
　　　　　　　那么，你要哪里去？哪里去？"
小　　　丑　我们自己马上来把这歌儿唱完它；我父亲跟两位大爷在认真讲话，我们不去麻烦他们：来，跟着我把你那包儿带来。姐儿们，我替你们两个都要买点东西。货郎，让我们来先挑。随我来，姑娘们。

　　　　　　　　　　　　　［与桃卡丝及珇泊沙下。］

奥托力革厮　［旁白］你得替她们出足价钱。
　　　　　［唱］　"你可要替你的披肩
　　　　　　　　买什么飘带或花边，
　　　　　　　俺娇小玲珑的小鸭儿，亲亲？
　　　　　　　　什么丝巾帕或线儿，
　　　　　　　　头上的什么玩意儿，
　　　　　　　最俏丽的式样，最美，最时新？
　　　　　　　　快来吧，来找货郎要；
　　　　　　　　好管闲事的是钱钞，

That doth utter all men's ware-a.

[*Exit.*]

[*Re-enter* Servant.]

Servant Master, there is three carters, three shepherds, three neat-herds, three swine-herds, that have made themselves all men of hair; they call themselves saltiers: and they have dance which the wenches say is a gallimaufry of gambols, because they are not in't; but they themselves are o' the mind (if it be not too rough for some that know little but bowling) it will please plentifully.

Shepherd Away! we'll none on't; here has been too much homely foolery already. —I know, sir, we weary you.

Polixenes You weary those that refresh us: pray, let's see these four threes of herdsmen.

Servant One three of them, by their own report, sir, hath danced before the king; and not the worst of the three but jumps twelve foot and a half by the squire.

Shepherd Leave your prating: since these good men are pleased, let them come in; but quickly now.

Servant Why, they stay at door, sir.

[*Exit.*]

[Here a dance of twelve Satyrs.]

Polixenes [*To* Shepherd]O, father, you'll know more of that hereafter. —

[*To* Camillo.] Is it not too far gone? — 'Tis time to part them. —

He's simple and tells much. [*To* Florizel.] How now, fair shepherd!
Your heart is full of something that does take
Your mind from feasting. Sooth, when I was young
And handed love as you do, I was wont
To load my she with knacks: I would have ransack'd
The pedlar's silken treasury and have pour'd it
To her acceptance; you have let him go,
And nothing marted with him. If your lass

它流通着天下人的货品。"

[下。

[仆人上。

仆　　　人　东家,有三个赶车的,三个牧羊人,三个牧牛人,三个牧猪人,都化装成了毛茸茸的毛人儿;他们自称是山羊人妖仙;他们会跳一个舞蹈娘儿们管它叫跳踢杂烩舞,因为她们自己不在里边;可是她们认为,——若是对于她们之中的有些个,只知道玩滚球的,那蹦跳不显得太粗鲁的话,——这跳踢会叫大家大乐一阵。

牧　羊　人　去!我们不要那个;这儿已经有太多粗俗的滑稽了。我知道,大人,我们叫您厌烦。

包列齐倪思　你叫那些个欢娱我们的人厌烦了;请你让我们看看这些个牧人的四个三人团吧。

仆　　　人　有一个三人团,据他们自己说,大爷,曾经在君王面前舞蹈过;三个人中最不行的一个,量尺码跳得有十二英尺半高。

牧　羊　人　别多话了:既然两位贵客高兴,让他们进来就是;可是快些个。

仆　　　人　哎也,他们就在门首等,主人。

[十二名山羊人妖仙之舞。]

包列齐倪思　[向牧羊人]啊,老人家!等一下你自会知道。
[向喀米罗]不是已进行得够久了吗?现在该
分开他们了。他单纯,讲得很多。
[向弗洛律采尔]怎么样,俊俏的牧羊后生?你的心
满盛着什么东西,使你没心绪
参加欢乐。说实话,当我年轻时,
如像你这般手握着姣娃,我怎把
小玩意送给我的她充怀满抱:
我会把货郎的所有丝绸宝藏,
倾倒给她请受领;你却让他走,
一点东西也没买。若是你那姑娘

Interpretation should abuse, and call this
Your lack of love or bounty, you were straited
For a reply, at least if you make a care
Of happy holding her.
Florizel　　　　　Old sir, I know
She prizes not such trifles as these are:
The gifts she looks from me are pack'd and lock'd
Up in my heart; which I have given already,
But not deliver'd. — O, hear me breathe my life
Before this ancient sir, who, it should seem,
Hath sometime lov'd, — I take thy hand! this hand,
As soft as dove's down, and as white as it,
Or Ethiopian's tooth, or the fann'd snow that's bolted
By the northern blasts twice o'er.
Polixenes　　　　　What follows this? —
How prettily the young swain seems to wash
The hand was fair before! — I have put you out:
But to your protestation; let me hear
What you profess.
Florizel　　　Do, and be witness to't.
Polixenes　And this my neighbour, too?
Florizel　　　　　　　　And he, and more
Than he, and men, — the earth, the heavens, and all: —
That, — were I crown'd the most imperial monarch,
Thereof most worthy; were I the fairest youth
That ever made eye swerve; had force and knowledge
More than was ever man's, — I would not prize them

	对你有误解,把这叫做你对她 没情爱,不慷慨大度,你将没有话 回答她,假使你真的关心要使她 快乐。
弗洛律采尔	老封君,我知道她并不看重 这样琐屑的小东西。她指望由我 赠与她的礼品都已经包扎停当, 锁在我心中,而且我已经给了她, 不过还未曾讲出来。啊!听我来 将我的性命当着这位老大伯 宣明,他哟,似乎年轻时也爱过: 我和你手搀着手订终身;这只手 像鸽子的绒毛一样软,也一样白, 或者好比埃昔屋比亚人的牙齿, 或者像搛来的白雪,两次被北风 筛到南边来——
包列齐倪思	这以后还有什么? 多么可爱,这后生的牧羊子像在 洗这只原来很干净的手!我把你 窘住了:还是来你那公开的声明吧: 让我们来听你郑重宣告些什么。
弗洛律采尔	请听,还请作证人。
包列齐倪思	也请我这位 同伴吗?
弗洛律采尔	也请他,不止请他,还要请 所有的人,请皇天,请后土,请一切; 我是说,我若被加冠当上了威灵 显赫的君王,而且该受之无愧, 我如果是个自来曾摄人注目 凝眸的最美的美少年,精力弥满, 学识充沛,超过任何人,我将会 不把它们当作一回事,假使我

Without her love; for her employ them all;
Commend them, and condemn them to her service,
Or to their own perdition.
Polixenes   Fairly offer'd.
Camillo   This shows a sound affection.
Shepherd   But, my daughter,
Say you the like to him?
Perdita   I cannot speak
So well, nothing so well; no, nor mean better:
By the pattern of mine own thoughts I cut out
The purity of his.
Shepherd   Take hands, a bargain! —
And, friends unknown, you shall bear witness to't:
I give my daughter to him, and will make
Her portion equal his.
Florizel   O, that must be
I' the virtue of your daughter: one being dead,
I shall have more than you can dream of yet;
Enough then for your wonder: but come on,
Contract us 'fore these witnesses.
Shepherd   Come, your hand; —
And, daughter, yours.
Polixenes   Soft, swain, awhile, beseech you;
Have you a father?
Florizel   I have; but what of him?
Polixenes   Knows he of this?
Florizel   He neither does nor shall.
Polixenes   Methinks a father
Is, at the nuptial of his son, a guest
That best becomes the table. Pray you, once more;
Is not your father grown incapable

	没有她的爱;为了她我会把它们 来使用;责令它们去为她服务, 或宣判它们去绝灭。
包列齐倪思	奉献得得体。
喀 米 罗	这显示有坚实的情爱。
牧 羊 人	可是,女儿, 你对他也这般说吗?
哀 笛 达	我不能说得 这样好,说不了这么好;不,用意 也不能比他好:凭我自己的思想 作模型,我雕刻他这片精醇当作 我的话。
牧 羊 人	挽手结姻缘;一言为定; 不知名的朋友,请你们两位作证: 我将女儿给了他,我给她的遗产 将跟他那份一样多。
弗洛律采尔	啊!那一定 是说你女儿的美德:有个人死了, 我有的将比你如今所能梦想的 还多;那时节就够你去诧异的了。 可是,来吧;在这些证人前,替我们 许下婚。
牧 羊 人	来,你的手;和你的,女儿。
包列齐倪思	且慢,牧羊子,请你等一下。你可有 父亲吗?
弗洛律采尔	我有;可是为什么要说他?
包列齐倪思	他知道这事吗?
弗洛律采尔	他没有知道,也不会。
包列齐倪思	据我看来,父亲 在他儿子的结婚筵席上乃是位 最相宜的宾客。再请问一声,是否 你父亲已变得不懂人情事理?

Of reasonable affairs? is he not stupid
With age and altering rheums? can he speak? hear?
Know man from man? dispute his own estate?
Lies he not bed-rid? and again does nothing
But what he did being childish?
Florizel   No, good sir;
He has his health, and ampler strength indeed
Than most have of his age.
Polixenes   By my white beard,
You offer him, if this be so, a wrong
Something unfilial: reason my son
Should choose himself a wife; but as good reason
The father, — all whose joy is nothing else
But fair posterity, — should hold some counsel
In such a business.
Florizel   I yield all this;
But, for some other reasons, my grave sir,
Which 'tis not fit you know, I not acquaint
My father of this business.
Polixenes   Let him know't.
Florizel   He shall not.
Polixenes   Pr'ythee let him.
Florizel   No, he must not.
Shepherd   Let him, my son: he shall not need to grieve
At knowing of thy choice.
Florizel   Come, come, he must not. —
Mark our contract.
Polixenes   [*Discovering himself.*] Mark your divorce, young sir,
Whom son I dare not call; thou art too base
To be acknowledged: thou a sceptre's heir,

　　　　　　　　他是否年迈力衰涕泗涟,体液
　　　　　　　　突变神情蠢?他能说话吗?能听?
　　　　　　　　分得清你和他?能谈他自己的事?
　　　　　　　　躺在床上起不来?跟从前一样,
　　　　　　　　回到了孩童时?
弗洛律采尔　　　　　　不对,亲爱的大伯:
　　　　　　　　他健康无恙,精力比好些他那样
　　　　　　　　年岁的老人要充沛。
包列齐倪思　　　　　　　　凭我这白须
　　　　　　　　假使事情是这样,你对他给予了
　　　　　　　　冒犯,有点儿不孝。很合乎公道,
　　　　　　　　为儿的应替他自己选一个妻子,
　　　　　　　　但同样公道那父亲,——他整个欢乐
　　　　　　　　只在有优秀的儿孙,——应在这事上
　　　　　　　　被征询意见。
弗洛律采尔　　　　　　这一切我都承认;
　　　　　　　　但为另一些理由,可敬的老大伯,
　　　　　　　　不便给你知道,我不曾把这事
　　　　　　　　告诉我父亲。
包列齐倪思　　　　　　让他知道。
弗洛律采尔　　　　　　　　　　他不能。
包列齐倪思　请你,给他知道吧。
弗洛律采尔　　　　　　不行,决不能。
牧　羊　人　让他知道了,我的孩子:他不会
　　　　　　　　知道了你这选中的娘子而悲伤。
弗洛律采尔　算了,算了,他决计不能。请听
　　　　　　　　我们的婚约。
包列齐倪思　　　　　　听你们的拆散,少君。

〔除去化装。〕

　　　　　　　　我不敢叫你儿子:你太卑鄙了,
　　　　　　　　没法使人承认你:你原本乃是位
　　　　　　　　王权宝仗的冢子,却这般立志

That thus affects a sheep-hook! — Thou, old traitor,
I am sorry that, by hanging thee, I can but
Shorten thy life one week. — And thou, fresh piece
Of excellent witchcraft, who of force must know
The royal fool thou cop'st with, —

Shepherd   O, my heart!

Polixenes   I'll have thy beauty scratch'd with briers,
    and made
More homely than thy state. For thee, fond boy, —
If I may ever know thou dost but sigh
That thou no more shalt see this knack, — as never
I mean thou shalt, — we'll bar thee from succession;
Not hold thee of our blood, no, not our kin,
Far than Deucalion off: — mark thou my words:
Follow us to the court. — Thou churl, for this time,
Though full of our displeasure, yet we free thee
From the dead blow of it. — And you, enchantment, —
Worthy enough a herdsman; yea, him too
That makes himself, but for our honour therein,
Unworthy thee, — if ever henceforth thou
These rural latches to his entrance open,
Or hoop his body more with thy embraces,
I will devise a death as cruel for thee
As thou art tender to't.
                                   [*Exit.*]

Perdita   Even here undone!
I was not much afeard: for once or twice
I was about to speak, and tell him plainly
The self-same sun that shines upon his court
Hides not his visage from our cottage, but
Looks on alike. — [*To* Florizel.] Will't please you, sir, be
    gone?
I told you what would come of this! Beseech you,
Of your own state take care: this dream of mine,

想执牧羊杖！你这老逆贼,我可惜
把你处绞了只能缩短你生命
一星期。而你,姣艳绝色的姝丽妖,
你定必知情相与这王家的蠢物,——

牧 羊 人
包列齐倪思 啊,我的心!
　　　　　　我会要把你的美貌
让野蔷薇枝子刮得比你的家世
还丑陋。对于你,蠢小子,你若知道
你只要为了不能见到这玩意儿
而叹息,——我决意使你永不再见她,——
我们将摈斥你不许你继承;把你
不当作我们的血胤,不,不算你
是我们的宗属,远超过杜凯良:
你得注意我这话:跟我们宫里去。
你啊,野老头,这回我们虽恼你,
可是且饶你,不给与致命的打击。
至于你,妖姑,——给个牧羊人很配得;
不错,对他也配得,若不是挂碍了
我们高华的家世,而他的行径
却不能跟你配,——假使以后你再把
这些田舍的柴门开给他进来,
或是将你的拥抱揽着他身躯,
我将设法叫你死得惨,那正好
给你去生受。　　　　　　　　　[下。

哀 笛 达　　　　这就给毁了！我并不
很怕;曾有一两次我几乎要说话,
对他分明讲,同一个太阳照到他
宫中,对我们的茅屋并不遮着脸,
也同样照见而放光。[向弗洛律采尔]殿下,您高兴
去了吧？我告诉过您结果会怎样:
请您对您自己的景况要留神:
我这梦——如今已醒了,我将不再

Being now awake, I'll queen it no inch further,
But milk my ewes, and weep.
Camillo   Why, how now, father!
Speak ere thou diest.
Shepherd   I cannot speak, nor think,
Nor dare to know that which I know. —[*To* Florizel.] O,
   sir,
You have undone a man of fourscore-three,
That thought to fill his grave in quiet; yea,
To die upon the bed my father died,
To lie close by his honest bones! but now
Some hangman must put on my shroud, and lay me
Where no priest shovels in dust. —[*To* Perdita.] O cursèd
   wretch,
That knew'st this was the prince, and wouldst adventure
To mingle faith with him! —Undone, undone!
If I might die within this hour, I have liv'd
To die when I desire.
                                              [*Exit.*]
Florizel   Why look you so upon me?
I am but sorry, not afeard; delay'd,
But nothing alt'red: what I was, I am:
More straining on for plucking back; not following
My leash unwillingly.
Camillo   Gracious, my lord,
You know your father's temper: at this time
He will allow no speech, —which I do guess
You do not purpose to him, —and as hardly
Will he endure your sight as yet, I fear:
Then, till the fury of his highness settle,
Come not before him.
Florizel   I not purpose it.
I think Camillo?
Camillo   Even he, my lord.

|||多演一忽儿王后的戏,只去挤
羊奶和哭泣。

喀米罗　　　　　　　哎也,怎样了,老人家?
你在死去前,说句话来。

牧羊人　　　　　　　　　我不能
说话,也不能思想,也不敢知道
我所知道的。[向弗洛律采尔]啊,叫你声太子爷!
你这可毁了个八十三岁的老人,
他原想安然入土,是啊,死在我
父亲死去的那只床上,躺在他
诚实的骨殖近旁:可是如今啊,
一定得由什么吊绞手来替我
穿上尸衣,且把我放在没牧师
铲土的穴里。[向衷笛达]啊,给诅咒的坏东西!
你知道这是王太子,竟敢跟他把
终身定。给毁了! 给毁了! 假使我在
这个钟点里早一刻死掉,我死得
也甘心。　　　　　　　　　　　　　　[下。

弗洛律采尔　　　为什么你这样对我望着?
我只是伤心,并不害怕;被延迟,
并未被改变。我仍和过去一样:
只因被拉回,更挣扎着向前;并不
跟着我那皮带走,就是勉强跟
也并不。

喀米罗　　　　　　殿下吾主,您知道您父亲
性情怎么样:他此刻不容人说话,
我猜想您不会想跟他交谈;我怕
他未必能容您去见他:所以,在他
那尊威的盛怒平息前,莫到他跟前。

弗洛律采尔　我不要见他。我想,喀米罗——
喀米罗　　　　　　　　　　　　就是他,
殿下。

Perdita How often have I told you 'twould be thus!
How often said my dignity would last
But till 'twere known!
Florizel   It cannot fail but by
The violation of my faith; and then
Let nature crush the sides o' the earth together
And mar the seeds within! — Lift up thy looks. —
From my succession wipe me, father; I
Am heir to my affection.
Camillo   Be advis'd.
Florizel I am, — and by my fancy; if my reason
Will thereto be obedient, I have reason;
If not, my senses, better pleas'd with madness,
Do bid it welcome.
Camillo   This is desperate, sir.
Florizel So call it: but it does fulfil my vow;
I needs must think it honesty. Camillo,
Not for Bohemia, nor the pomp that may
Be thereat glean'd; for all the sun sees or
The close earth wombs, or the profound seas hide
In unknown fathoms, will I break my oath
To this my fair belov'd: therefore, I pray you,
As you have ever been my father's honour'd friend
When he shall miss me, — as, in faith, I mean not
To see him any more, — cast your good counsels
Upon his passion: let myself and fortune
Tug for the time to come. This you may know,
And so deliver, — I am put to sea
With her, whom here I cannot hold on shore;
And, most opportune to her need, I have
A vessel rides fast by, but not prepar'd

哀笛达	我告诉过您多少次,结果会这样!说过多少次我的高位只能维持到大家知道前!
弗洛律采尔	它不能完结,除非我对你的忠诚被摧折;那时节让造化压烂大地的方圆,把里边的种子全毁灭!举眼向前:抹掉我名下的继承权利,父亲;我是我情爱的宗嗣。
喀米罗	听人的劝告。
弗洛律采尔	我听;听爱情的劝告;若我的理智能对它服从,我能有理智;如果不,我的心神它更喜欢的是疯癫,会对它欢迎。
喀米罗	这可真绝望了,殿下。
弗洛律采尔	就说是吧;但这样能符合我的誓言;我一准认为是真诚老实。喀米罗,不为了波希米亚,也不为在这里所能获得的尊荣,也不为太阳所照见的一切、密闭的地母之所包容,汪洋大海隐藏在万丈深渊里的一切,不为这种种我会肯对我这明艳的爱人毁弃信誓。所以,我请你,既然你一向是我父亲所敬重的友人,当他将不见而想念我时,——当真,我不想再见他,——把你优良的劝告安抚他的激动:让我去跟命运一同对将来奋斗。这件事你可以知道而且去报告,我和她跨海去了,因为我不能在岸上保有她;对我们的需要最为适合时宜,我有条船儿停泊在

For this design. What course I mean to hold
Shall nothing benefit your knowledge, nor
Concern me the reporting.
Camillo   O, my lord,
I would your spirit were easier for advice,
Or stronger for your need.
Florizel   Hark, Perdita. —[*Takes her aside.*]
[*To* Camillo.] I'll hear you by and by.
Camillo   He's irremovable,
Resolv'd for flight. Now were I happy if
His going I could frame to serve my turn;
Save him from danger, do him love and honour;
Purchase the sight again of dear Sicilia
And that unhappy king, my master, whom
I so much thirst to see.
Florizel   Now, good Camillo,
I am so fraught with curious business that
I leave out ceremony.
Camillo   Sir, I think
You have heard of my poor services, i' the love
That I have borne your father?
Florizel   Very nobly
Have you deserv'd: it is my father's music
To speak your deeds; not little of his care
To have them recompens'd as thought on.
Camillo   Well, my lord,
If you may please to think I love the king,
And, through him, what's nearest to him, which is
Your gracious self, embrace but my direction, —
If your more ponderous and settled project
May suffer alteration, — on mine honour,

近旁海上,但本非备得为这件事。
我将如何去行事将无益让你
去知晓,我也毋须来向你报。

喀米罗 啊,
殿下!我但愿您那性情和英锐
柔和得能听谆劝,或者坚强得
符合您的需要。

弗洛律采尔 听我来说,哀笛达。

[携伊至一旁。]

[向喀米罗]等一下再跟你谈。

喀米罗 他不会动摇,
决心要逃亡。如今我也许会快乐,
假如能使他的出奔正合我的意,
救他免危险,致他于眷爱和光荣,
得能再见到西西利亚和那位
不幸的君王,我的故主,想见他
我这般渴望。

弗洛律采尔 现在,亲爱的喀米罗,
我手上满都是麻烦的事,以致
对礼数有亏。

喀米罗 殿下,我想您听说过
我在对令尊效忠时所尽的微劳?

弗洛律采尔 你应受恢弘的感谢:我父亲说起
你对他的义举,就如同八音齐鸣,
他不小一部分殷勤的关注是在
想到它们时便对你酬谢。

喀米罗 很好,
殿下,假如您高兴想起我眷爱
君王,以及因他而爱他的至亲者,
那便是您储君殿下,请听我指引。
倘使您那较强劲而已定的计划
可容许变更,凭我的荣誉我将

I'll point you where you shall have such receiving
As shall become your highness; where you may
Enjoy your mistress, — from the whom, I see,
There's no disjunction to be made, but by,
As heavens forfend! your ruin, — marry her;
And, — with my best endeavours in your absence —
Your discontenting father strive to qualify,
And bring him up to liking.
Florizel   How, Camillo,
May this, almost a miracle, be done?
That I may call thee something more than man,
And, after that, trust to thee.
Camillo   Have you thought on
A place whereto you'll go?
Florizel   Not any yet;
But as the unthought-on accident is guilty
To what we wildly do; so we profess
Ourselves to be the slaves of chance, and flies
Of every wind that blows.
Camillo   Then list to me:
This follows, — if you will not change your purpose,
But undergo this flight, — make for Sicilia;
And there present yourself and your fair princess, —
For so, I see, she must be, — 'fore Leontes:
She shall be habited as it becomes
The partner of your bed. Methinks I see
Leontes opening his free arms, and weeping
His welcomes forth; asks thee, the son, forgiveness,
As 'twere i' the father's person; kisses the hands
Of your fresh princess; o'er and o'er divides him
'Twixt his unkindness and his kindness, — the one
He chides to hell, and bids the other grow

　　　　　　　　指点您前往您准会获得适合您
　　　　　　　　殿下身份接待的地方去；那里，
　　　　　　　　您可以享有您这位情娘，——我知道
　　　　　　　　您没法跟她分离，除非是，上天
　　　　　　　　决不准！您遇到不测，——和她成婚；
　　　　　　　　当您不在时我将尽最大的奋勉，
　　　　　　　　努力去缓和您恼怒的严亲，使他
　　　　　　　　开怀畅意于您这太子妃。
弗洛律采尔　　　　　　　　　　这几乎
　　　　　　　　是奇迹，喀米罗，怎样去做？那我可
　　　　　　　　真要叫你作超人，而且从此后
　　　　　　　　任何事都对你信赖。
喀　米　罗　　　　　　　您想到没有，
　　　　　　　　你们将前往何处去？
弗洛律采尔　　　　　　　　　还不曾想起；
　　　　　　　　由于这未曾想起的偶然事出于
　　　　　　　　我们一时的冲动，所以我们得
　　　　　　　　承认，我们是机运的奴隶，每一阵
　　　　　　　　刮起的风里的飞蝇。
喀　米　罗　　　　　　　那就听我说：
　　　　　　　　接着便这样；若是您决意不变动，
　　　　　　　　还是要逃跑，就到西西利亚去，
　　　　　　　　介绍您自己和您这端丽的公主，——
　　　　　　　　因为据我看她准是，——给里杭底斯；
　　　　　　　　她将会冠带衣袍穿戴齐，适合
　　　　　　　　作您的新娘。我看来，似乎已见到
　　　　　　　　里杭底斯张开他热切的两臂
　　　　　　　　流泪表欢迎；向您，您父亲的儿子，
　　　　　　　　求原谅，仿佛您便是令高尊；吻您
　　　　　　　　这朱颜公主的手；且将他自己
　　　　　　　　再三又再四剖分给苛酷与仁和：
　　　　　　　　将苛酷咒到地狱里，叫仁和日滋

Faster than thought or time.
Florizel　　　　　　　　Worthy Camillo,
What colour for my visitation shall I
Hold up before him?
Camillo　　　　　　Sent by the king your father
To greet him and to give him comforts. Sir,
The manner of your bearing towards him, with
What you as from your father, shall deliver,
Things known betwixt us three, I'll write you down;
The which shall point you forth at every sitting,
What you must say; that he shall not perceive
But that you have your father's bosom there,
And speak his very heart.
Florizel　　　　　　　I am bound to you:
There is some sap in this.
Camillo　　　　　　A course more promising
Than a wild dedication of yourselves
To unpath'd waters, undream'd shores, most certain
To miseries enough: no hope to help you;
But as you shake off one to take another:
Nothing so certain as your anchors; who
Do their best office if they can but stay you
Where you'll be loath to be: besides, you know
Prosperity's the very bond of love,
Whose fresh complexion and whose heart together
Affliction alters.
Perdita　　　One of these is true:
I think affliction may subdue the cheek,
But not take in the mind.
Camillo　　　　　　Yea, say you so?
There shall not at your father's house, these seven years
Be born another such.
Florizel　　　　　My good Camillo,
She is as forward of her breeding as

	又夜长，比思想和时间还长得快。
弗洛律采尔	卓绝的喀米罗，什么堂皇的托辞 我将为我的拜谒陈展在他跟前？
喀 米 罗	奉您父王的谕旨，差您去向他 致敬意，并存问安好。殿下，您对他 如何去举止，以及仿佛您父亲叫 传的话，我们三人间所共知的事， 我会替您写下来；那将会指点您 每次面见时您该说什么话；使他 不能不见到您在那上头有您 父亲的心里话，诉说他的真情意。
弗洛律采尔	我对你感激不尽。这里头有希望。
喀 米 罗	比较将你们自己胡乱委身于 没路的海上，未曾梦见过的岸滩， 一定无疑去遭受够多的灾祸， 我这条前程可要较为有把握： 由你们自己去乱闯，没有希望 帮得了你们的忙，当一个灾祸 刚摔掉，又去捡起另一个；还不如 你们的船锚般可靠，它们只要 能使人待在不愿待的地方，就算 尽到了它们最好的作用。而况， 您知道昌隆是恋爱不可少的胶漆， 痛苦却能改变它的红颜与情意。
哀 笛 达	两件事里一件说得对：我想痛苦 也许会使容颜憔悴，但不能征服 人的心。
喀 米 罗	是哟，你这么说吗？在多少 年之内，你父亲屋里不会再生 你这样的孩子了。
弗洛律采尔	我亲爱的喀米罗， 她远远超越她的教养，正如出身

She is i' the rear our birth.
Camillo   I cannot say 'tis pity
She lacks instruction; for she seems a mistress
To most that teach.
Perdita   Your pardon, sir; for this:
I'll blush you thanks.
Florizel   My prettiest Perdita! —
But, O, the thorns we stand upon! — Camillo, —
Preserver of my father, now of me;
The medicine of our house! — how shall we do?
We are not furnish'd like Bohemia's son;
Nor shall appear in Sicilia.
Camillo   My lord,
Fear none of this: I think you know my fortunes
Do all lie there: it shall be so my care
To have you royally appointed as if
The scene you play were mine. For instance, sir,
That you may know you shall not want, — one word.
            [*They talk aside.*]
            [*Re-enter* Autolycus.]
Autolycus Ha, ha! what a fool Honesty is! and *Trust*, his sworn brother, a very simple gentleman! I have sold all my trumpery; not a counterfeit stone, not a riband, glass, pomander, brooch, table-book, ballad, knife, tape, glove, shoe-tie, bracelet, horn-ring, to keep my pack from fasting; — they throng who should buy first, as if my trinkets had been hallowed, and brought a benediction to the buyer: by which means I saw whose purse was best in picture; and what I saw, to my good use I remembered. My clown (who wants but something to be a reasonable man) grew so in love with the wenches' song that he would not stir his pettitoes till he had both tune and words; which so drew the rest of the herd to me that all their other senses stuck in ears:

远在我之后。

喀 米 罗　　　　　　　我不说可惜她缺少
教训,因为和好些教师相比时,
她好像是位女教师。

哀 笛 达　　　　　　　　　请你原谅,
老伯伯;为这个,我红着脸向你多谢。

弗洛律采尔　我最最明艳的哀笛达!不过,啊!
我们是站在荆棘上。喀米罗,救过
我父亲,如今是我的救命恩公,
我们一家的医生,我们将怎么办?
我们穿戴得不像个波希米亚
王子,在西西利亚时也将不像是。

喀 米 罗　殿下,请不用担心:我想您知道
我所有的财产都在那边:我准会
设法好叫您衣冠显焕,仿佛您
表演的这场戏是我的。比如,殿下,
为让您知道您不得缺少,说句话。

〔两人旁语。〕

〔奥托力革厮上。〕

奥托力革厮　哈,哈!"老实"真是好一个傻瓜!而"信赖",他的把兄弟,是位脑筋多简单的相公!俺把俺这些哄人的小玩意儿全卖了:不留一块假宝石,一根缎带,一面镜子,一个香球,一块帽镇,一本日记本儿,一支歌曲,一柄小洋刀,一根毛线带,一双手套,一副皮鞋带,一只手镯,一枚牛角戒指,好叫俺这货色不空着肚子:他们挤拢来抢先买,仿佛俺这些小玩意儿是神圣的,买了它们能得天父赐福似的:就用那手段俺瞧见谁的钱包儿最好;而且俺把瞧到的就记在肚里派最好的用处。俺那乡下佬儿,——他只少了点儿东西成为个懂事的人,——那么爱上了娘儿们的歌曲,在他把曲调和歌词都学到手以前,他干脆不肯把脚蹄移动;这样一来,就把其余的头口都引到了俺

you might have pinched a placket, — it was senseless; 'twas nothing to geld a codpiece of a purse; I would have filed keys off that hung in chains: no hearing, no feeling, but my sir's song, and admiring the nothing of it. So that, in this time of lethargy, I picked and cut most of their festival purses; and had not the old man come in with whoobub against his daughter and the king's son, and scared my choughs from the chaff, I had not left a purse alive in the whole army.

[Camillo, Florizel, *and* Perdita *come forward.*]

Camillo   Nay, but my letters, by this means being there
So soon as you arrive, shall clear that doubt.

Florizel   And those that you'll procure from king Leontes, —

Camillo   Shall satisfy your father.

Perdita   Happy be you!
All that you speak shows fair.

Camillo   [*Seeing* Autolycus.] Who have we here?
We'll make an instrument of this; omit
Nothing may give us aid.

Autolycus   [*Aside.*] If they have overheard me now, — why, hanging.

Camillo   How now, good fellow! why shakest thou so? Fear not, man; here's no harm intended to thee.

Autolycus   I am a poor fellow, sir.

Camillo   Why, be so still; here's nobody will steal that from thee: yet, for the outside of thy poverty we must make an exchange; therefore discase thee instantly, — thou must think there's a necessity in't, — and change garments with this gentleman: though the pennyworth on his side be the worst, yet hold thee, there's some boot. [*Giving money.*]

Autolycus   I am a poor fellow, sir: — [*Aside.*] I know ye well enough.

身旁来,而且把他所有其他的感觉都聚到了耳朵里去:你可以手捻一条女裙,它一点知觉也没有;往裤子遮阳里去摸一只钱包,一点不费劲儿;俺尽可以用锉刀锉掉挂在链儿上的成串的钥匙:没耳朵,没感觉,只有俺那相公的歌儿,把它那不值一个屁崇拜得五体投地;结果是,在这无知无觉的当儿,叫俺摸了他们大伙儿的节日口袋,剪了钱包儿的绺;若不是那老头儿进来叱喝他女儿和那王子,把俺这群穴乌从稃糠堆上吓走了的话,俺在这一大伙里要来个一网打尽,掏得一只钱包也不剩。

[喀米罗、弗洛律采尔与衷笛达上前。

喀　米　罗	不,可是我的信,这么样送到了那里,一等您到达,将扫除那疑虑。
弗洛律采尔	而那些你将从里杭底斯国王处得来——
喀　米　罗	准使您父亲满意。
衷　笛　达	乐了你!你说的一切都显得合适。 　　　[见奥托力革厮。]是谁在这里?我们来利用一下吧:凡是能帮我们忙的,且莫放过。
奥托力革厮	[旁白]若他们在旁听到了俺说话,哎也,会给绞死。
喀　米　罗	怎么样,好人儿?你为什么这样发抖?不用害怕,人儿;不会来伤害你。
奥托力革厮	俺是个穷人哪,大爷。
喀　米　罗	哎也,还那样好了;没有人会把你那个偷起走;可是,你那穷苦的外貌,我们得交换一下;因此上,马上把衣服脱下,——你得认为这件事有需要,——跟这位相公掉换着穿:虽说他得到的不上算,可是你拿着,这儿还有点好处给你。

[给他钱。

奥托力革厮	俺是个穷人哪,大爷。——[旁白]俺挺认得你。

Camillo Nay, pr'ythee dispatch: the gentleman is half flay'd already.
Autolycus Are you in earnest, sir?—[*Aside.*] I smell the trick on't.
Florizel Dispatch, I pr'ythee.
Autolycus Indeed, I have had earnest; but I cannot with conscience take it.
Camillo Unbuckle, unbuckle.

[Florizel *and* Autolycus *exchange garments.*]

Fortunate mistress,—let my prophecy
Come home to you!—you must retire yourself
Into some covert; take your sweetheart's hat
And pluck it o'er your brows, muffle your face,
Dismantle you; and, as you can, disliken
The truth of your own seeming; that you may,—
For I do fear eyes over,—to shipboard
Get undescried.

Perdita   I see the play so lies
That I must bear a part.

Camillo   No remedy. —
Have you done there?

Florizel   Should I now meet my father,
He would not call me son.

Camillo   Nay, you shall have no hat. —[*Giving it to* Perdita.]
Come, lady, come. —Farewell, my friend.

Autolycus   Adieu, sir.

Florizel O Perdita, what have we twain forgot!
Pray you a word.

[*They converse apart.*]

Camillo [*Aside.*] What I do next, shall be to tell the king
Of this escape, and whither they are bound;
Wherein, my hope is, I shall so prevail
To force him after: in whose company
I shall re-view Sicilia; for whose sight
I have a woman's longing.

Florizel   Fortune speed us! —

喀　米　罗	莫那样,请你,要快些:这位相公已经脱掉了一半衣裳。
奥托力革厮	您可是认真说吗,大爷?〔旁白〕俺嗅到这里头有花样叫俺上当。
弗洛律采尔	赶快,我请你。
奥托力革厮	当真,俺拿了定钱;可是俺拿它有亏良心。
喀　米　罗	脱下来,脱下来。——

　　　　　　　　〔弗洛律采尔与奥托力革厮交换衣服。〕

　　　　　　交运的姑娘,——让我的预言对你
　　　　　　能应验!——你得退到什么树丛里:
　　　　　　拿着你意中人这顶帽子,把它
　　　　　　盖住了你的双眉;遮着你的脸;
　　　　　　您把衣服脱下来,若能够的话,
　　　　　　装得不像您自己的模样;那样
　　　　　　您就能,——因为我怕有人睃着您,——
　　　　　　上船不给人看破。

哀　笛　达	我见到这出戏

　　　　　　演到这田地,我一定得扮个脚色。

喀　米　罗	没办法。您好了没有?
弗洛律采尔	我现在碰到

　　　　　　我父亲的话,他不会叫我是儿子。

喀　米　罗	不行,您不能戴帽子。　　〔将帽授与哀笛达。〕

　　　　　　　　来吧,小姐,
　　　　　　来吧。再会了,朋友。

奥托力革厮	再会了,大爷。
弗洛律采尔	啊,哀笛达,我们两个人忘记了

　　　　　　什么哟?请你,说句话。　　〔彼等至一旁低语。〕

喀　米　罗	〔旁白〕接下来我将去禀报君王这逃跑,

　　　　　　以及他们到那里去;在这件事里,
　　　　　　我的希望是要能达到我的目的,
　　　　　　逼得他追赶去:跟着他一起,我将
　　　　　　重新见西西利亚,想见那乡邦
　　　　　　我像个妇人般渴慕。

弗洛律采尔	幸运保佑

Thus we set on, Camillo, to the sea-side.
Camillo The swifter speed the better.
            [*Exeunt* Florizel, Perdita, *and* Camillo.]
Autolycus I understand the business, I hear it: — to have an open ear, a quick eye, and a nimble hand, is necessary for a cut-purse; a good nose is requisite also, to smell out work for the other senses. I see this is the time that the unjust man doth thrive. What an exchange had this been without boot? what a boot is here with this exchange? Sure, the gods do this year connive at us, and we may do anything extempore. The prince himself is about a piece of iniquity, — stealing away from his father with his clog at his heels: if I thought it were a piece of honesty to acquaint the king withal, I would not do't: I hold it the more knavery to conceal it; and therein am I constant to my profession. Aside, aside; — here is more matter for a hot brain: every lane's end, every shop, church, session, hanging, yields a careful man work.
            [*Re-enter* Clown *and* Shepherd.]
Clown See, see; what a man you are now! There is no other way but to tell the king she's a changeling, and none of your flesh and blood.
Shepherd Nay, but hear me.
Clown Nay, but hear me.
Shepherd Go to, then.
Clown She being none of your flesh and blood, your flesh and blood has not offended the king; and so your flesh and blood is not to be punished by him. Show those things you found about her; those secret things, — all but what she has with her: this being done, let the law go whistle; I warrant you.
Shepherd I will tell the king all, every word, — yea, and his son's pranks too; who, I may say, is no honest man neither to his father nor to me, to go about to make me the king's brother-in-law.
Clown Indeed, brother-in-law was the farthest off you could have been to him; and then your blood had

我们！便这样，喀米罗，我们去海边。
喀 米 罗　　愈快愈好。　　　　　　〔与弗洛律采尔及哀笛达下。
奥托力革厮　俺懂得这桩事；俺听到了。耳朵敞开，眼睛尖，手脚灵活，是个扒手少不了的本领；一个好鼻子也是必需的，去替其他的感觉把工作嗅出来。俺见到这回可是不老实的人儿交了运。若没有补偿，这是够多好一笔交换！有了这笔交换，这是够多好一注补偿！准是的，天神们今年对咱们眼开眼闭，所以咱们能不用先动脑筋随便做什么。那王太子本身便差不多是一片罪恶；打他父亲那儿逃走，脚跟上还拖着那拖累的石头。若是俺以为去告诉国王是件老实事；俺就不去报：俺认为把它瞒着不报倒更是桩坏事情，在那行止里俺对俺这行业尽忠。站开，站开：这儿又有点事儿要动动热脑筋。每条小径的尽头，每家铺子，每座教堂，每回审判庭，每次行绞刑，都对用心思的人提供活儿。
　　　　　　　　〔小丑与牧羊人上。
小　　　丑　瞧，瞧，你现在是怎样的一个人儿！没有别的办法只能告诉国王她是个捡来的女孩儿，不是你的亲骨肉。
牧 羊 人　不，听我说。
小　　　丑　不，听我说。
牧 羊 人　你去讲，那么。
小　　　丑　她既然不是你的亲骨肉，你的亲骨肉便没有得罪国王；所以你的亲骨肉不该受他的责罚。把你在她身上找到的那些东西给他看；那些秘密东西，除掉她身上带着的东西之外的所有的东西：这事做了以后，法律动不了你一根毫毛：我向你保证。
牧 羊 人　我要把一切东西都告诉国王，每句话，是的，他儿子捣的蛋也讲；那孩子，我可以说，对他父亲，对我，都不老实，想叫我去做国王的亲家公。
小　　　丑　当真，亲家公是你跟他最天差地远的事了，不过假使

been the dearer by I know how much an ounce.

Autolycus [*Aside.*] Very wisely, puppies!

Shepherd Well, let us to the king: there is that in this fardel will make him scratch his beard!

Autolycus [*Aside.*] I know not what impediment this complaint may be to the flight of my master.

Clown Pray heartily he be at palace.

Autolycus [*Aside.*] Though I am not naturally honest, I am so sometimes by chance. Let me pocket up my pedlar's excrement. [*Takes off his false beard.*] — How now, rustics! whither are you bound?

Shepherd To the palace, an it like your worship.

Autolycus Your affairs there, what, with whom, the condition of that fardel, the place of your dwelling, your names, your ages, of what having, breeding, and anything that is fitting to be known? discover.

Clown We are but plain fellows, sir.

Autolycus A lie; you are rough and hairy. Let me have no lying; it becomes none but tradesmen, and they often give us soldiers the lie: but we pay them for it with stamped coin, not stabbing steel; therefore they do not give us the lie.

Clown Your worship had like to have given us one, if you had not taken yourself with the manner.

Shepherd Are you a courtier, an't like you, sir?

Autolycus Whether it like me or no, I am a courtier. Seest thou not the air of the court in these enfoldings? hath not my gait in it the measure of the court? receives not thy nose court-odour from me? reflect I not on thy baseness court-contempt? Think'st thou, for that I insinuate, or toaze from thee thy business, I am therefore no courtier? I am courtier cap-à-pie, and one that will either push on or pluck back thy business there: whereupon

	是真的话,我不知道你的血每盎司要贵起多少来。
奥托力革厮	[旁白]很聪明,巧驴儿们!
牧　羊　人	很好,让我们去见国王:这包袱里有东西会叫他搔他的胡须。
奥托力革厮	[旁白]我不知要是他们这么说了会不会妨碍我那主人的逃走。
小　　　丑	希望他在宫里。
奥托力革厮	[旁白]虽然俺生性并不老实,俺有时却会碰巧变得老实:让俺来把咱这货郎的毛毛放在口袋里。[将假须拉去。]什么事,乡下佬儿们? 你们上哪儿去?
牧　羊　人	上王宫里去,您老爷若是高兴。
奥托力革厮	你们上那儿有什么事,去找谁,那包袱是怎么回事,你们住在哪儿,叫什么名字,多大岁数,有什么家财,是什么家世? 还有该给知道的什么别的东西,讲出来。
小　　　丑	我们只是两个简单的小百姓。
奥托力革厮	胡说;你们不简单,头发长得毛茸茸的。莫对俺撒谎;那只跟做买卖的合适,他们常给俺们当军人的上当;可是俺们为了这个付给他们的倒是打印的洋钱,不是戳人的刀尖;因此上他们就不再给俺们上当了。
小　　　丑	您相公几乎对我们撒了一个谎,若是您没有把话缩回去的话。
牧　羊　人	您可是位朝廷官员吗,您若是高兴说的话,老爷?
奥托力革厮	不管俺高兴不高兴,俺反正是位朝廷命官。你不见这些衣装上有朝廷气概吗? 俺穿着它走起路来,没朝廷上的官派模样吗? 你鼻子嗅不到俺身上的朝廷味道吗? 俺不把你这身家低贱当作藐视朝廷官员吗? 你可是以为,因为俺管了你的闲事,或者把你的事情拉出来,俺便不是朝廷官员吗? 俺确是朝廷官员,从脑袋一直到脚上,而且是个会把你那事儿推上去或拉下来的主儿:因此上,俺命令你把事情说

I command thee to open thy affair.
Shepherd My business, sir, is to the king.
Autolycus What advocate hast thou to him?
Shepherd I know not, an't like you.
Clown Advocate's the court-word for a pheasant; say you have none.
Shepherd None, sir; I have no pheasant, cock nor hen.
Autolycus How bless'd are we that are not simple men!
Yet nature might have made me as these are,
Therefore I will not disdain.
Clown This cannot be but a great courtier.
Shepherd His garments are rich, but he wears them not handsomely.
Clown He seems to be the more noble in being fantastical: a great man, I'll warrant; I know by the picking on's teeth.
Autolycus The fardel there? what's i' the fardel? Wherefore that box?
Shepherd Sir, there lies such secrets in this fardel and box which none must know but the king; and which he shall know within this hour, if I may come to the speech of him.
Autolycus Age, thou hast lost thy labour.
Shepherd Why, sir?
Autolycus The king is not at the palace; he is gone aboard a new ship to purge melancholy and air himself: for, if thou beest capable of things serious, thou must know the king is full of grief.
Shepherd So 'tis said, sir, — about his son, that should have married a shepherd's daughter.
Autolycus If that shepherd be not in hand-fast, let him fly: the curses he shall have, the tortures he shall feel, will break the back of man, the heart of monster.
Clown Think you so, sir?
Autolycus Not he alone shall suffer what wit can make heavy and vengeance bitter; but those that are germane to him, though removed fifty times,

	出来。
牧　羊　人	我的事情,老爷,是去见国王。
奥托力革厮	你对他可有什么代言人?
牧　羊　人	我不懂,若是您高兴的话。
小　　丑	代言人是朝廷上叫一只野鸡的说法:你就说你没有。
牧　羊　人	没有,老爷;我没有野鸡,公的母的都没有。
奥托力革厮	俺们脑筋不简单真天赐宏恩! 但造化也可能把俺造成跟这些 一个样,所以俺不去鄙视。
小　　丑	这不能不是位朝廷大官儿。
牧　羊　人	他的衣服是富丽的,可是他穿着它们不怎么体面。
小　　丑	他这么怪模怪样更显得高贵:是一位大人物,我敢保证;我从他剔牙齿上看得出来。
奥托力革厮	那边那包袱? 包袱里有什么东西? 那只箱子是做什么的?
牧　羊　人	老爷,这包袱和箱子里有这样的秘密,除国王外任何人不能知道;而且他就在这个钟点里准会知道,若是我能跟他说话的话。
奥托力革厮	老头儿,你白辛苦了。
牧　羊　人	为什么,老爷?
奥托力革厮	国王不在宫廷里;他上了一条新船去排解郁闷,透透空气:因为,假使你能感受到什么严肃的事情的话,你一定知道国王心里很忧愁。
牧　羊　人	听人这么说,老爷,说起他的儿子,说是差点跟牧羊人的姑娘结了亲。
奥托力革厮	若是那个牧羊人如今还没有给看管起来,让他逃走吧:他准会有的诅咒,准会吃到的苦楚,会叫人的脊梁给压断,妖怪的心都碎掉。
小　　丑	你以为是这样吗,老爷?
奥托力革厮	不光他一个人将遭受机灵所想得出来的最重要的和报复所施的最苦的刑罚;而且凡是跟他关着亲的,即

shall all come under the hangman: which, though it be great pity, yet it is necessary. An old sheep-whistling rogue, a ram-tender, to offer to have his daughter come into grace! Some say he shall be stoned; but that death is too soft for him, say I. Draw our throne into a sheep-cote! — all deaths are too few, the sharpest too easy.

Clown Has the old man e'er a son, sir, do you hear, an't like you, sir?

Autolycus He has a son, — who shall be flayed alive; then 'nointed over with honey, set on the head of a wasp's nest; then stand till he be three quarters and a dram dead; then recovered again with aqua-vit? or some other hot infusion; then, raw as he is, and in the hottest day prognostication proclaims, shall he be set against a brick wall, the sun looking with a southward eye upon him, — where he is to behold him with flies blown to death. But what talk we of these traitorly rascals, whose miseries are to be smiled at, their offences being so capital? Tell me, — for you seem to be honest plain men, — what you have to the king: being something gently considered, I'll bring you where he is aboard, tender your persons to his presence, whisper him in your behalfs; and if it be in man besides the king to effect your suits, here is man shall do it.

Clown He seems to be of great authority: close with him, give him gold; and though authority be a stubborn bear, yet he is oft led by the nose with gold: show the inside of your purse to the outside of his hand, and no more ado. Remember, — ston'd and flayed alive.

Shepherd An't please you, sir, to undertake the business for us, here is that gold I have: I'll make it as much more, and leave this young man in pawn till I bring it you.

Autolycus After I have done what I promised?

Shepherd Ay, sir.

使相隔有二十重,也准会逃不掉吊绞手的手掌;这虽然很可怜,可是不能不这样办。一个吹羊哨子的老流氓,一个看羊的家伙,想要叫他的姑娘沾到王恩!有人说他准会给用石头来砸死;可是那样死法对他太便宜了,俺说:要把俺们的君王宝座吸引到牧羊人茅棚里去!各种各样的死法一起来还嫌太少,最凶的死法还是太轻松。

小　　丑　　这老头儿曾有个儿子吧,老爷,你听说过没有,若是您高兴的话,老爷?

奥托力革厮　　他有个儿子,那准会给活剥皮;然后给涂上了蜂蜜,放在胡蜂窠顶上;在那里给放到死掉了四分之三多一点儿;再用火酒或有些别的热药汁灌醒回来;接下来,他的皮剥得精光的,在历书里所预言的最热的日子,他将被斜倚在一堵砖墙上,南面的太阳晒着他,就在那太阳光里他将给苍蝇用臭粪玷死。可是咱们何必去谈这些谋反叛逆的恶棍呢?他们吃的苦头该当做笑料,他们犯的罪这么该杀。告诉俺,——因为你们看来是老实的简单的小百姓,——你们去见王上有什么事:你们只要对俺送一点私礼,俺能把你们带到他船上,引到他面前,凑着他耳朵低声替你们说句话儿;假使除掉国王自己之外有另外的人能替你们打关节走门路的话,咱家就是能干这件事的人。

小　　丑　　他像是权力很大:跟他约定了吧,给他黄金;权力是头粗暴的熊,可是用黄金可以牵着它的鼻子走。把你钱包里头的东西亮给他的手外头去看,别再多噜哧了。记住,"砸死"和"活剥"!

牧　羊　人　　您若是高兴,老爷,替我们承揽这件事,这里是我有的那黄金;我还有这么多给您,现在把这小伙子押给您,等我再把它拿来向您领赎。

奥托力革厮　　等俺把答应你的做了之后吗?

牧　羊　人　　是啊,老爷。

Autolycus Well, give me the moiety. Are you a party in this business?

Clown In some sort, sir: but though my case be a pitiful one, I hope I shall not be flayed out of it.

Autolycus O, that's the case of the shepherd's son. Hang him, he'll be made an example.

Clown Comfort, good comfort! We must to the king and show our strange sights. He must know 'tis none of your daughter nor my sister; we are gone else. Sir, I will give you as much as this old man does, when the business is performed; and remain, as he says, your pawn till it be brought you.

Autolycus I will trust you. Walk before toward the seaside; go on the right-hand; I will but look upon the hedge, and follow you.

Clown We are blessed in this man, as I may say, even blessed.

Shepherd Let's before, as he bids us: he was provided to do us good.

[*Exeunt* Shepherd *and* Clown.]

Autolycus If I had a mind to be honest, I see Fortune would not suffer me: she drops booties in my mouth. I am courted now with a double occasion,—gold, and a means to do the prince my master good; which who knows how that may turn back to my advancement? I will bring these two moles, these blind ones, aboard him: if he think it fit to shore them again, and that the complaint they have to the king concerns him nothing, let him call me rogue for being so far officious; for I am proof against that title, and what shame else belongs to't. To him will I present them: there may be matter in it.

[*Exit.*]

奥托力革厮	很好,给俺一半。你是这件事里的一方吗?
小　　丑	差不多,老爷;不过,虽然我的境况很可怜,我希望我不会给活剥。
奥托力革厮	啊!那是这牧羊人的儿子的境况:绞死他,他会被当作一个榜样。
小　　丑	安慰,多好的安慰!我们一定得去见国王,给他看我们这值得他看看的东西:他一定得知道这不是你姑娘,也不是我妹子;不然的话,我们可完了。老爷,事情办好以后,我会送给您跟这老人给你的一般多;而且留给您,正如他所说的,作抵押,直等到东西交给了您。
奥托力革厮	俺相信你们。在头里走,对着海边;靠右手边走;俺在这矮树丛里小便一下,就跟你们来。
小　　丑	我们碰到这人算交了运,正如我说的,简直交了运。
牧　羊　人	让我们先走,正如他关照我们的那样。他是老天爷安排好叫指引我们的。

　　　　　　　　　　　　　　　　　　[牧羊人与小丑同下。

奥托力革厮	俺若是有心要老实的话,俺如今却见到命运不叫俺那样:她把赃物落在俺嘴里。俺如今给使出双重机会来招惹,用黄金,而且还有办法使得俺主人太子爷有利;这件事谁知道也许会回过来又叫俺能得升迁?俺要把这两只瞎眼的地老鼠带到他船上去;若是国王认为把他们放回岸上来合适,而且觉得他们对他告的状和他没有关系,让他去叫咱流氓好了,说俺狗颠屁股瞎忙;因为俺对那称呼已经皮老得满不在乎,再也不怕什么害臊了。俺要引他们去见他:这件事里也许有把戏好做。

　　　　　　　　　　　　　　　　　　　　　　　　[下。

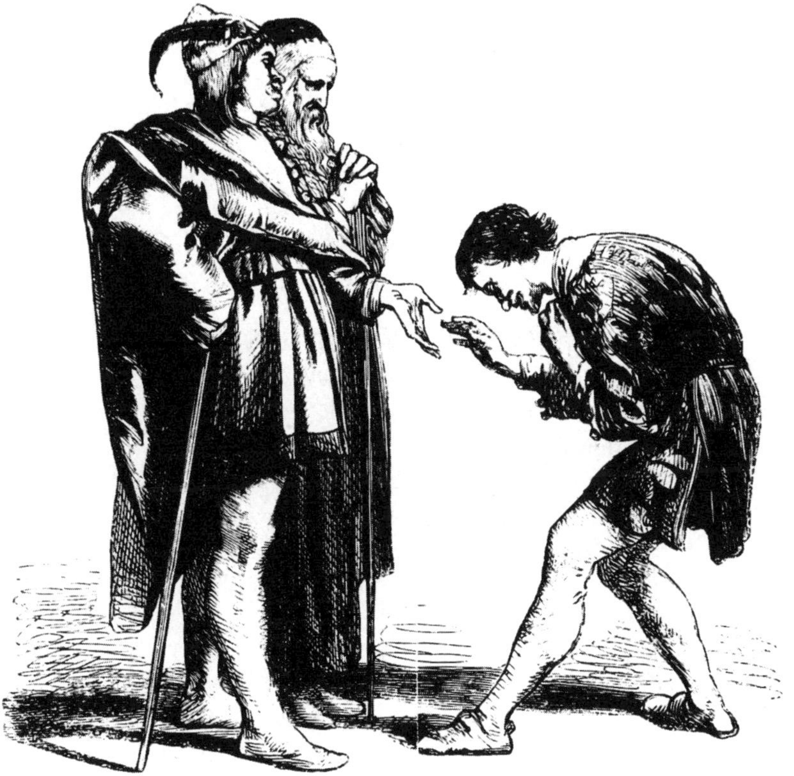

ACT V.

SCENE I. Sicilia. *A Room in the palace of* Leontes.

[*Enter* Leontes, Cleomenes, Dion, Paulina, *and Servants.*]

Cleomenes Sir, you have done enough, and have perform'd
A saint-like sorrow: no fault could you make
Which you have not redeem'd; indeed, paid down
More penitence than done trespass: at the last,
Do as the heavens have done, forget your evil;
With them, forgive yourself.
Leontes Whilst I remember
Her and her virtues, I cannot forget
My blemishes in them; and so still think of
The wrong I did myself: which was so much
That heirless it hath made my kingdom, and
Destroy'd the sweet'st companion that e'er man
Bred his hopes out of.
Paulina True, too true, my lord;
If, one by one, you wedded all the world,
Or from the all that are took something good,
To make a perfect woman, she you kill'd
Would be unparallel'd.
Leontes I think so. — *Kill'd!*

第 五 幕

第 一 景

［西西利亚。里杭底斯宫中一室］
［里杭底斯、克廖弥尼司、第盎、宝理娜与仆人等上。

克廖弥尼司 王上，您做得已够，已经尽到了
圣徒一般的悲伤；不可能犯过
什么样罪辜，您尚未赎尽前愆；
当真，您所付的忏悔已超过咎戾。
最后，跟上天似的，请将那邪恶
忘怀；和上天一样，宽恕您自己。

里杭底斯 只要想起她和她的美德，
我便不能忘掉我自己的过错，
所以总想起我自己铸成的枉曲；
那是这么多，以致使我的王国
没有了后裔，而且摧折了人自来
所曾寄托希望的最亲密的同伴。

宝理娜 果真，太对了，吾主；假使您跟
举世一个个女子都结婚，或者从
所有的女子身上都采取一点儿
优良，去造个白璧无瑕的良妻，
曾被您杀死的她，仍将独绝而无双。

里杭底斯 我也这么想。杀死的！我杀死的她！

She I *kill'd*! I did so; but thou strik'st me
Sorely, to say I did; it is as bitter
Upon thy tongue as in my thought; now, good now,
Say so but seldom.
Cleomenes   Not at all, good lady;
You might have spoken a thousand things that would
Have done the time more benefit, and grac'd
Your kindness better.
Paulina   You are one of those
Would have him wed again.
Dion   If you would not so,
You pity not the state, nor the remembrance
Of his most sovereign name; consider little
What dangers, by his highness' fail of issue,
May drop upon his kingdom, and devour
Incertain lookers-on. What were more holy
Than to rejoice the former queen is well?
What holier than, — for royalty's repair,
For present comfort, and for future good, —
To bless the bed of majesty again
With a sweet fellow to't?
Paulina   There is none worthy,
Respecting her that's gone. Besides, the gods
Will have fulfill'd their secret purposes;
For has not the divine Apollo said,
Is't not the tenour of his oracle,
That king Leontes shall not have an heir
Till his lost child be found? which that it shall,
Is all as monstrous to our human reason
As my Antigonus to break his grave
And come again to me; who, on my life,

我确曾如此；但你说到这上头
打得我很痛：在你唇舌间道出，
跟在我思想里想着，同样奇苦。
如今，请你，要少说为是。

克廖弥尼司 好夫人，
一次也别说：您说一千桩别的事，
会对那事有好处，使您的温蔼
更能增光彩。

宝　理　娜 你也是那些个愿他
再婚的人中的一个。

第　盎 你若是不愿
这般，您对于邦国便不存怜爱，
对于他至尊的名声的忆念也没
顾惜；未曾考虑到，因王上子嗣
空虚，什么样危难会降落到邦中，
把犹豫不定的旁观者悉数毁灭。
什么事能比庆贺旧时的王后
健好无恙，更清纯圣洁？什么事
能比欢庆王统的更新，同时为
目今的慰藉，也为将来的福绥，
去祝贺御榻上又有了亲密的同伴，
更清纯圣洁？

宝　理　娜 与去世的娘娘相比，
没有谁堪供匹配。而况，天神们
将会要完成他们那秘奥的计划，
因为神灵的阿波罗不是说过吗，
他那神谕的用意不是曾明言，
说国王里杭底斯，他失去的孩子
找到前，不会有后嗣？假使有的话，
那真和我们人类的理智不相容，
正如我的安铁冈纳施破开坟墓
到我跟前来；他呀，凭我的生命，

Did perish with the infant. 'Tis your counsel
My lord should to the heavens be contrary,
Oppose against their wills. — [*To* Leontes.] Care not for
   issue;
The crown will find an heir: great Alexander
Left his to the worthiest; so his successor
Was like to be the best.
Leontes   Good Paulina, —
Who hast the memory of Hermione,
I know, in honour, — O that ever I
Had squar'd me to thy counsel! — then, even now,
I might have look'd upon my queen's full eyes,
Have taken treasure from her lips, —
Paulina   And left them
More rich for what they yielded.
Leontes   Thou speak'st truth.
No more such wives; therefore, no wife: one worse,
And better us'd, would make her sainted spirit
Again possess her corpse; and on this stage, —
Where we offend her now, — appear soul-vexed,
And begin *Why to me*?
Paulina   Had she such power,
She had just cause.
Leontes   She had; and would incense me
To murder her I married.
Paulina   I should so.
Were I the ghost that walk'd, I'd bid you mark
Her eye, and tell me for what dull part in't
You chose her: then I'd shriek, that even your ears
Should rift to hear me; and the words that follow'd
Should be *Remember mine*!
Leontes   Stars, stars,
And all eyes else dead coals! — fear thou no wife;

　　　　　　已和那孩婴同归于尽。你想劝
　　　　　　主上乖天心,违逆天神们的意志。——
　　　　　　[向里杭底斯]不必为后嗣多顾虑;宝祚自会
　　　　　　找到后继人:伟大的亚历山大
　　　　　　将他的大宝遗给堪当其位者,
　　　　　　故而他的继承人该是最好的。
里杭底斯　亲爱的宝理娜,我知道你是耿耿
　　　　　　怀念着候妙霓;啊!但愿我采取了
　　　　　　你的谏诤去行事!那样时,到如今,
　　　　　　我尽可举目凝望我王后的明眸,
　　　　　　从她那唇边得到无穷的宝藏,——
宝　理　娜　哦,她唇边的宝藏,取之无尽而
　　　　　　用之不竭。
里杭底斯　　　　　　你说得极是。再没有
　　　　　　这样的妻子了;所以,不再要妻子:
　　　　　　一个不如她而能得较优待遇的,
　　　　　　会使她已成为神圣的亡灵重据
　　　　　　她的尸骸,而在这舞台上,——这里
　　　　　　我们如今都有罪,——现形,且愤激
　　　　　　难禁地问道,"为什么你对我如此?"
宝　理　娜　她若能这样做,自有充分的原因。
里杭底斯　她很有原因;且将激得我性起,
　　　　　　凶杀那新妇。
宝　理　娜　　　　　　我当会那么做:假如
　　　　　　我是那还魂的幽灵,我会叫您
　　　　　　注视她的眼瞳,看了对我说您可
　　　　　　看中她那里边的什么迟钝部分,
　　　　　　所以选中她;然后我将发锐唳,
　　　　　　而您的耳鼓会破裂;接着我还会
　　　　　　对您说,"记得我的眼睛"。
里杭底斯　　　　　　　　　　　星星,星星!
　　　　　　别的眼睛全都是熄了火的焦炭。

I'll have no wife, Paulina.
Paulina   Will you swear
Never to marry but by my free leave?
Leontes Never, Paulina; so be bless'd my spirit!
Paulina Then, good my lords, bear witness to his oath.
Cleomenes You tempt him over-much.
Paulina   Unless another,
As like Hermione as is her picture,
Affront his eye.
Cleomenes Good madam, —
Paulina   I have done.
Yet, if my lord will marry, — if you will, sir,
No remedy but you will, — give me the office
To choose you a queen: she shall not be so young
As was your former; but she shall be such
As, walk'd your first queen's ghost, it should take joy
To see her in your arms.
Leontes   My true Paulina,
We shall not marry till thou bidd'st us.
Paulina   That
Shall be when your first queen's again in breath;
Never till then.
             [*Enter a* Gentleman.]
Gentleman One that gives out himself Prince Florizel,
Son of Polixenes, with his princess, — she
The fairest I have yet beheld, — desires access
To your high presence.
Leontes   What with him? he comes not

　　　　　　你不用害怕我娶妻；我将不再有
　　　　　　妻子，宝理娜。
宝　理　娜　　　　　　　您可肯宣誓吗，决不
　　　　　　再结婚，除非得我的同意？
里杭底斯　　　　　　　　　　　宝理娜，
　　　　　　我决不：让我的灵魂得福！
宝　理　娜　　　　　　　　　　　那么，
　　　　　　亲爱的贵人们，对他这誓言作证。
克廖弥尼司　您使他过于奋激。
宝　理　娜　　　　　　　　除非又有位，
　　　　　　好比画像般与候妙霓一模一样，
　　　　　　为他所目击。
克廖弥尼司　　　　　　亲爱的夫人，——
宝　理　娜　　　　　　　　　　　我的话
　　　　　　已说完。可是，主君如果要结婚，——
　　　　　　若是您要的话，吾王，毫无办法，
　　　　　　您准要，——给我那任务为您选一位
　　　　　　后妃，她定得不如您先前的那位
　　　　　　那样年轻；但她将是这样的人儿，
　　　　　　假使您先前的王后的幽灵在此，
　　　　　　她将乐意见她在您的臂抱中。
里杭底斯　　真诚不假的宝理娜，在你叫我们
　　　　　　结婚前，我们将不结。
宝　理　娜　　　　　　　　那将会是在
　　　　　　您那第一位王后重复呼吸时；
　　　　　　不到那时候决不会。
　　　　　　　　　　〔一近侍上。
近　　　侍　有一位自言是弗洛律采尔亲王，
　　　　　　包列齐倪思的儿子，同他的妃子，——
　　　　　　我从未见过这样的美人，——愿求
　　　　　　王驾对他们赐见。
里杭底斯　　　　　　　　谁和他在一起？

Like to his father's greatness: his approach,
So out of circumstance and sudden, tells us
'Tis not a visitation fram'd, but forc'd
By need and accident. What train?
Gentleman　　　　　　　　But few,
And those but mean.
Leontes　　　　　His princess, say you, with him?
Gentleman　Ay; the most peerless piece of earth, I think,
That e'er the sun shone bright on.
Paulina　　　　　　　　O Hermione,
As every present time doth boast itself
Above a better gone, so must thy grave
Give way to what's seen now! Sir, you yourself
Have said and writ so, — but your writing now
Is colder than that theme, — *'She had not been,
Nor was not to be equall'd'*; thus your verse
Flow'd with her beauty once; 'tis shrewdly ebb'd,
To say you have seen a better.
Gentleman　　　　　　Pardon, madam:
The one I have almost forgot, — your pardon; —
The other, when she has obtain'd your eye,
Will have your tongue too. This is a creature,
Would she begin a sect, might quench the zeal
Of all professors else; make proselytes
Of who she but bid follow.
Paulina　　　　　　　How! not women?
Gentleman　Women will love her that she is a woman
More worth than any man; men, that she is

他到来不像他父亲,车水马龙
旗幡拥;他这下来到,仪从清简
又仓猝,告诉我们这不是预先
计议来相访,而是为需要与偶然
所促使。有什么随从?

近　　侍　　　　　　　　　只少数,而且
也寒伧。

里杭底斯　　　你说有他的妃子一同来?
近　　侍　是啊,那该是,我想,从来太阳曾
照亮的最绝的一块土。

宝 理 娜　　　　　　　　啊,候妙霓!
既然每一刻现今总夸耀它自己
超迈了较好的过往,你的坟墓
也就一定得让位于此刻之所见。
先生,您自己曾说过、写过这句话,——
但您那大作如今已比那话题
还要冷,——"她,人中绝,再也无人能
相比";便这般您诗中曾一度流过
她的美:要说您曾见佼好的美人,
这话已时过而境迁,不堪再回忆。

近　　侍　请原谅,夫人:那一位我几已忘掉——
望你原谅——这一位您一经目注,
将无不心仪而舌赞。这是这样
一个人,只要她开创一支教派,
所有其他教派里的信徒的热诚
都会被她熄灭掉,只要她叫谁
跟她、谁就会成她的皈依者。

宝 理 娜　　　　　　　　　怎样?
不是女人吧?

近　　侍　　　　　　女人会爱她,因为她
是个比任何男子更宝贵的女人;
男子会爱她,因为她是个女人中

The rarest of all women.
Leontes   Go, Cleomenes;
Yourself, assisted with your honour'd friends,
Bring them to our embracement. — Still, 'tis strange
          [*Exeunt* Cleomenes *and* others.]
He thus should steal upon us.
Paulina   Had our prince, —
Jewel of children, — seen this hour, he had pair'd
Well with this lord: there was not full a month
Between their births.
Leontes Pr'ythee no more; cease; Thou know'st
He dies to me again when talk'd of: sure,
When I shall see this gentleman, thy speeches
Will bring me to consider that which may
Unfurnish me of reason. — They are come. —
          [*Re-enter*, Florizel, Perdita,
               Cleomenes *and* others.]
Your mother was most true to wedlock, prince;
For she did print your royal father off,
Conceiving you: were I but twenty-one,
Your father's image is so hit in you,
His very air, that I should call you brother,
As I did him, and speak of something wildly
By us perform'd before. Most dearly welcome!
And your fair princess, — goddess! O, alas!
I lost a couple that 'twixt heaven and earth
Might thus have stood, begetting wonder, as
You, gracious couple, do! And then I lost, —
All mine own folly, — the society,
Amity too, of your brave father, whom,
Though bearing misery, I desire my life
Once more to look on him.

最登峰造极的。

里杭底斯　　　　　　　　你去,克廖弥尼司;
你自己,你的荣誉的同僚们帮着,
将他们带来入我们的怀抱。还是
很奇怪,　　　　　　　[克廖弥尼司与余众下。
　　他会这样偷偷的来访。

宝　理　娜　若我们的王子——孩子中的宝——见到
这时辰,他会跟这位殿下成一双:
他们的生日相差不到一足月。

里杭底斯　请你莫说了:住口吧! 你知道一经
提起他,对于我,就是再死了一遭:
当我见到这位少君时,你的话
准会使我想起那情事,那许会
叫我丧神而失智。他们已来了。

　　　[弗洛律采尔、衷笛达、克廖弥尼司与余众上。]
你母亲何等精贞于婚媾,亲王;
因为她将你怀孕时,把你的父王
印版一般地打印了出来。我此刻
假如是二十一岁,令尊的形象在你
眉宇间丝毫不爽,这气概跟他
一模一样,我会像以前称呼他,
那么,叫你作王兄;且跟你谈起
我们从前轻率地一同做的事。
最最亲爱的欢迎! 美好的妃子,
还有你,——天仙! 啊,唉哟! 我失掉了
儿女一双,若他们在天上和人间,
会引得神仙与下界都赞叹,正和
你们,尊荣的贤伉俪,一个样:另外
我也失掉了——都因我自己的愚蠢——
你堂堂父王的友伴和友爱,对他,
我挨着衷心的惨痛,愿在此生中
再见他一面。

Florizel   By his command
Have I here touch'd Sicilia, and from him
Give you all greetings that a king, at friend,
Can send his brother: and, but infirmity, —
Which waits upon worn times, — hath something seiz'd
His wish'd ability, he had himself
The lands and waters 'twixt your throne and his
Measur'd, to look upon you; whom he loves,
He bade me say so, — more than all the sceptres
And those that bear them, living.
Leontes   O my brother, —
Good gentleman! — the wrongs I have done thee stir
Afresh within me; and these thy offices,
So rarely kind, are as interpreters
Of my behind-hand slackness! — Welcome hither,
As is the spring to the earth. And hath he too
Expos'd this paragon to the fearful usage, —
At least ungentle, — of the dreadful Neptune,
To greet a man not worth her pains, much less
The adventure of her person?
Florizel   Good, my lord,
She came from Libya.
Leontes   Where the warlike Smalus,
That noble honour'd lord, is fear'd and lov'd?
Florizel   Most royal sir, from thence; from him whose
    daughter
His tears proclaim'd his, parting with her: thence, —
A prosperous south-wind friendly, we have cross'd,
To execute the charge my father gave me,
For visiting your highness: my best train
I have from your Sicilian shores dismiss'd;
Who for Bohemia bend, to signify

弗洛律采尔	奉着他的命,我在西西利亚登了岸;为他尽敬礼,问安好于君王,这乃是一位国君怀着友情能致他王兄的至意:若不是衰颓,——那跟老年一同来,——有点制服了他愿有的能力,他会迈越过您和他御座之间的海陆相距亲自来见您,他爱您——他要我对您这么说——甚于爱一切王权,和活着的君王。
里杭底斯	啊,我的王兄啊!——亲爱的君子,——我对您所行的不义重复在我心中内疚,而您的这些周章斡旋,这么样无比地亲仁恳挚,只能说明我多拖延迟滞,多疏懈怠忽!欢迎你来到此间,如欢迎春来大地。而他还竟然促使这位琼绝的天人,冒着那可怕的奈泼钧的可畏之威——至少不温柔,来敬礼一个不值她麻烦,更不堪她冒逆生命危险的人吗?
弗洛律采尔	亲爱的吾王,她来自利比亚。
里杭底斯	是否在那里,那勇武的司马勒,高贵与光荣两全之主,为人所畏惧而敬爱?
弗洛律采尔	至尊的伯父,是从那方来;来自他那边,他流泪与他的爱女道别:我们打那里过海来——一路是南风友好地顺送——执行我家父给我,叫拜谒尊颜之命:我最好的扈从我自西西利亚海边已解散回家;他们已转向波希米亚去,不仅去

Not only my success in Libya, sir,
But my arrival, and my wife's, in safety
Here, where we are.

Leontes The blessèd gods
Purge all infection from our air whilst you
Do climate here! You have a holy father,
A graceful gentleman; against whose person,
So sacred as it is, I have done sin:
For which the heavens, taking angry note,
Have left me issueless; and your father's bless'd, —
As he from heaven merits it, — with you
Worthy his goodness. What might I have been,
Might I a son and daughter now have look'd on,
Such goodly things as you!

[*Enter a* Lord.]

Lord Most noble sir,
That which I shall report will bear no credit,
Were not the proof so nigh. Please you, great sir,
Bohemia greets you from himself by me;
Desires you to attach his son, who has, —
His dignity and duty both cast off, —
Fled from his father, from his hopes, and with
A shepherd's daughter.

Leontes Where's Bohemia? speak.

Lord Here in your city; I now came from him:
I speak amazedly; and it becomes
My marvel and my message. To your court
Whiles he was hast'ning, — in the chase, it seems,
Of this fair couple, — meets he on the way
The father of this seeming lady and
Her brother, having both their country quitted
With this young prince.

Florizel Camillo has betray'd me;

　　　　　　汇报我在利比亚的成功,大伯父,
　　　　　　也为去陈禀我与妃子的安全
　　　　　　到达了此间我们如今之所在。

里杭底斯　愿众位神圣的天神将空中疫气
　　　　　　清扫尽,当你在此作客时!你有位
　　　　　　清纯圣洁的尊亲,一位懋德而
　　　　　　获天佑的君子;对他的福体,那是
　　　　　　如此地神圣,我犯过罪戾:为那个,
　　　　　　上苍心怀着恼怒,使我无子嗣;
　　　　　　而令尊却得福——他应受天恩呵护——
　　　　　　有了你,堪当他的盛德。我若现今
　　　　　　能眼望儿女双双在眼前,如同
　　　　　　你这样的佳儿,我将多么心情爽!

〔一贵人上。

贵　　人　至尊的明君,我待禀报的将不邀
　　　　　　信任,假使凭证不来得这么近。
　　　　　　您许会高兴,大王,波希米亚王
　　　　　　御驾亲自命我向尊座致问候;
　　　　　　愿您将他的王子逮捕住,他把
　　　　　　高位、名分都抛弃而不顾,打从他
　　　　　　父王,打从他的希望逃遁,而且是
　　　　　　和个牧羊人的女儿一同出奔。

里杭底斯　波希米亚在哪里?快说。
贵　　人　　　　　　　　　　他在您
　　　　　　这城中;我此刻是从他那里来此:
　　　　　　我出言慌乱,这正和我的惊愕
　　　　　　与传言相符契。当他赶来您宫中,——
　　　　　　看来是来追这俊俏的一双,——路上
　　　　　　被他撞见了这个像千金的父亲
　　　　　　和她的哥哥,他们都随同这位
　　　　　　年轻的王子背离了他们的乡井。

弗洛律采尔　喀米罗出卖了我了;他的荣誉

Whose honour and whose honesty, till now,
Endur'd all weathers.
Lord   Lay't so to his charge;
He's with the king your father.
Leontes   Who? Camillo?
Lord   Camillo, sir; I spake with him; who now
Has these poor men in question. Never saw I
Wretches so quake: they kneel, they kiss the earth;
Forswear themselves as often as they speak:
Bohemia stops his ears, and threatens them
With divers deaths in death.
Perdita   O my poor father! —
The heaven sets spies upon us, will not have
Our contract celebrated.
Leontes   You are married?
Florizel   We are not, sir, nor are we like to be;
The stars, I see, will kiss the valleys first: —
The odds for high and low's alike.
Leontes   My lord,
Is this the daughter of a king?
Florizel   She is,
When once she is my wife.
Leontes   That once, I see by your good father's speed,
Will come on very slowly. I am sorry,
Most sorry, you have broken from his liking,
Where you were tied in duty; and as sorry
Your choice is not so rich in worth as beauty,
That you might well enjoy her.
Florizel   Dear, look up:
Though Fortune, visible an enemy,
Should chase us with my father, power no jot

　　　　　　　　　和他的诚实到此为止,还能够
　　　　　　　　　经受住一切风波云雾。
贵　　　人　　　　　　　　　　　将这事
　　　　　　　　　归罪于他吧:他和您父王在一起。
里杭底斯　是谁？喀米罗？
贵　　　人　　　　　　　正是喀米罗,君王:
　　　　　　　　　我刚和他说过话,他现在正跟这
　　　　　　　　　两个可怜的人儿在打话。我从未
　　　　　　　　　见过遭际狼狈的家伙这么样
　　　　　　　　　颤抖:他们下着跪,叩着头请罪,
　　　　　　　　　每说一会话便诅咒一下自己:
　　　　　　　　　波希米亚手掩着自己的耳朵,
　　　　　　　　　用各种各样的死法威吓他们。
哀笛达　啊,我可怜的父亲！天公差密探
　　　　　　　　　跟随着我们,不叫我们的婚事
　　　　　　　　　庆合欢。
里杭底斯　　　　　　你们结过婚吗？
弗洛律采尔　　　　　　　　　　我们没,
　　　　　　　　　大伯父,看来不见得成功了;星星,
　　　　　　　　　我看来,要先吻过了山谷才成:
　　　　　　　　　中彩头对于位高位低都一样。
里杭底斯　我的亲王,这是位国王的女儿吗？
弗洛律采尔　她是的,只要一做了我的妃子。
里杭底斯　那个"一做了",我看来,只因你父亲
　　　　　　　　　来得太快,恐怕要延宕。我抱憾,
　　　　　　　　　非常抱憾,你打破了他的喜爱,
　　　　　　　　　挣脱本分的维系走出来;我同样
　　　　　　　　　抱憾的是你这选中的偶俪品位
　　　　　　　　　敌不上美貌,好叫你得能消受她。
弗洛律采尔　心爱的,抬头望:虽然命运,如今
　　　　　　　　　显得是敌人,同我的父亲一起来
　　　　　　　　　追我们,她却没有一点点力量

Hath she to change our loves. —Beseech you, sir,
Remember since you ow'd no more to time
Than I do now: with thought of such affections,
Step forth mine advocate; at your request
My father will grant precious things as trifles.
Leontes Would he do so, I'd beg your precious mistress,
Which he counts but a trifle.
Paulina   Sir, my liege,
Your eye hath too much youth in't: not a month
'Fore your queen died, she was more worth such gazes
Than what you look on now.
Leontes   I thought of her
Even in these looks I made. —[*To* Florizel.] But your petition
Is yet unanswer'd. I will to your father.
Your honour not o'erthrown by your desires,
I am friend to them and you: upon which errand
I now go toward him; therefore, follow me,
And mark what way I make. Come, good my lord.
                                                    [*Exeunt.*]

SCENE II. *Before the Palace.*

[*Enter* Autolycus *and* a Gentleman.]

Autolycus Beseech you, sir, were you present at this relation?

First Gentleman I was by at the opening of the fardel, heard the old shepherd deliver the manner how he found it: whereupon, after a little amazedness, we were all commanded out of the chamber; only this, methought I heard the shepherd say he found the child.

Autolycus I would most gladly know the issue of it.

First Gentleman I make a broken delivery of the business; but the changes I perceived in the king and Camillo were very notes of admiration. They seem'd almost, with staring on one another, to tear the cases

　　　　　　　来改变我们的爱情。恳求您,伯父,
　　　　　　　请回忆从前您和我如今一样,
　　　　　　　那年轻时节;回想到这样的情爱,
　　　　　　　请您站出来替我作主张;在您
　　　　　　　申请下,我父亲会给珍宝如草芥。
里杭底斯　　若果真如此,我讨要你这位
　　　　　　　宝贝的姑娘,他会把她当草芥
　　　　　　　来给予。
宝　理　娜　　　　　　　王上,我的主君,您这双
　　　　　　　眼睛里还太多青春的光焰:王后
　　　　　　　过世前不满一个月,她更配领受
　　　　　　　您此刻眼端端所投的凝视。
里杭底斯　　　　　　　　　　　　　　就在
　　　　　　　这些顾视中,我想起了她来。[向弗]可是
　　　　　　　我还未回答你的恳请。我要去看
　　　　　　　你父亲:你的荣誉若未被欲念
　　　　　　　所推翻,我愿为它们,愿为你尽力;
　　　　　　　去求情,我现在要看他。所以来吧,
　　　　　　　看我的成就如何:跟我来,好贤侄。

　　　　　　　　　　　　　　　　　　　　　〔同下。

第　二　景

〔王宫前〕
〔奥托力革厮与一士夫上。

奥托力革厮　请问您,大人,讲那经过情形时您在场吗?
士　夫　甲　打开那包裹时我在,听到那牧羊老人讲起他是怎样
　　　　　　　捡到的:诧异了一会之后,我们被吩咐离开那房间;
　　　　　　　不过我似乎听到牧羊人说,他是捡到那孩子的。
奥托力革厮　俺倒挺乐意知道那事情结果如何。
士　夫　甲　我传报这件事可说不齐全;不过我看到国王和喀米
　　　　　　　罗脸色变了,一派的惊奇:他们彼此互相瞪着,好似

of their eyes; there was speech in their dumbness, language in their very gesture; they looked as they had heard of a world ransomed, or one destroyed: a notable passion of wonder appeared in them; but the wisest beholder, that knew no more but seeing could not say if the importance were joy or sorrow; — but in the extremity of the one, it must needs be. [*Enter* another Gentleman.] Here comes a gentleman that happily knows more. The news, Rogero?

Second Gentleman Nothing but bonfires: the oracle is fulfilled: the king's daughter is found: such a deal of wonder is broken out within this hour that balladmakers cannot be able to express it. [*Enter* a third Gentleman.] Here comes the Lady Paulina's steward: he can deliver you more. How goes it now, sir? This news, which is called true, is so like an old tale that the verity of it is in strong suspicion. Has the king found his heir?

Third Gentleman Most true, if ever truth were pregnant by circumstance. That which you hear you'll swear you see, there is such unity in the proofs. The mantle of Queen Hermione; her jewel about the neck of it; the letters of Antigonus, found with it, which they know to be his character; the majesty of the creature in resemblance of the mother; the affection of nobleness, which nature shows above her breeding; and many other evidences, — proclaim her with all certainty to be the king's daughter. Did you see the meeting of the two kings?

Second Gentleman No.

Third Gentleman Then you have lost a sight which was to be seen, cannot be spoken of. There might you have beheld one joy crown another, so and in such manner that it seemed sorrow wept to take leave of them; for their joy waded in tears. There was casting up of eyes, holding up of hands, with countenance of such distraction that they were to be known

要瞪破眼眶似的；他们不说话中间有话，光那姿态里就有言语；他们那神情里像是听到了整个世界得救了，或是给毁了：一阵异乎寻常的诧愕的激情在他们形容间透露出来；可是即使最聪明的旁观者，只凭眼看，不知道内情，也说不上那是什么意思，是欢乐还是悲哀；不过总不出这两桩里的一桩，且准是到了极点。

〔又一士夫上。

这里来了位士夫，也许会多知道些。有什么新闻，罗格罗？

士　夫　乙　什么也没有，只有祝火；神谕是应验了；公主是找到了：这么多惊人的奇事在这一响发生出来，小曲家们还来不及编造歌曲呢。

〔又一士夫上。

宝理娜夫人的家宰来了：他能多给你些消息。现在怎样了，先生？这新闻据说是真实的，但跟个老故事一样，它的真不真很有点可疑：国王找到了他的胤嗣吗？

士　夫　三　千真万确，假使真情能叫一些情况的细节充实而坐证的话：你听到的一些事你可以发誓你看到过，证据是这么完全一致。候妙霓王后的斗篷，挂在孩子颈上的那颗宝石，和它一起捡到的安铁冈纳施的信件，那个他们认得是他的笔迹；那姑娘的气概举止庄严宏大一如她母亲，天生成性情高贵远超过她所受的教养，还有许多其他的证据宣明她毫无疑问是国王的女儿。你看到两位国王彼此相见吗？

士　夫　乙　没有。

士　夫　三　那你就损失掉一场奇观了，那是要眼睛看的，嘴巴说不像。那里你能见到欢乐之上又加欢乐，以致，且到了这般模样，看来像"悲哀"离开他们时哭得不可开交，因为他们的"欢乐"是徒涉着眼泪互相拥抱的。他们眼睛往上望，手臂高举着，仓皇混乱做一团，你

by garment, not by favour. Our king, being ready to leap out of himself for joy of his found daughter, as if that joy were now become a loss, cries O, *thy mother, thy mother*! then asks Bohemia forgiveness; then embraces his son-in-law; then again worries he his daughter with clipping her; now he thanks the old shepherd, which stands by like a weather-bitten conduit of many kings' reigns. I never heard of such another encounter, which lames report to follow it, and undoes description to do it.

Second Gentleman   What, pray you, became of Antigonus, that carried hence the child?

Third Gentleman   Like an old tale still, which will have matter to rehearse, though credit be asleep and not an ear open. He was torn to pieces with a bear: this avouches the shepherd's son, who has not only his innocence, — which seems much, — to justify him, but a handkerchief and rings of his, that Paulina knows.

First Gentleman   What became of his bark and his followers?

Third Gentleman   Wrecked the same instant of their master's death, and in the view of the shepherd: so that all the instruments which aided to expose the child were even then lost when it was found. But, O, the noble combat that 'twixt joy and sorrow was fought in Paulina! She had one eye declined for the loss of her husband, another elevated that the oracle was fulfilled: she lifted the princess from the earth, and so locks her in embracing, as if she would pin her to her heart, that she might no more be in danger of losing.

First Gentleman   The dignity of this act was worth the audience of kings and princes; for by such was it acted.

Third Gentleman   One of the prettiest touches of all, and that which angled for mine eyes, — caught the water, though not the fish, — was, when at the relation of the queen's death, with the manner how she came to it, — bravely confessed and lamented by the king, — how attentivenes wounded his daughter; till, from one sign of dolour to another, she did with an *Alas*! —

只能分辨出衣袍,不能凭眉眼面相辨认他们了。我们的王上,为了找到他女儿而狂欢,几乎要跳起来,乐极生悲,叫道,"啊,你母亲,你母亲!"跟着就请求波希米亚对他宽恕;接下来便拥抱他的女婿;再就是去搂抱他女儿;然后去感谢那牧羊老人,他站在一旁像个经过了好多代王朝的喷泉上的石人儿似的。我从未听说过这样的相会,这真是传报会蹩着腿跟不上,描画会变成哑巴说不出来。

士 夫 乙　安铁冈纳施,是他把这孩子送去的,请问你,他怎么样了?

士 夫 三　还是像个老故事那样,那想要把事情说出来,可是没有人会相信。他给一头大熊撕烂了:牧羊人的儿子肯定地这样说,而他则不光有他的蠢拙——那好像很厉害——证明他不诳,而且还有他的一方手帕和几只戒指宝理娜认得出来。

士 夫 甲　他那条船和他的随从们怎样了?

士 夫 三　船破了,跟他们主子的死是同一个时刻,而且牧羊人还看到:所有帮同他抛弃那孩子的所有的人手就在她给捡到的那一刻都给消灭了。可是,啊!那狂欢和极痛在宝理娜心中那场严肃的搏斗可真了不起!她为她丈夫的死低垂着一只眼睛,为神谕的应验高举着另一只:她把公主从地上举了起来,拥抱她得这么紧,仿佛要把她钉住在心上似的,好使她不再遭失掉的危险。

士 夫 甲　这个动作的庄严是值得君王们、太子公主他们观看的,因为那就在他们面前表演。

士 夫 三　在一切情状里最可爱的,而那是来钓我的眼睛的,——钓到了眼泪,不是鱼,——是正当讲起王后的死的时候,说到她怎样会死,——那件事国王自己勇于认罪而悼伤,——他女儿非常注意听,那可真伤了她的心;等到,悲伤的征象一个接着一个来,最后她叫声

I would fain say, bleed tears; for I am sure my heart wept blood. Who was most marble there changed colour; some swooned, all sorrowed: if all the world could have seen it, the woe had been universal.

First Gentleman Are they returned to the court?

Third Gentleman No: the princess hearing of her mother's statue, which is in the keeping of Paulina, — a piece many years in doing and now newly performed by that rare Italian master, Julio Romano, who, had he himself eternity, and could put breath into his work, would beguile nature of her custom, so perfectly he is her ape: he so near to Hermione hath done Hermione that they say one would speak to her and stand in hope of answer: — thither with all greediness of affection are they gone; and there they intend to sup.

Second Gentleman I thought she had some great matter there in hand; for she hath privately twice or thrice a day, ever since the death of Hermione, visited that removed house. Shall we thither, and with our company piece the rejoicing?

First Gentleman Who would be thence that has the benefit of access? every wink of an eye some new grace will be born: our absence makes us unthrifty to our knowledge. Let's along.

[*Exeunt* Gentlemen.]

Autolycus Now, had I not the dash of my former life in me, would preferment drop on my head. I brought the old man and his son aboard the prince; told him I heard them talk of a fardel and I know not what; but he at that time over-fond of the shepherd's daughter, — so he then took her to be, — who began to be much sea-sick, and himself little better, extremity of weather continuing, this mystery remained undiscover'd. But 'tis all one to me; for had I been the finder-out of this secret, it would not have relish'd among my other discredits. Here come those I have done good to against my will, and already appearing in the blossoms of their fortune.

"唉哟"！我愿说，哭出的眼泪似流血，因为我敢肯定我心里的血也像眼泪在泉涌。谁在那里就是最铁石心肠的也会脸上变色；有人昏晕过去了，大家都哭了：假使全世界的人能来看到，那悲哀就会是普天下的了。

士　夫　甲　他们回到王宫里去了吗？

士　夫　三　没有；公主听说了她母亲的雕像，那是宝理娜保管着的——一尊雕了好多年，现在才由那位卓越的意大利大师巨利奥·罗马诺新完成的杰作；他若是有永恒把握，能把呼吸放进他作品里去的话，他会把造化的主顾抢走，竟能模仿她到这么一丝不爽：他把候妙霓雕刻得这么像候妙霓本人，他们说人们能对她说话而站着等她回答：他们都怀着满腔热爱去到了那里，预备在那里进晚餐。

士　夫　乙　我想她在那里当有什么大事情在做，因为自从候妙霓死后，她总是一天两三回独白一人去到那隐僻的房屋里去。我们也到那里，凑着伴儿跟他们一起去欢庆如何？

士　夫　甲　能给进去的谁愿意不去？眼睛每一霎，就会有什么新的恩福会产生：我们不在那里使我们的闻见减少。一块儿走吧。

〔三士夫同下。

奥托力革厮　如今，俺若是没有以前生活里的那点儿缺德的话，升官发财会能掉到咱头上来。俺把那老头儿和他儿子带上太子爷的船：告诉他俺听到他们讲起一个包裹，不过俺不知道是怎么一回事；可是他在那时节，太迷恋着那牧羊老儿的姑娘，——那一晌他以为她确是那样个人，——她开始晕船晕得很凶，他自己稍微好一点，风浪不断地很厉害，这秘密便没有给发现。不过这对俺是一样的；因为如果俺发现了这秘密的话，这不会同俺的丢脸事一起被当作好事儿的。这儿来了两个俺违背自己的意愿去讨好的人儿，他们已经鸿运高照。

[*Enter* Shepherd *and* Clown.]

Shepherd Come, boy; I am past more children, but thy sons and daughters will be all gentlemen born.

Clown You are well met, sir: you denied to fight with me this other day, because I was no gentleman born. See you these clothes? say you see them not and think me still no gentleman born: you were best say these robes are not gentlemen born. Give me the lie, do; and try whether I am not now a gentleman born.

Autolycus I know you are now, sir, a gentleman born.

Clown Ay, and have been so any time these four hours.

Shepherd And so have I, boy!

Clown So you have:—but I was a gentleman born before my father; for the king's son took me by the hand and called me brother; and then the two kings called my father brother; and then the prince, my brother, and the princess, my sister, called my father father; and so we wept; and there was the first gentleman-like tears that ever we shed.

Shepherd We may live, son, to shed many more.

Clown Ay; or else 'twere hard luck, being in so preposterous estate as we are.

Autolycus I humbly beseech you, sir, to pardon me all the faults I have committed to your worship, and to give me your good report to the prince my master.

Shepherd Pr'ythee, son, do; for we must be gentle, now we are gentlemen.

Clown Thou wilt amend thy life?

Autolycus Ay, an it like your good worship.

Clown Give me thy hand: I will swear to the prince thou art as honest a true fellow as any is in Bohemia.

Shepherd You may say it, but not swear it.

Clown Not swear it, now I am a gentleman? Let boors and franklins say it, I'll swear it.

［牧羊人与小丑上。

牧 羊 人　来吧,孩子;我是不会再有孩子的了,不过你的儿子女儿会都是大户人家的儿女了。

小　　　丑　碰到您很高兴,您家。您那天拒绝跟我决斗,因为我不是大户人家子弟;您看到这些衣服吗?您若是还说没见到它们,还把我当作不是大户人家子弟;您最好还是说这些锦袍不是大户人家做的。侮辱我一下,说我撒谎,来呀,试一下,看我现在是不是一位大户人家子弟了呢?

奥托力革厮　俺知道您现在是,大爷,一位大户人家的子弟了。

小　　　丑　是呀,我这四个钟头里随时都是的。

牧 羊 人　不错,是我生下了你的,儿子。

小　　　丑　是你生的;可是我父亲没有生我时,我就是个大户人家的子弟了;因为那国王的儿子拉着我的手叫我哥哥;跟着两位国王都叫我父亲亲家;下来那王太子我的兄弟和公主我的妹子叫我父亲作父亲;我们大家便这么哭起来:那是我们第一次流相公式的眼泪。

牧 羊 人　我们这辈子,儿子,还会流好多次呢。

小　　　丑　是呀;不然的话就是运气不好,眼见到我们如今景况这么乖戾。

奥托力革厮　俺恭恭敬敬恳求您,大爷,饶了俺对您大相公所犯的过错吧,请您对太子爷俺主人要讲咱的好话。

牧 羊 人　请你,儿子,就那么办;因为我们是相公官人了,我们便得文雅温存些。

小　　　丑　你会改过自新吗?

奥托力革厮　是的,若是您大相公高兴的话。

小　　　丑　把手伸给我;我会对太子赌咒,你是个在波希米亚比不拘那个真正老实人还要忠厚的人。

牧 羊 人　你说就是了,可不要赌咒。

小　　　丑　不得赌咒,为了我如今是个士子了?让野汉和乡下佬去说这话,我要赌咒。

Shepherd How if it be false, son?

Clown If it be ne'er so false, a true gentleman may swear it in the behalf of his friend. — And I'll swear to the prince thou art a tall fellow of thy hands and that thou wilt not be drunk; but I know thou art no tall fellow of thy hands and that thou wilt be drunk: but I'll swear it; and I would thou wouldst be a tall fellow of thy hands.

Autolycus I will prove so, sir, to my power.

Clown Ay, by any means, prove a tall fellow: if I do not wonder how thou darest venture to be drunk, not being a tall fellow, trust me not. — Hark! the kings and the princes, our kindred, are going to see the queen's picture. Come, follow us: we'll be thy good masters.

[Exeunt.]

SCENE III. *A Chapel in Paulina's house.*

[*Enter* Leontes, Polixenes, Florizel, Perdita, Camillo, Paulina, Lords *and* Attendants.]

Leontes O grave and good Paulina, the great comfort
That I have had of thee!

Paulina   What, sovereign sir,
I did not well, I meant well. All my services
You have paid home: but that you have vouchsaf'd,
With your crown'd brother and these your contracted
Heirs of your kingdoms, my poor house to visit,
It is a surplus of your grace which never
My life may last to answer.

Leontes   O Paulina,
We honour you with trouble: — but we came
To see the statue of our queen: your gallery
Have we pass'd through, not without much content
In many singularities; but we saw not

牧 羊 人　若这话是假的,那怎么办,儿子?
小　　丑　不管它多假,一位真的士子可以替他的朋友赌咒:而我要对太子赌咒,说你是个能干有胆量的人,又说你不会喝醉;可是我知道你并不能干有胆量,而且会喝醉:不过我会赌咒,而且愿意你是个能干有胆量的人。
奥托力革厮　俺要尽量那么做,大爷。
小　　丑　是啊,无论如何要成个能干有胆量的人:若是我不奇怪怎么你敢冒险喝醉,且不去做个能干有胆量的人,就不要相信我。听!两位国王和太子公主他们,我们的自家人,正在去看王后的像了。来吧,跟我们来:我们可以做你的好主人。

〔同下。

第 三 景

〔宝理娜府中小教堂〕
〔里杭底斯、包列齐倪思、弗洛律采尔、哀笛达、喀米罗、宝理娜、贵人数人、侍从数人上。

里杭底斯　啊,可敬而亲爱的宝理娜,我从
你那里得到多大的安慰!
宝 理 娜　　　　　　　　什么事,
君王,我做得不好,我用意却美。
我所效的辛勤,您已充分酬报;
您能和您的王兄,与你们两座
王国的联姻宝胄,都屈尊下顾
蓬荜,这便是恩宠逾盈,尽我这
一生也休想能报答。
里 杭 底 斯　　　　　　　　啊,宝理娜!
我们前来打扰你:可是我们来
是要看我们王后的雕像:我们
走过了你的行廊,很欣赏许多
珍奇的宝器,但我们还未曾见到

That which my daughter came to look upon,
The statue of her mother.
Paulina　　　　　　　As she liv'd peerless,
So her dead likeness, I do well believe,
Excels whatever yet you look'd upon
Or hand of man hath done; therefore I keep it
Lonely, apart. But here it is: prepare
To see the life as lively mock'd as ever
Still sleep mock'd death: behold; and say 'tis well.
　　　　[Paulina *undraws a curtain, and discovers*
　　　　　　Hermione, *standing as a statue.*]
I like your silence, — it the more shows off
Your wonder: but yet speak; — first, you, my liege.
Comes it not something near?
Leontes　　　　　　　Her natural posture! —
Chide me, dear stone, that I may say indeed
Thou art Hermione; or rather, thou art she
In thy not chiding; for she was as tender
As infancy and grace. — But yet, Paulina,
Hermione was not so much wrinkled; nothing
So agèd, as this seems.
Polixenes　　　　　　O, not by much!
Paulina　So much the more our carver's excellence;
Which lets go by some sixteen years, and makes her
As she liv'd now.
Leontes　　　　　As now she might have done,
So much to my good comfort, as it is
Now piercing to my soul. O, thus she stood,
Even with such life of majesty, — warm life,
As now it coldly stands, — when first I woo'd her!
I am asham'd: does not the stone rebuke me

我女儿特来参拜的她母亲的像。

宝　理　娜　　正如她在世时没有匹敌,故而她
死后的造像,我很相信,超过了
您所曾见过或是人的手所能
做到的任何东西;所以我将它
单独安放着。但它在这里:请准备
来看那生人给仿造得活灵活现,
仿如沉静的睡眠模仿着死亡:
看吧！您说,多好。

　　　　　　　[宝理娜拽启帷幕,显候妙霓为一雕像。]
我爱您的沉默:
这更显得您在赞赏;可还是说吧:
首先请您,主君,这有点像真的吗?

里杭底斯　　是她自然的姿势！将我呵责吧,
亲爱的石像,好使我说道,你当真
就是候妙霓;或者更也许,因你
不呵责而正就是她,因为她温柔
和煦,如婴稚与仁慈一样。可是,
宝理娜,候妙霓还没这般皱纹多;
并没有这样衰老。

包列齐倪思　　　　　　　　啊,没衰老得
恁厉害。

宝　理　娜　　　　　这更显得我们的雕刻师
多卓越;他使得几乎十六年流过,
而将她雕成如今还活着的一般。

里杭底斯　　像她如今还活着般,那真是好不
令我安慰,正如它如今却刺入
我灵魂。啊,她当时也这般站立着,
也正像这样庄严地活灵活现,——
暖呼呼满是生气,它如今却冷冷
站立着,——当我初次向她求爱时。
我感到惭愧:这石像不骂我比它

For being more stone than it? — O royal piece,
There's magic in thy majesty; which has
My evils conjur'd to remembrance; and
From thy admiring daughter took the spirits,
Standing like stone with thee!

Perdita And give me leave;
And do not say 'tis superstition, that
I kneel, and then implore her blessing. — Lady,
Dear queen, that ended when I but began,
Give me that hand of yours to kiss.

Paulina O, patience!
The statue is but newly fix'd, the colour's
Not dry.

Camillo My lord, your sorrow was too sore laid on,
Which sixteen winters cannot blow away,
So many summers dry; scarce any joy
Did ever so long live; no sorrow
But kill'd itself much sooner.

Polixenes Dear my brother,
Let him that was the cause of this have power
To take off so much grief from you as he
Will piece up in himself.

Paulina Indeed, my lord,
If I had thought the sight of my poor image
Would thus have wrought you, — for the stone is mine, —
I'd not have show'd it.

Leontes Do not draw the curtain.

Paulina No longer shall you gaze on't; lest your fancy
May think anon it moves.

Leontes Let be, let be. —
Would I were dead, but that, methinks, already—
What was he that did make it? See, my lord,
Would you not deem it breath'd, and that those veins

更冥顽甚于石？啊，石雕的王后！
你这庄严里有魔法，将我的罪恶
咒召得重新记起来，且从你又惊
又喜的女儿身上摄取了生气，
她和你并峙着，石头一般。

哀笛达　　　　　　　　　准许我，
请别说这是迷信，我要跪下来，
且这么请求她祝福。亲爱的王后，
娘亲，当我入世时你便已逝去，
你那只手给我来吻。

宝理娜　　　　　　　　啊，莫性急！
这石像还只新放下，色彩还没干。

喀米罗　吾王，您这悲伤太漫羡宽广了，
十六个寒冬还不能吹去，十六个
炎夏也不能使它干：不见得有欢乐
活得这么久；再没有悲哀不自行
早已殒灭。

包列齐倪思　　　　我亲爱的王兄，让我，
这悲伤的因由，能从您身上分去
如许多，来增加我衷心的负担。

宝理娜　　　　　　　　　　当真，
吾主，我若能意想到给您看见了
我这可怜的造像，——石头是我的，——
会使您这么激动，我不会来陈展。

里杭底斯　莫拉拢幔幕。
宝理娜　　　　　　您不能再定睛凝望，
否则您那幻想会以为它就要
行动。

里杭底斯　　　让它去，让它去！我愿意死掉，
若不是，我看来，已经——那造像的人
是谁？看啊，王兄，您不以为它
在呼吸，而且那些血管里果真

Did verily bear blood?
Polixenes Masterly done;
The very life seems warm upon her lip.
Leontes The fixture of her eye has motion in't,
As we are mock'd with art.
Paulina I'll draw the curtain;
My lord's almost so far transported that
He'll think anon it lives.
Leontes O sweet Paulina,
Make me to think so twenty years together!
No settled senses of the world can match
The pleasure of that madness. Let't alone.
Paulina I am sorry, sir, I have thus far stirr'd you; but
I could afflict you further.
Leontes Do, Paulina;
For this affliction has a taste as sweet
As any cordial comfort. — Still, methinks,
There is an air comes from her; what fine chisel
Could ever yet cut breath? Let no man mock me,
For I will kiss her!
Paulina Good my lord, forbear;
The ruddiness upon her lip is wet;
You'll mar it if you kiss it; stain your own
With oily painting. Shall I draw the curtain?
Leontes No, not these twenty years.
Perdita So long could I
Stand by, a looker on.
Paulina Either forbear,
Quit presently the chapel, or resolve you
For more amazement. If you can behold it,

有血液在流？
宝 理 娜　　　　　　　雕得真出色：就在她
　　　　　唇边像是暖乎乎有生气。
里杭底斯　　　　　　　　　　她那
　　　　　目光的凝注里有颤动，想我们该是
　　　　　被绝艺所欺罔。
宝 理 娜　　　　　　　我要把幔幕拉上；
　　　　　君王差一点要这么神飞而心动，
　　　　　不久他会以为这像是活的了。
里杭底斯　啊，亲爱的宝理娜！让我去这么
　　　　　"以为"它二十年：我想世间不可能
　　　　　有甚静定的思想，能和那疯狂
　　　　　比愉快。让它去。
宝 理 娜　　　　　　　对不起，王上，我竟
　　　　　使您激动到这地步：但我能使您
　　　　　更苦恼。
里杭底斯　　　　　来吧，宝理娜；因为这苦恼，
　　　　　它的滋味跟任何爽心的乐事
　　　　　一般甜。可还是，我看来，有阵气息
　　　　　飘下来：自来有什么神妙的凿子
　　　　　能雕刻呼吸？莫让谁来嘲笑我，
　　　　　因为我要和她接吻了。
宝 理 娜　　　　　　　　别那样，
　　　　　亲爱的主上。她嘴上的红色还潮：
　　　　　您若去接吻，会把它弄坏；把油彩
　　　　　粘在您嘴上。我好来拉上幔幕吗？
里杭底斯　不行，这二十年里不能拉。
哀 笛 达　　　　　　　我能够
　　　　　站得那么久，在旁观看着。
宝 理 娜　　　　　　　您如果
　　　　　不引退，立即离开这小教堂，就请
　　　　　准备看更多的惊奇。您若能看着，

I'll make the statue move indeed, descend,
And take you by the hand, but then you'll think, —
Which I protest against, — I am assisted
By wicked powers.

Leontes What you can make her do
I am content to look on: what to speak,
I am content to hear; for 'tis as easy
To make her speak as move.

Paulina It is requir'd
You do awake your faith. Then all stand still;
Or those that think it is unlawful business
I am about, let them depart.

Leontes Proceed:
No foot shall stir.

Paulina Music, awake her: strike. —[*Music.*]
'Tis time; descend; be stone no more; approach;
Strike all that look upon with marvel. Come;
I'll fill your grave up: stir; nay, come away;
Bequeath to death your numbness, for from him
Dear life redeems you. — You perceive she stirs.

[Hermione *comes down.*]

Start not; her actions shall be holy as
You hear my spell is lawful: do not shun her
Until you see her die again; for then
You kill her double. Nay, present your hand:
When she was young you woo'd her; now in age
Is she become the suitor?

Leontes [*Embracing her.*] O, she's warm!
If this be magic, let it be an art
Lawful as eating.

　　　　　　　我会叫这石像当真来移动,下来,
　　　　　　　搀着您的手;不过那时节您会想,——
　　　　　　　那个我可要反对,——我有魔法
　　　　　　　帮助我。
里杭底斯　　　　　　你能使她做的事,我乐意
　　　　　　　来观看;说的话,我乐意来听;因为
　　　　　　　使她说话跟行动同样地容易。
宝 理 娜　　那就需要您振奋起精诚。然后,
　　　　　　　大家都立定;或者,什么人以为
　　　　　　　我正要做的是不法的事,让他们
　　　　　　　就离开。
里杭底斯　　　　　　进行:不许有脚步移动。
宝 理 娜　　音乐声,鸣醒她:奏响!　　　　　　　[乐声起。]
　　　　　　　　　　时间已到;
　　　　　　　下来;莫再是石头了:这里来,震惊
　　　　　　　所有看的人,叫他们大家都讶异。
　　　　　　　来吧,我要把您的坟墓封起来:
　　　　　　　移动;别那么,走下来;将您的麻痹
　　　　　　　遗留给死亡,因为亲爱的生命
　　　　　　　救您离开他。你们见到她在动了:
　　　　　　　　　　　　　　　　　　　　　　　[候妙霓下降。]

　　　　　　　莫畏缩;她的行动将会都圣洁
　　　　　　　而清纯,一如您所听到的我这些
　　　　　　　咒辞全合法:莫要回避她,除非您
　　　　　　　见到第二回她又死去后,因为,
　　　　　　　假使那样时,您便双重杀死了她。
　　　　　　　别那样,把您的手伸出来:当她
　　　　　　　年轻时,您向她求爱;如今年老了,
　　　　　　　要她做求爱者?
里杭底斯　　[拥抱伊]啊! 她身上是温暖的。
　　　　　　　假使这算是魔法,当它跟吃东西
　　　　　　　同样是一种合法的巫术好了。

Polixenes She embraces him.
Camillo She hangs about his neck:
If she pertain to life, let her speak too.
Polixenes Ay, and make it manifest where she has liv'd,
Or how stol'n from the dead.
Paulina That she is living,
Were it but told you, should be hooted at
Like an old tale; but it appears she lives,
Though yet she speak not. Mark a little while. —
Please you to interpose, fair madam: kneel,
And pray your mother's blessing. — Turn, good lady;
Our Perdita is found.

[*Presenting* Perdita, *who kneels to* Hermione.]

Hermione You gods, look down,
And from your sacred vials pour your graces
Upon my daughter's head! — Tell me, mine own,
Where hast thou been preserv'd? where liv'd? how found
Thy father's court? for thou shalt hear that I, —
Knowing by Paulina that the oracle
Gave hope thou wast in being, — have preserv'd
Myself to see the issue.
Paulina There's time enough for that;
Lest they desire upon this push to trouble
Your joys with like relation. — Go together,
You precious winners all; your exultation
Partake to every one. I, an old turtle,
Will wing me to some wither'd bough, and there
My mate, that's never to be found again,
Lament till I am lost.
Leontes O peace, Paulina!
Thou shouldst a husband take by my consent,

包列齐倪思　她在拥抱他。
喀　米　罗　　　　　她围着他的脖子：
她如果活着的话,让她也开口。
包列齐倪思　是啊;让她说明她一向在哪里
过活,或者怎样从死人处偷出来。
宝　理　娜　说她是活着的,只要告诉您,就会被
嘲骂,像个老故事一般;这样子
却显得她是活的,虽然还没说话。
再看上一会。请您来居间,美小娘：
跪下来请您母亲来祝福。转过来,
亲爱的娘娘;我们的哀笛达找到了。

　　　　　　　　［引见哀笛达,伊跪向候妙霓。］

候　妙　霓　众位天神,请向下俯视,从你们
神圣的樽中将你们的神恩向下
倾注,倾在我女儿头上！告诉我,
我的亲儿,你在哪里被确保着
安全？在哪里过的活？怎样会找到
你父亲的宫阙？因为你将会听说,
我从宝理娜那里得知了神谕
说你有希望还活着,我便将自己
保存着来看这结局。
宝　理　娜　　　　　　　　有的是时间
来谈那些事;我怕在这样的时会
有人会想用同样的叙述来打断
你们这欢乐。都一同去吧,你们
全是大好的得胜者：你们的大喜
让大家分享。我嗷,一头老雉鸠,
会独自飞上一枝枯树枝,那里去
悼伤我永远不再能找到的老伴,
直等到我自己也亡故。
里杭底斯　　　　　　　　啊！且住,
宝理娜。你应当听我的劝告,接纳

As I by thine a wife: this is a match,
And made between's by vows. Thou hast found mine;
But how, is to be question'd: for I saw her,
As I thought, dead; and have, in vain, said many
A prayer upon her grave. I'll not seek far, —
For him, I partly know his mind, — to find thee
An honourable husband. — Come, Camillo,
And take her by the hand, whose worth and honesty
Is richly noted, and here justified
By us, a pair of kings. — Let's from this place. —
What! look upon my brother: — both your pardons,
That e'er I put between your holy looks
My ill suspicion. — This your son-in-law,
And son unto the king, whom heavens directing,
Is troth-plight to your daughter. — Good Paulina,
Lead us from hence; where we may leisurely
Each one demand, and answer to his part
Perform'd in this wide gap of time, since first
We were dissever'd: hastily lead away!

[Exeunt.]

一位夫君,如同我听你而迎一位
贤妻:这是个相约,我们双方来
起誓把它定。你找到了我的;但怎样
会找到,我要来问你;因为我见她,
我以为是死了,而且在她那墓上
徒然地作了好多次祈祷。我毋须
远觅,——关于他,我知道他心意的大较,——
去为你寻一位荣誉的夫君。来吧,
喀米罗,跟她手挽手;他的品德
和荣誉大家都知道,而且在这里,
我们两君王能证实。让我们
离此回宫吧。什么!望着我的王兄:
请你们都对我宽恕,只怪我不该
在你们圣洁的顾视间妄投我那
恶劣的狐疑。这是你我的子婿,
兄台君王的儿子,——蒙上苍指引,
已和你女儿订婚。亲爱的宝理娜,
领我们离开此间,去到那所在,
我们好安闲地每人发问和回答,
他在这么一大段时间的空缺里
曾做过什么事,自从我们彼此
相互分离后:快快领我们离开。

〔同下。

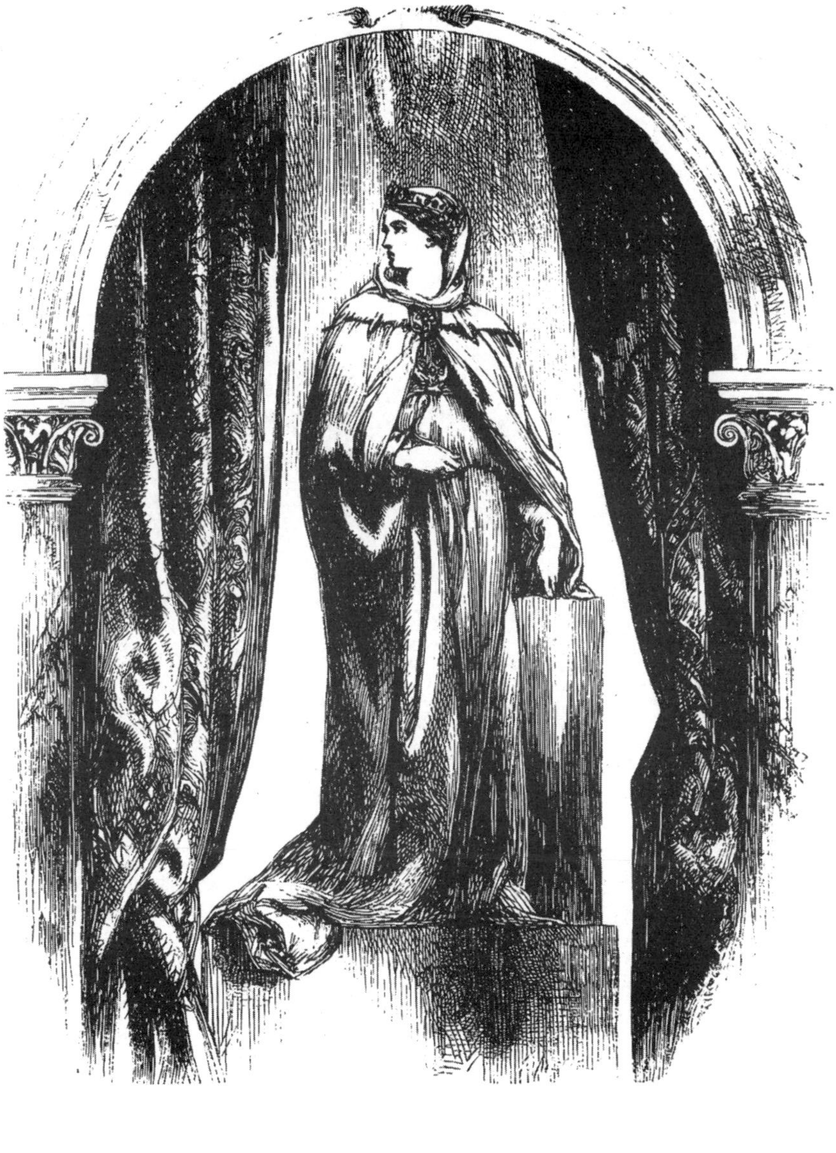

图书在版编目(CIP)数据

冬日故事/[英]莎士比亚著；孙大雨译.
—上海：上海三联书店，2018.
ISBN 978-7-5426-6171-5

Ⅰ.①冬… Ⅱ.①莎… ②孙… Ⅲ.①诗剧—剧本—
英国—中世纪 Ⅳ.①I561.33

中国版本图书馆CIP数据核字(2017)第320867号

冬日故事(中英文双语对照)

著　　者　[英]威廉·莎士比亚
译　　者　孙大雨

责任编辑　钱震华
装帧设计　陈益平

出版发行　上海三联书店
　　　　　(201199)中国上海市都市路4855号
印　　刷　上海昌鑫龙印务有限公司

版　　次　2018年4月第1版
印　　次　2018年4月第1次印刷
开　　本　890×1240　1/32
字　　数　220千字
印　　张　7.75
书　　号　ISBN 978-7-5426-6171-5/I·1358
定　　价　30.00元